I0582679

PRAISE FOR CHELSEA MUELLER

Casual Conversations About Love and Murder

"Emma's righteous anger, frustration, and determination are palpable, making for a take-charge heroine. **Mueller's winding thriller will enthrall.**" — Publisher's Weekly

"…will keep you guessing and on the **edge of your seat** until the big reveal." — @dreaminginpages

Prom House

A 2022 YALSA Quick Pick!

"Those **addicted** to teen drama will be **hooked.**" — Kirkus

"This book is a **fun, blood-filled young adult thriller** that can be gulped down in one day." — Lish McBride, author of Hold Me Closer, Necromancer

Borrowed Souls

"…**readers who like dark worlds and compelling heroines** will enjoy this smooth read" —Booklist

"Mueller explores an intriguing concept in a seedy, visceral setting that **pops to life on the page.**" — Publisher's Weekly

CLOUD NINE

CLOUD NINE
BOOK 1

CHELSEA MUELLER

CLOUD NINE

Copyright © 2023 by Chelsea Mueller

All rights reserved.

No part of this book may be reproduced in any form or by any electronic or mechanical means, including information storage and retrieval systems, without written permission from the author, except for the use of brief quotations in a book review.

Cover Design by Murphy Rae

Copy Editing by Catharine Lindsey / Heart Full of Ink

❀ Created with Vellum

CHAPTER 1
I'M NOT MOVING

No way would I move to Cloud Nine.

I stormed into the entryway of my house and threw my shoes across the room. My sister Leah had told everyone I was going to ditch my family and friends for some stupid government project in the sky. It didn't matter if she was lying. Her betrayal demanded an apology and then some.

Minutes passed. While the decontamination chamber did its thing, I bottled my emotions, stockpiling them until the opportune moment to explode.

I left my boots outside the air-locked door. It was overkill, but Mom disagreed. My bare feet clapping against the hardwood floors didn't muffle the sound of her and Leah whispering in the kitchen. I stomped down the hallway, past family photos last updated a decade ago. It was easy to trust when you were seven. Not so much anymore.

My presence silenced them, but it was the way Mom looked at me that converted my legs to string cheese.

"Ally, honey, I'm glad you're home." I'd been around her for seventeen years. I knew what her smile looked like, and that wasn't it.

"Is it true?" I blurted, and it was like I'd thrown up on the Thanksgiving table. Leah stared at her feet like they could answer my question. Mom's eyes narrowed. Her anger was beginning to boil. We had that in common.

"Sit down." Mom pointed at the chair to her right. My chair. I ignored her.

"Answer the question." I crossed my arms. I was solid. A tree. Rooted to the kitchen floor.

Her sigh shook my soul. The urge to run or collapse or something to not have to deal with this fluttered in my mind, but they weren't real options.

I stay. I fight.

"Leah? Tell me you lied to the guys at school." I'd already locked my abs tight in preparation for the verbal gut shot. She turned in her seat as though her profile would make her disappear.

"You are moving to Cloud Nine." Mom rested her forearms on the table. She forced sincerity at me like a weapon. "You and your sister deserve something better. The Clean Air Development pods provide a chance for you to live a better life."

She maintained the straight face while the news broadcast on the screen behind her showed Greece's president sidestepping fault for the death of twenty-two teenaged botanists working on their own de-pollution program. No one had died in the U.S. program, but we hadn't seen any good news either.

"They provide a chance to have the government make me their slave while they do jack down here to fix problems." Air sucks so bad on Earth that we'll move the kids up a few miles. They're the only ones able to adapt. "Shipping kids to the stratosphere doesn't exactly solve things."

"You know better than that. There are opportunities there, and you'll be helping with something really important."

"Important, my ass." It was a cop-out. One she expected me to be a part of.

"Language."

I gave her my best you've-got-to-be-kidding-me look. Like that was our biggest problem right now. I had 'important' things here, too. People needed me. Mr. Jordan would miss me in self-defense classes. My best friend Sarah would be lost without me reminding her which guys were useless. I had a life here, and my mom didn't care.

"Allison, stop. The papers are already signed. You are going to Cloud Nine."

I mentally flipped through arguments. I doubted any would motivate Mom to change her mind, and I wasn't brave enough to mention how the government had failed Dad. Besides, that still didn't answer the real question.

"How did I get in?"

Mom rolled her eyes this time. "That's a silly question. You won the Centorcelli Prize for Chemistry the last two years. They take notice of national awards, honey."

No. Everyone received letters from the EPA saying, "You, too, could be chosen." I should know. I had thrown each copy we received into the black trash bin in the corner. They equated the silly thing to the moon landing and said we were all special and they only wanted the best of the best. What they really wanted was for everyone to pay the twenty-five dollars to apply. It's the same reason they agreed to take any siblings along with the kid who aced the test. Application fees made the package deal worth it.

Mom continued like she couldn't hear my groan. The same way we both pretended not to hear one another when she came home late from work. It was often simpler for us to avoid each other. "They need more experienced people, women especially, with strong chemistry skills."

"It doesn't matter, because I'm not going." Folding my arms across my chest kept me from slamming a fist into the wall adorned with the aprons we never used.

"You are."

Oh, no, I wasn't. That earlier need to flee reared again. Little Box in the Sky was not the place for me. Phoenix at Ground Level was my home. I wasn't going to leave Sarah or any of my other friends for the sake of a politician's platform. They let their own die before, who was to say they wouldn't do it again?

This time I heeded the urge and bolted for the front door. I stopped past the first airlock to slam my feet back into my boots. Industrial grade rubber, safe even if it rained. My desperate need to escape was slowed by the necessity of outdoor prep. Normally I didn't mind, but today it was just one more thing stifling me. I tucked the edges of my pants in and strapped the laces, pulling tighter than necessary. How could she make these huge choices without even talking to me?

This was worse than being kicked out. My mom was shipping me off to work for a government with ideals that diverged from mine in glaring ways. I was sure she'd send letters, even though I wouldn't be allowed to reply. She'd accepted it. She'd bought into their package deal of foregoing contact with your kid in the name of a better life.

I zipped my jacket up to my chin, pulled my goggles down over my eyes, blinked a few times to adjust to the tint. Now I was ready to storm off. I jerked the handle of our front door to the left, yanked it open, and ran.

CHAPTER 2
SARAH SAVE ME

A hint of green still skimmed the horizon, but the sky had already shifted to charcoal gray. The winds picked up as evening set in, and I was glad I took the time to suit up. Sure, raging out the door might have been more effective in pissing my parent off, but it wasn't worth the chemical burn because I hadn't taken the time to cinch my jacket.

The slivers of exposed skin just below my goggles tingled a bit, but I had another good hour of this before any discoloration would set in. I needed the sensation after this kind of day.

My boots disappeared against the black tar of the asphalt as I walked in the middle of the already empty street. Everything in my view was tinged with black. Even the soil of my neighbors' yards had bits of coal crusted onto its grit. I understood why people like my mom wanted to believe in Cloud Nine. Just forty years ago the world had been vibrant—blue skies, green trees, pink flowers. Now it's tarnished.

I just wished they would want to fix it here, for my mom and for friends who don't understand covalent bonds. Instead they rounded up the smart kids and the strong kids and took them above. They'd made it clear adolescent bodies could adapt to the air changes necessary for the Clean Air pods, but what good did that do for everyone else?

EPA Director Abrams claimed the work on Cloud Nine was about trying to reverse the problems at Ground Level. Maybe it was, but they'd had three years and I hadn't seen anything change. The rain still burned my hair. The wind still razed my skin. And I was one of only two girls and four boys in my grade who could run a mile.

Cloud Nine was a cheat. It was a ploy to make us feel better. To try and get people to forget we were still churning out more sulfur dioxide into the air—the very reason I wore the stupid goggles—instead of, you know, changing our behavior. You didn't need to be a rocket scientist to figure out when something burned your eyes, you should stop doing it.

No one told the government, I guessed.

Now I was supposed to work for them? Not happening.

The emerald tinge of the old house's windows muted any light from inside, but Sarah was home. What little illumination managed past the glass was so muted it acted as a nightlight, that dull hum of safety that didn't scare away the bad guys but made us think we had a fighting chance.

I bypassed the front door and skirted behind the metal bushes lining the house. Sarah's dad was determined to make his house look like one from an old-school Christmas card. He kept welding together metal versions of government-banned plants to stick in his yard. His artwork wasn't so bad, but the whole concept was depressing. No point in longing for things that no longer existed. Like my home on Ground Level, apparently. I tried to furrow my brow, but it only made my goggles pinch the bridge of my nose.

Three raps on the side door told Sarah I was coming in. It'd been our code for the last couple years.

I still had to spend the five minutes getting dusted for chemicals and stripping out of my outdoor gear, but this back entrance was just a few steps from Sarah's room. For such control freaks, you'd think her parents would be a bit more concerned about easy access to Sarah's room. Then again, sneaking in was second nature for me.

She stood in the hallway, lounge pants rolled up to mid-calf, hip cocked. "You're up to something, Miss Ramsey."

My throat squeezed. How could I leave Sarah? I licked my lips. Stalling. Man, bad news was just not my thing.

Her hand dropped from her hip. "Ally, what's up?" Her voice softened like she was talking down a scared animal. How had one day turned me into the frightened kitten?

"My mom did something really stupid."

"That's not news." Leave it to Sarah to try to lighten the mood even when she knew crap was about to rain on us.

"She wants to send me and Leah to Cloud Nine."

"You? Has she met you?" She pivoted on bare feet and led me into her room. After closing the door, she continued, "Besides, you have to apply for that and be tested for magical DNA or a fairy brain or whatever."

"Apparently it's a done deal." I sat on the carpeted floor, pulling my knees against my chest.

Sarah scrunched her face. "Still, no tests equal no admittance, right?"

"She said they wanted me. Maybe she found pixy dust in my hair at night and mailed it in?"

"Dude. She so would, too." We laughed. My mom may not have been home a lot, but she seriously loved snooping. Anything I wanted to keep from her stayed at Sarah's place or my locker at school. It was as though her way to know me was via my things. I couldn't blame her for the creepy behavior, either. She wasn't around and I wasn't forthcoming, so I'd accepted it.

My smile evaporated. "She didn't even tell me, Sar. I found out from a jerk outside school."

"How the hell did he know?" Before I could answer, she figured it out. "Leah knew?"

"Apparently." I stared at the ceiling for a bit. Sarah allowed me the respite. "Mom isn't even giving me a choice."

"Is Leah going with you? Siblings get a free pass, yeah?"

"Yeah, I think so. I was too focused on her sending me away to listen to the details." I didn't need to tell her about the disappointment on Mom's face when I bailed. It wouldn't help me.

"At least you'll have her there with you, though, right?" She sounded so sure.

"Kid sister plus giant bubble filled with a bunch of people I don't know does not equal a good time."

"You could be wrong. Maybe it's badass. No bossy parents. High probability of hot dudes. Decent food. Plus, you might get to see the sun. Can you imagine?"

Ugh. I forgot about Sarah's thing about the sun. I'd spent years and years not seeing it. I knew that when it was up, the sky was green and when it set, things went black. I wasn't sure I was missing out on anything.

"The hot guy part is enticing, but the doing what you're told part isn't real high on my list of awesome." I didn't have the heart to tell her guys were not on the top of my priority list, either. The chances I'd meet someone who hated being there and liked girls who hated makeup was slim. After all, I hadn't had much luck on Ground Level.

"What will you be doing?"

My stomach sank. "No clue. That tidbit hasn't been shared either."

We were both quiet at that.

Sarah's voice was so hushed it barely broke the silence. "I could apply."

So. Tempting. She could apply and be there in a few months. The Cloud Nine ideal wasn't for me, but with Sarah there maybe I could endure it.

But what if they said no? Or worse, said yes and she was given a job scooping poop?

Fears aside, I knew she wouldn't do it. She would never leave this city block, much less Ground Level entirely. "That would be awesome, Sar."

CHAPTER 3
DOES IT MAKE A
DIFFERENCE?

Talking to Sarah calmed me, but the sharp stab in my stomach wouldn't go away as I stood on the sidewalk in front of my house ten minutes later. The bricks still showed a hint of red through the soot, but staring at them didn't ease the ache of leaving home. If I could turn this into a good-riddance moment, I could make this work.

Unfortunately, I liked my life. I didn't mind layering clothing or being covered up. I liked the color black. I even thought the cargo pants did a little something for my butt while letting me move around. I was accustomed to the bite of the morning air and the spark on my tongue when talking on the walk to school. My house was warm and vibrant with wood and bamboo and all those remnants of life inside.

Mom was forcing me to leave all of that. To live in plastic and do 'assigned tasks.' I could see myself locked in a tiny, white room. I'd mark checkboxes on paperwork for hours on end. There would only be space to stretch as far as needed to hand in completed files and accept new ones. How long would it take before my muscles failed me? A few months and lifting a gallon jug would be my only fight.

I vomited there at the corner. I hadn't eaten much, so it was an empty gesture. Chemicals scraped the back of my throat as I gasped after the last heave. I had to go in for water or risk losing my voice for a week.

That meant talking to Mom. It meant accepting moving to Cloud Nine.

I stayed outside another five minutes. I would have stayed there all night, but a coughing fit drove me toward the house.

Mom was waiting just inside the door with a big glass of water. She was just as stubborn as me. The woman stood there, watching me puke and choke until I caved and came inside. For the best. I would have stayed out there longer if she'd tried to force me inside. I was mad she was sending me away, but would be mad if she made me come closer. The irony was not lost on me.

I drained the glass, gulping so quickly rivulets of water trickled over my chin. I wiped them away with my sleeve.

"Get changed. I'll have another glass for you when you get inside." She left off the obvious follow-up that she expected us to talk then.

Knowing the chat was coming didn't slow me down. The water took away the worst of the grit from my mouth and throat, but I tasted sickness. I took the time to brush my teeth and chug another two glasses of water before facing her.

Mom waited for me in my room.

She sat on my bed, an empty gray duffle bag, obviously meant for me, gaped open on the bed next to her. I glared at it as though my eyes could set it ablaze. No such luck. Instead it just sat there limply until my mom shoved it backward and patted the vacated space.

"It's going to be okay." That was easy for her to say. She wasn't being sent away.

I shook my head. "It doesn't feel that way."

When I sat, she slipped an arm around me and pulled me close. "I know it, baby. I do. But this is an amazing chance for you."

"What if I don't want it?"

"You need to trust me, Ally. This is going to change your life."

"That's the problem." I pushed back from her. My eyes burned, and it didn't have anything to do with microscopic metals in the air. "I like my life now."

"I'm thinking about the big picture. This is your chance to be healthy—"

"I'm already healthy. I'm one of the strongest and fastest in my grade."

"Yes, for here you're healthy. Because you struggle to be. There was a time when it was normal for people to run miles and miles outdoors for recreation. Or ride bicycles. Your lungs take in a tiny percentage of what they used to." I knew this, but the way her voice shook stopped me from saying something sharp. "You're a star here, but you could be extraordinary if you had the opportunities they have up there. When you're above, you'll be able to breathe, Ally. Really breathe. You'll have access to all the research that might be able to improve the air down here."

"Dad wouldn't want me working for them." The words slid out my mouth as a hiss. They were the ones I knew I shouldn't say, but if left inside would furrow into my heart.

She bit her lip. I'd hurt her. Guilt panged me, but I stayed quiet while she spoke. "Wrong. He would want you making a difference. Cloud Nine will let you help people. That mattered to him."

A ball of guilt the size of a hockey puck lodged itself inside my throat. "We don't know what kind of job I'll get," I muttered.

"They want you for the research division." She rubbed her hand in small circles on my back. The soothing touch didn't go deep enough. "I told you. They came to me about this."

They came to her? Like agents at the front door asking Ms. Ramsey if they could have a word? Doubtful. "How would they even know?"

"The standardized tests you take come from the government. Did you think they didn't look at them?" She gave me her best smile. This one was real. Why did she have to be so proud of me? My chest ached. I wanted to hug her for thinking I was better than I was, but I wasn't willing to be done being mad yet. Sometimes it's easier to be angry than to be honest.

I pulled back from her embrace. "You don't think that's weird?"

Her mouth tightened for a flash. She was good at that: immediately covering her feelings. She probably wanted to give me a long 'don't be stupid' look, but knew it'd be counterproductive.

"It's not weird, and you know that." She let out a long sigh and rested her palms on her knees. She wasn't looking at me now, and that worked for me. "I'm not up for debating this with you. The shuttle leaves at seven tomorrow morning. I love you."

She got up and walked out the door before I said it back.

CHAPTER 4
THIS WILL CHANGE OUR LIVES? NO, THANK YOU.

surveyed my bedroom. As much as I didn't want to leave, packing felt like the only thing to do. How much of my life could I cram into a two-foot by one-foot bag? The best I could do was pack reminders of it.

Unframed pictures of Sarah and me lay in an unruly pile on the dresser. We'd gone ice-skating at the Vente mall. She was awful at it. I mean awful. I think her butt must have been as black as the ice by the time we were done. Not to say I didn't fall. I did. I was just a more experienced faller. Less injuries for me.

I picked up my favorite of the bunch. She and I were leaning forward, our cheeks smushed together. My hair had fallen out of its ponytail and did this wavy thing around my face while hers frizzed out everywhere. I decided something that honest needed to come with me. We looked busted and sweaty, but so happy. I wanted to take that feeling to Cloud Nine.

I picked up the black wooden picture frame on my desk. It held two pictures. On the right was Mom, Leah and I at the holidays. Leah was wearing an ugly sweater. I chose to keep that one. On the right was an older picture of Sarah and me with Leah photo bombing a silly face in the background.

There used to be such a bigger age gap between Leah and I. Not in years, of course. That never changed. If you asked Leah we're two years apart. I tended to say three, but the truth was exactly in the middle. Still, there's a big difference between ten and twelve. Less so now that I edged toward eighteen and she'd been fifteen for months. I used to help her get to school safely. Now I spent more time punching the guys who couldn't take a hint from my little sister.

I slid open the back of the frame and placed the newer picture of Sarah and me inside. I let the old one stay behind it, though. Just in case.

After placing the updated picture frame on my bed, I kept looking for special things to take with me. I had a small porcelain doll that used to be my grandmother's. It was about eight inches tall and one hundred years old. Even after a century, the paint was vibrant. It was the only place I've ever seen a true yellow. The little girl's blonde curls looked like they'd be springy if they were real. Her porcelain body was adorned with a fluffy dress in cream, though I've often wondered if it was originally white and, like fabric, the glaze tinged with age.

I decided not to bring it with me. Breaking it would kill me. I loved it because my grandmother and my mom trusted me with it. It could stay safe here on Ground Level. The program hadn't been in place long enough for us to see people come home, but surely after I passed the 21-year age mark, they'd let me come back to visit. Those were the rules, right?

Four years was a long time. My dad had been gone seven. His bosses at the Environmental Protection Agency had taken his seismograph and the good microscopes, and our house had been left with dated pictures and the echoes of a fun, if too trusting, scientist.

I shuffled to my bookcase, thinking I would find something important there. Instead of books it was full of photo albums and track trophies. It wasn't worth taking the awards with me. They wouldn't mean anything up there. It's hard to run a mile at Ground Level and I'd trained relentlessly to be able to do so, but I suspected everyone on the station could do it.

The way they talked about it at school, our lungs got stronger with cleaner air and that whole place was hyper filtered. I didn't know if it was true or more propaganda, but considering they were actually recruiting for this thing, I'd bet there were some strong and fast types there. Sarah might be right about the hot dude prospects. I'd bet they even had a gym up there. Not that I was excited about moving to Cloud Nine, but I wouldn't mind full-time access to good workout equipment.

There was an optional self-defense class at my school. I took it every semester as it was the ultimate outlet for my stress. Mr. Jordan would shake his head each time I showed up and tease me about being too stubborn for my own good. Still, he'd let me come in early and practice on the heavy bag each morning. My stomach sank. He'd be there tomorrow morning waiting for me to train, and I'd be leaving without saying goodbye.

Narrowing down your possessions should not be done in a single night. I kicked the edge of my bed, and immediately regretted it. The throbbing pain wasn't worth the momentary release of whacking my foot at something. You'd think I'd know better. I really didn't.

Packing my clothes was easy, at least. I wore black. A lot of black. It let me fade in. It matched everything. Sometimes I wished my hair was black just to complete the tough look. Washed-out brown didn't exactly fit the monochromatic style.

I threw my two nicest pairs of nylon cargo pants into the bag first. Three tee shirts flew across the room next. My aim was good and they softly thunked against the inside of the back of the bag. Tees go with everything. We always had to layer up to be outside, but nine times out of ten, I had something short-sleeved on underneath. Freedom to move is important.

Despite my love for exposed arms, I also added a long-sleeve thermal and a track jacket to the pile. What if it's cold up there? There wasn't a guidebook for this thing. No one gave me a pamphlet with some happy kids on the front explaining what to expect when you move to the stratosphere.

I jammed the rest of the essentials—socks, underwear, toiletries, another pair of shoes—into the bag with less care than usual. If they didn't like what I brought, then they could send me home. I used one of the tee shirts to carefully wrap the picture frame. Wood frames weren't legal to purchase anymore, but I loved the feel the real grain against my fingers when I smoothed them along its edge. The faux wood frames were okay, but they didn't feel the same in your hands.

Leah distracted me from dwelling on my distaste for plastic by knocking on my door. She usually just barged in, so maybe she did feel guilty about selling me out. I tilted my chin up quickly to admit her, then turned to shuffle things about in my bag. It would have been easier to yell at her. To be mad and stomp and scare her out of the room. Wouldn't be the first time I'd done it, but I didn't have the energy to be angry anymore tonight. That didn't mean I had the energy to talk about it, though. Avoiding her gaze was my only recourse.

"I'm sorry—"

"Nope." I cut her off. "We're not doing that."

"But I should have told you." I could hear her toes digging into the little area rug I kept near the door. I didn't have to look to know she was staring at her feet. I wanted the guilt to turn her face red, but I didn't look to confirm either way. It was better to pretend she was actually ashamed of selling me out.

"How long did you know?" I stopped myself. There wasn't a point in learning how much she'd known and when. "Wait, don't tell me. It's done."

"But I'm really sorry." The sincerity rang like a bell. I believed her, but I still didn't like it.

"Heard you the first time." I took the picture frame out again, then rewrapped it in my track jacket. I needed something to do with my hands. Anything to keep myself calm and focused elsewhere. I didn't even want to be pissed at Leah. She did stupid things; she ran her mouth. That's just how my sister was. I knew this. Being mad didn't change that.

"It's going to be great." She was wrong. We only had wood floors because the government didn't rip them out of houses from before the turn of the century. Did she really want to work for the same people who stole the bamboo from her friend Kim's house?

"Maybe it will be for you." I said it quietly, but she heard me. Her toes stopped grating across the thick pile of the rug.

Leah stayed silent for almost thirty seconds. Possibly a record. "It will be for both of us." She swallowed hard enough I was impressed she was able to talk again afterward. "Trust Mom. She knows this is going to change our lives."

That's exactly what I was afraid of.

CHAPTER 5
HELLO, DECLAN

Even with family at your side, eighteen-foot fences with razor wire will turn the most stoic girl's stomach.

Mom escorted Leah and I as close to the shuttle as patrol allowed. In this case, it was to the chain-link gates set into the aforementioned steel walls. For a place the flyers touted as "a heaven just above Earth," it looked a lot like a prison.

Leah flashed a smile at one of the guards and he gave her a small one back in kind. Maybe she didn't notice the gun at his hip. I did. Had anyone ever tried to break into Cloud Nine? Was it worth all the gates-and-guards hurrah?

Mom nudged me with her shoulder. "Quit staring at them like that. They are protecting you." She kept her voice soft while she admonished me.

I was far less sure they were at the gates to keep people out and not hold others in, but this definitely wasn't the place to argue about it. I nodded to acknowledge I heard her, but kept my mouth shut.

We couldn't stand around for long. Mom hugged me and whispered, "Please give it a chance," in my ear.

I gave a noncommittal grunt, but Mom read it as the compromise I'd intended.

"Buck up, Buttercup." I don't know if she said it to make me cry, but I almost wanted to. She had to know my dad's favorite words for his precocious daughter would spark something. I gave her a sharp nod and ignored the pinpricks at the corners of my eyes.

Leah did cry, but then she was much more of the sort. Mom hugged her longer on account of the tears. I doubted she shared the 'don't screw it up' message with her.

When the guards opened the gates, eight others crowded up with Leah and me. I didn't know any of them, but maybe that was for the best. The ten of us were corralled into a line of dark, little ducklings. Each person outfitted in heavy rubber boots, bulky goggles that made them look like bugs and jackets that made our bodies lose all shape.

Our guard—scratch that—escort kept us moving at a quick pace. I might have liked him if he weren't wearing a weapon like some sort of prison guard. Five minutes of quick footing it and we arrived at a set of thick doors on a squat, grey building with no hard angles. Impressive that they kept the building from getting much darker than a heavy, ash color. They probably made someone whitewash it once a week.

The doors opened with a heavy swish and a new guard emerged from within. He was a foot taller than me and nearly twice as wide. His hand dwarfed the clipboard he gripped.

We shuffled forward single file. Each step I took closer to the doorway made my muscles tighten. My quads were about to snap my legs in half by the time I made it to Clipboard Guy.

"Name?" He didn't bother lifting his gaze from the sheet pinned to the board. Was he so tall he could see the paper and me at once?

"Allison Ramsey." I sounded far more confident than I felt. Could he tell I was staring at his gun? Would there be guns up in Cloud Nine? Unlikely. It's a plastic bubble with fancy filtered air. They didn't need anyone puncturing it with willy-nilly gunfire.

He grunted. "Clear. Take a right, then you're in seat No. 8."

Assigned seating on move-in day? I'd ask if he was kidding me, but something told me this man had never even heard a joke.

As soon as I crossed the threshold, goosebumps broke out across my skin. The double layers didn't stop the refrigeration feeling. I slowed after a few steps in the white corridor, waiting for Leah. I glanced back to see her coming through the door and looking far more pleased about her exchange with Clipboard Guy than I had been.

Little bits of black dust marked the path from the entrance to the pod we'd been directed to enter. I tapped the tip of my boot against the white tile and watched sooty gravel fall from its tread. At least I wouldn't have to clean that up.

Leah vaulted toward me, bouncing on the balls of her feet. I had to fight not to roll my eyes at her. Tears faded fast for her, while an ache was just settling deep in my stomach. Her palms landed on my shoulders and she sprung up a bit, using me for leverage before landing next to me. All the smiling kids on the Clean Air Development posters at our high school made Leah believe Cloud Nine would a party without any adult supervision.

"I'm in seat No. 2. Are you sitting by me?" My springy sister confused a shuttle ride to the stratosphere with the lunchroom.

"I'm in No. 8." The bounce left her step, and I wondered how much handholding I'd be doing over the next few weeks.

The pod turned out to be a small tube with a row of six seats on each side. A slim aisle separated the two. This pleased Leah as it meant I was directly across from her. I, however, was less thrilled by being squished between people I didn't know. Ones who hadn't even been decontaminated yet. Shouldn't that be like step one of this thing? Maybe they did need me on that station to give them some logical protocols.

Once everyone was seated, Clipboard Guy tromped in. His gun was gone, but he didn't look like the administrative type. In addition to being a big dude, he was also young. Maybe two years older than me. Wearing the requisite guard uniform of charcoal grey didn't disguise the fact this guy worked out a lot. It made sense for him to be a soldier, not a pencil pusher. His grey-blue eyes scanned each seated person. I didn't know what he was looking for, but he must have seen it because he closed the door and dropped the latch into place.

"Welcome to Cloud Nine processing." They only did these transports once every few months, but the weary tone in Clipboard Guy's voice made me think he was sick of shuttling kids to the station.

"Today's going to be a long day, so I will need you to follow directions explicitly in order to get things done in a timely fashion."

Oh yeah, he was over this whole thing. Perhaps not everyone loved Cloud Nine. The thought was promising.

"My name is Declan. I'll be running the show today." He looked up from the clipboard finally—and met my eyes directly. I swallowed. Hard. The full force of this guy's gaze was like a sucker punch to the liver. "You are the lucky few chosen to live on regional designation 42's Clean Air Development station, better known as Cloud Nine. We take care of food, shelter, water, and all other basic necessities. In exchange, we request your help in making our world stronger."

There was a propaganda line if I ever heard it. His eyes tightened infinitesimally, but I caught the reaction. Like he knew I was internally calling him on his bull.

"Until you've lived above, you can't understand exactly what we do. I understand that may make some of you skeptical about our intentions. Know that the work being done here has the chance to save lives. Your parents, your friends, everyone."

Why did his stare have to pin me like a butterfly to a wall? I wanted to root around in his brain and find out what about me was setting off his radar. Maybe the clipboard, which nearly disappeared in his hand at his hip, had a note about me. Maybe I already had a file in this new world above the earth. Perhaps someone had jotted a memo warning the processing team to keep an eye on Ally, because she's crafty and didn't want to be there.

I didn't, but at least they were offering some rather interesting people to keep me on my toes. I wasn't sure if I was scared of Declan or impressed. Regardless, I knew three things: One, they wanted me to be scared of him; two, I wanted to touch his biceps no matter now many levels of wrong it was; and, three, Cloud Nine was going to be far more complicated if there were people like Declan filling the halls.

"You will each be assigned a duty based on your strengths." He paused and smiled like he was in on some hidden joke. "That won't happen today."

Oh. That's surprising. I'd thought they'd want to set us to work immediately. Well, I could use a little adjustment period without punching my card for The Man.

"In a moment, this shuttle will take us up twenty miles to the base of Cloud Nine. There, you will participate in a thorough decontamination process." He smiled for real this time. "I won't lie to you: It sucks. However, once you do it, you won't have to ever do decontamination again unless you leave Cloud Nine."

I rather liked that. I liked it even more if it meant not having to wear the bug-eyed goggles anymore. I understood their purpose, and picked ones that made me look the least like an arthropod, but that didn't stop the hate.

"Seatbelts buckled, please."

I snapped the nylon tether around my hips and waited. He walked down the aisle, glancing at the waist of each person as he passed. His eyes met mine again, briefly, and he appeared more intrigued than murderous. So the notes about me weren't all bad.

Declan took a seat at the very end of my row. He wrapped his hand around a shiny pole at his left and instructed us to hold on.

CHAPTER 6
IT'S A GOOD PAIN

A second later, all my organs were vying for the chance to reside between my hips. It should have been a horrifying sensation, but I grinned.

The rush didn't last long enough. Maybe ten seconds had passed and we were stopping. Declan was up immediately clomping his way back to the entrance hatch. He was wearing thick combat boots. I didn't think they were necessary to keep out chemicals up here—no decontamination!—which meant either he got in fights a lot and wanted tough shoes or he just enjoyed playing the part of badass. Either way, I approved.

He opened the door and whispered with someone on the other side. I might have been able to run longer than most people, but there were times when Leah's eavesdropping skills would come in handy.

"Everybody up." He was all business now, voice gruff enough to raze. I fought the instinct to touch my ears.

I unlocked the seatbelt. Normally, I liked to be the first through doors. Not today. Any hint of a smile had been scoured from Declan's face the moment he unlatched the pod door, and I was not about to be the first person to know why.

"Make sure to stay close to me. It's time to get you cleaned up." He wasn't looking back at us, but his words vibrated against the walls.

We exited single file again. It was better than the holding-hands-style buddy system. Small favors. Declan led us down three bare white corridors. I wanted doorways or people to pass, but it was solely pristine tile and the echoes of our feet colliding with them. When we finally stopped it was so abrupt I almost slammed into the girl in front of me. I still ended up close enough to know she used a strawberry shampoo. Too frou-frou for me.

Declan instructed the women to head to the right, the men to the left. Another military type was waiting on the other side of that door. She was bulky, too. I expected the female guards to be built more like me, lean muscle and a touch lanky. Her body had more in common with Declan's than with mine. She pointed us to shower stalls. "We need you to remove all potentially contaminated clothing."

I took off the same things I always took off, stripping down to my base tee and panties. The other girls in the room had the same thought, but according to the guard we did it wrong.

"Sorry, ladies. We have to run all your clothing through the ionizer, just like your bags are going through now. You'll get the clothing back once we've ensured it and you are contagion and toxin free."

That did not sound promising. At all.

I didn't like being naked. Natural state and all that was lovely, but it's cold and exposed. Chemical burns, cuts, and toxic nastiness get in through your skin. Why would I want it unprotected and ready for assault?

The other girls looked less than thrilled as well, but everyone complied. I shut my eyes tightly and began to do the same. It was easier if I pretended I wasn't here and there wasn't a cold breeze coming from somewhere—there weren't windows in this room and I sure didn't see fans in the ceiling—making me shiver involuntarily.

I sensed motion in front of me, and my eyes snapped open. Distaste for this process wouldn't make me drop my guard. Another woman, this one not in a guard uniform, passed each of our stalls and took our clothing.

It screamed prank. *We've shot you in the air, stolen your clothes and now you can find your own way home, suckers!* Was it awful that part of me wished that were the case? If it meant going home today, I'd let a bunch of people see my bare ass as I went streaking past.

"Stand on the black square within your stall. This will ensure all the proper cleansing occurs. If you move from your mark, we will have to do it all over again." This guard didn't sound tired like Declan. She did, however, sound like she didn't have time for screw-ups.

No prank. I faced the wall and stepped forward onto the painted block. While the shower flooring had bumps all over it—I assumed to keep us from falling down mid-shower and spilling contaminated blood everywhere—it was like the rest of the tile in the room: cold. Even after a few seconds of standing on my makeshift platform, it didn't warm to my body temperature. It just leeched heat from me. I shivered again.

"All right, ladies, eyes closed." The guard's order bounced off the walls and resonated in my chest. "Remember not to move. This first part is a bit of a shock."

She didn't give us time to process that. Probably smart on her part. Others would have spent the time thinking of the worst. I didn't have time to question why their process would include something requiring that type of warning.

Just as the last syllable left her mouth scalding water smacked me in the face. I caught myself before I leaped out of the burning deluge. It wasn't like being caught out in a chemical rainstorm. This was a different kind of burn. Our shower at home could never make water this hot. I could almost smell my skin searing, but refused to open my eyes and see what colors my flesh had shifted to. Like I needed blistered eyes, too.

As abruptly as the water started flowing, it ceased. I cracked my eyelids open, hopeful they wouldn't want to peel away after the scorching shower. White powder shot at me from a nozzle to the left. At least it wasn't hot. It did however smell like three-day-old breakfast —rotten eggs, stale sausage—and the dusting process made me feel like I was about to be breaded for dinner. At least oil wasn't involved thus far.

"Halfway there, ladies," the guard yelled out. What, was she a gym teacher in another life? I could picture her in a weight-lifting room. 'Just thirty more seconds. I know it hurts, girls, but it's a good pain. Fight through it.' Ugh. That's not what I needed.

I tried to think of it as an E.T.A. on when I'd get my clothes back, but I wasn't sure that was what she was talking about. Was it halfway through the powder process that caked my hair and made me want to sneeze, or halfway through being naked and letting people spray secret substances on me? I nearly wished she meant we were at the halfway point to being situated on Cloud Nine.

Oh God. Oh God. Oh God. The process officially became disgusting the second the powder free fall switched over to coating my body with thick, warm goo. It felt like warm peanut butter only stickier and something—my eyes were shut and I scrunched my face to keep any of whatever this was out—drizzled it over me. It traveled slowly downward until all of my skin was covered in a thick layer. It felt filthy. I didn't want to breathe. My pores were stifled and my lungs wanted to join them in solidarity. Instead I took slow, even breaths through my nose and prayed none of the sticky stuff would sneak up my nostrils. At least it didn't smell bad, though the scent of the last round of detoxification chemicals still sat heavy in the air.

With the drizzling complete, I stood there waiting for the next step. The others had been so rapid-fire there hadn't been time to think about anything. Now, I stayed on my black square, feet in a pool of tacky goo.

Seconds passed. Maybe minutes. I didn't know. When you were exposed and gross, time moved slower.

Finally our hostess gave us a little warning, "Hold your breaths. It's about to get hot right by your faces."

Why on earth did I see that as good news? Maybe this whole cleaning process was a big mind screw. A way to get you eager to do whatever pathetic thing they had planned because at least it was better than being doused with all sorts of weird substances while standing naked in a room full of strangers.

Clever folk.

She wasn't lying about the heat. The scalding water cut through the slime coating my face. If I hadn't felt the spray, I could have mistaken it for having marbles shot at my cheeks via pellet gun. The high-pressure water continued to assault me, working from my scalp all the way down to my toes. The pain was worth it to get that nasty stuff off my body.

Three loud beeps shook the room. "All clear. You may open your eyes." Our escort was back to a monotone voice. "Towels are at the end of each stall."

I snatched the towel off the closest hook, and then gave my hair a cursory drying before wrapping it around my torso. It was by far the softest fabric I'd ever felt. There were tiny loops of thread making it fluffy. The water pulled away from my body so quickly. I didn't know what the material was, but I wanted more.

The girl in the stall to the right commented on how white the towel was. She was right. I hadn't seen anything so bright in, well, ever. Given the bleached look to this place, that was less impressive than the functionality of the thing. How did we not have this at Ground Level? Was it something they made exclusively on Cloud Nine? If so, I'd take one as long as no one expected me to sit at a loom to make it.

I caught Leah's eyes across the room. She was running her fingers back and forth along the towel wrapped around her. She mouthed, "Awesome," at me. Leah would love making stuff like this.

Maybe there would be perks to this place. Or that pain shower addled my brain. Regardless, I was ready to get out of this room and put on some clothing.

Wrapped in our super soft towels, we exited through a door on the opposite side of the room. It opened silently at our approach and slid closed once our group had passed. My clothing, like all the other girls', was laid out on a chair for me. By the time I laced my boots, I was back to being angry about this place. If I was this supposed hot commodity worthy of recruitment, then why would they just order me around all day? Inwardly, I swore. This better be a one-day thing. I had a cap on asshole-tax-free days. This one already pushed my limits.

None of us bothered putting on jackets or goggles. I rather liked the less layered look, and from the reactions around the room, I wasn't alone. Once our group was suited up again, we went through another gateway and found the guys already waiting for us in an amphitheater.

Everyone aside from the four guards in the room had damp hair. At least we weren't the only ones subjected to that debacle. It's not that I took joy in the suffering of others, but I appreciated the potential for solidarity. After the torture we'd just endured, I knew the second we were without a protective detail I wouldn't be the only one saying, "Screw these guys."

If I was the only one, I had bigger problems ahead.

CHAPTER 7
BIGGER PROBLEMS AHEAD

Declan was back in charge. He towered above a lectern at the front of the room. The peak of the black, plastic stand hit just below his belt buckle. If I hadn't been so close to him earlier, I would have thought he was in a kids' room. Miniature lectern for six-year-olds, right this way.

Leah grabbed my arm and held tight. Maybe the shower burned a little fear into her. It wasn't the time to be smug, so I patted her hand and let her cling to me. We took seats in the second row. Leah sat as far back into her seat as possible, while I barely had my butt on the cushion. She still managed to keep her hand on my biceps though.

"Welcome to Cloud Nine: Orientation Level." Declan launched into a prepared speech. There was no inflection. He had the spiel memorized and, again, I was caught by how tired he sounded. Or maybe it was carelessness I heard. Either way, he didn't look happy to be here.

"You will not be moving into Cloud Nine proper for a few days." What? Do not tell me I went through a detox process that may have removed a few layers of epidermis to not even get to the stupid pod. "The oxygen levels are much higher in the actual station, and over the next few days, we will slowly increase the levels here. This will allow you to acclimate without feeling like someone is choking you out."

Hmm. That couldn't have been scripted and put Declan back firmly in my "you could be useful" file.

I had to admit, I was surprised to hear the air quality was so much better that we'd damn near suffocate if we went directly into it. I leaned over to Leah and whispered, "Did you know about this?"

She nodded, but kept her eyes fixed forward.

"Like about the delay in actually getting to Cloud Nine?"

She shushed me and muttered about talking later. Declan was watching me again, but he never stopped his monologue. Nice not to get called out, I supposed.

They dimmed the lights and showed the same film I'd seen twice a year for the last three years: The official Clean Air Development Act video. It used phrases like "Hope of Tomorrow" like the words alone would change lives. It showed maps of the pod locations across North America, with the biggest in New York, Chicago, and Dallas. Any place with high population density. Not a one was near mountains, which I always found odd. Seemed like if you're trying to get up high, it's worth starting at a place with real altitude. Instead they went for places like Phoenix, where I lived, because deep in a valley is the place you want to start building things that need to reach the stratosphere.

The video digressed into educational blather about the differences between the troposphere (Ground Level) and the stratosphere (Cloud Nine) and why we chose not to cross into the third layer of the atmosphere. That mesosphere was sketchy, if the video was to be believed.

I understood it was easier to build at this level. Twenty miles up put us about as close to the mesosphere as we could get without getting too toasty. It still required us gulping down huge amounts of energy to run air filters, but we got the benefit of living within a layer of ozone, which filtered out some of the nasty effects of the sun. Supposedly.

Everything I knew about the big ball of gas made me not want to see it. Seriously. Stare at it and it'll burn your retinas. It can sear your flesh; it just does it slower than acid rain. It makes you all sweaty. It was supposed to let you grow natural food, but textbooks always left out that history also told us it could torch crops, too. I was skeptical of the sun.

The video relied on subtle guilt, too. The first CAD pods had been filled with adults before they discovered that fully developed lungs were unable to adapt to the extreme changes in air quality. So not only were teens the only ones who could do the job, but we were tasked with finding a way to make it possible for adults to enjoy the fresh air, as it were.

The film wrapped up by telling us it took five years to build this station, but we had the power to give Earth hundreds of years back in return. The CAD program had been running for three years. Nothing had changed at Ground Level. In the safety of low lighting I rolled my eyes. Hard.

We can change things, but it's not like there's a magic wand to erase decades and decades of pollution and general environmental asshatery. My stance aside, I was game to play with their cool research toys. I bet they had excellent lab equipment. I could make use of that if they'd let me roam free. The longer I sat in the stadium seating, the less likely I thought any sort of fun was.

Declan returned to his puny lectern. The lights stayed dim, and he pulled a whisper-yell, "Turn on the damn lights, Steve." If there was contention, then these people were actually human. Hope reigned eternal.

As the lights flickered to luminescence, Declan was back on topic. "You've seen the video before. Not exactly new information. That's where I come in." He almost smiled. His face wanted to pull the corners of his mouth up, but the lock of his jaw wouldn't allow it. "It should come as no surprise to you that you'll have a duty on Cloud Nine. We all have tasks, which are primarily divided into four groups. The first is mine, Security and Order. This includes all the escorts you've met today, anyone else in these uniforms." He gestured to himself and the lapel of his shirt tightened at his chest. I probably shouldn't have been looking. "It also includes the community leaders. All your on-site leaders will have lived on Cloud Nine for at least two years and have been handpicked by governmental personnel at Ground Level. Don't expect that job."

I thought he might try to smile again. He didn't, but then neither did I.

"The next group is also obvious: Research. It's divided, for the most part, into teams focused on technology and biology/botany elements. Sometimes they work together. You may be assigned to either, and then switched back and forth at random. Research tasks vary widely based on your skill set."

Ominous much?

"The other two areas are less talked about, but vital to the success of Cloud Nine. Procurement focuses on the creation and distribution of items needed to live here. That means food, textiles, goods, and the like. Maintenance does exactly what you think."

I wondered if he made his bed every morning. Would I be required to make my bed? A bit of a wasted effort, if you asked me. What would Declan's reaction be if I asked him to make my bed for me? Would he laugh or try to deck me? I didn't know the protocol up here, and testing boundaries sounded like more and more fun the longer I had to sit through some dumb lecture.

"While your test scores are on file, we like to verify everything here, too. Our tests are slightly different than what you may have done at school. Not only are we looking for the areas of greatest aptitude, but we actually care what you might enjoy." He pierced me with his stare. Like bolts of steel had been shot through my shoulders, I pressed back against the chair and held damn still. "I know that may be surprising to some of you."

What did this guy have on me? It's not like I was some sort of vigilante. Yes, my school records would show fights. I didn't like people touching me. I didn't like them messing with my sister. But on the whole, they weren't my fault. I didn't start fights, as they say, I finished them. My grades were rock-star quality and I was sure if they had notes from my teachers they'd say nice things. I may not have liked being told what to do, but I greedily accepted any morsel of information anyone was willing to give. The smarter I was, the more in control I was. I wanted to be in charge of myself and to do that you had to be smarter or faster. I had every intention of being both.

A few minutes later they spaced everyone throughout the room and the standardized test forms came out. There was a nice block on chemistry and what should and shouldn't be combined in the making of everything from simple plastics to nerve gas.

The science section spilled over into how plants work. I regurgitated what I remembered from the small excursions to the greenhouse farms. Few plants lived even in those controlled conditions, so they were limited mostly to grains. Thinking about forcing chlorophyll to absorb artificial light made me yawn. Declan probably noticed, but I didn't look up to verify. His bird-of-prey style only made me more determined to find out what kind of warning these folks had about me.

After a couple of hours filling in tiny bubbles with a pencil, they deemed the science portion complete. Thank goodness because that meant lunch. This was one of those times when I was pleased my body held anxiety in places other than my stomach. Leah might complain about my knee bouncing nonstop, but I was going to scarf whatever food they put in front of me.

Transferring to Cloud Nine was already proving to be a huge energy suck.

CHAPTER 8
TOO TRUSTING

So much for epic food.

The fancy towels had gotten my hopes up. When I stared down into the plastic bowl, I wondered where they found this stuff. Some kind of ground meat with flecks of red and green to it—what could make it speckled like that?—sat atop white rice and chunks of green stuff.

It wasn't the dehydrated clumps they'd transitioned into the schools two years ago. The letters sent home noted the change was due to limited crops in our local greenhouses. The last broadcast from the governor's ball showed them eating real food, though. Now I was part of their cabal and still being served sketchy food.

When others filled the seats at my table there was only minor hesitation before digging in. Even Leah shrugged at my questioning look and pushed her fork into the food.

When did she become the brave one?

I gave the food a chance, and it made my eyes want to water. In a good way. Sparks ignited on my tongue and I crossed my fingers all the food was going to be celebratory like this. I struggled to remember the last time I ate something with any type of spice.

"You two sisters?" The girl directly across the round table from me held her fork mid-air; crumbles of firework meat fell back down into her bowl.

My mouth was full. Leah took advantage to provide an enthusiastic response.

"Right on. That's my brother over there." The girl pointed to a short boy with shaggy black hair sitting at the other round table. "Day one and he's already trying to distance himself from his big sister."

"Maybe he just didn't want to be at a table with girls," Leah suggested. Always the one to try to find a happy medium.

I finally swallowed my forkful of awesome. "He's, what, four years younger than you? He's probably over there bragging to those guys that he has the in with you."

We shared a conspiratorial big sister smile. Leah pretended she was in on it. She wasn't.

"I'm Charlie." She had to be seventeen or eighteen, which was great because my survey of the room put me a little on the old side.

"I'm Ally." I wanted to ask what she was in for, as though Cloud Nine was a punishment. There were times when you met people and clicked. I hoped that was true with Charlie, but I wasn't going to risk it by calling out how much I didn't want to be there. As she pointed out, it was still day one.

Our name exchange got the others to join in. The first-day awkwardness wouldn't fully dissipate, but we could make it ebb a bit. Aside from Leah, Charlie, and me, there was another girl and a guy at our table. The girl's name was Roseann. She seemed nice enough, but I immediately identified her as someone to avoid. I didn't want to be that jerk who told her to shut up because her rodent-chirp voice drove me crazy. I would absolutely end up doing that.

The brave guy sitting with the four girls was Dave. He was my age, but the way he poked at his food made him appear younger. I'd considered he was skeptical of the cooking, but he'd had a few bites. He stayed sullen and didn't seem to care one way or another what we chittered about.

"Were you surprised we're not going to be in the real Cloud Nine for a few days?" Charlie asked the question I'd been too chicken to say aloud.

Leah answered before I had the chance. Again. "Totally. It wasn't in the enrollment papers, but makes sense, right?"

No, sister, it didn't make sense to keep a standard process a secret. I shook my head slightly and saw Charlie's lips quirk up. Glad someone else knew what it was like to have a blurt-y kid sister, I joined the conversation. "Right." What was I supposed to say? "I'm more curious what the plans are for the next few days. We haven't seen where we'll be sleeping yet."

Roseann chimed in. "I think I saw a room with bunks when I escaped for the bathroom earlier." Maybe she sounded more like a bird than a rodent. Or I was just giving her extra credit for scouting the sleeping arrangements.

"I could do bunks." Dave's voice was deeper than I expected. For some reason that made Leah look at him more closely. She should aim for a guy with more than sulking skills.

"I can handle that temporarily, but you know there's going to be at least one snorer in the bunch." This felt almost normal. Eating weird, tear-inducing food and talking with other teenagers. Normal.

They laughed and something in my chest relaxed.

"Laugh now. Ally snores real loud." Leah tried to follow up on my laugh, but it only won her smiles.

"We both do, actually. On the upside, we're sound sleepers."

"So you're saying it's best if we force you two to share a room for the sake of the group?" Charlie grinned. "How noble."

"You can crash with us, but you need to be able to sleep through drilling on metal. I mean if you have that skill, you're more than welcome."

"I bet there is a test for that." Charlie quipped. Was she talking about the damn fill-in-the-dot ones or the kind that required an ointment afterward?

"After two days of walking, I thought they'd at least give us decent beds." Enter Dave the Mood Killer.

My sister reached out to him. Her hand grazed his arm before he could pull back. "That sucks. Where did you have to come from?"

"Prescott." He didn't look up.

I wanted Leah to look at me. My eyes probably blinked yellow hazard lights.

But, of course, she just trudged on.

"In three days? That's kind of amazing." Why was she beaming at this dolt?

"Light rail down into the valley first." I stared holes in the back of Leah's head, but still managed to see Dave shifting his weight. Either he was as uncomfortable with these questions as I was, or he was lying. Maybe both.

"Oh, that makes sense." Really, Leah? No, it didn't. "We just had a short walk." She was about to say more when I kicked the back of her calf. She shot me a dirty look, but kept her mouth shut.

Leah didn't understand how people could use information against you. There's a reason she wouldn't have been admitted to Cloud Nine without me and it had nothing to do with her age. She's smart enough, but didn't get that knowledge puts people in control. If these people knew where we were from, they'd know more than how far we had to walk. They'd know about our tolerance to air exposure. They'd know how much money we made. They'd know what kind of schools we'd attended. And they'd have a damn good idea if we contributed to the horrific toxins in the air.

I didn't want anyone to know those things. Maybe these people were just being friendly like Leah. Maybe they didn't want leverage on us. Maybe they wouldn't guess that our families still had organic materials in our houses. Maybe they wouldn't figure out the government had used our house as an apology for failing our family seven years ago. I wasn't ready to give anyone that kind of trust.

Leah slumped in her chair. If she jutted out her bottom lip, everyone would have seen the pout. I wished for an easy way to make her understand the danger. She was too trusting, and that didn't put only her at risk.

Back home when new friends discovered I lived in the historic district they asked questions. Never fail, one would come over and misread the bamboo and oak in our home for wealth and not understand why I couldn't share. It wouldn't take long before they'd pull away, before they'd taunt the girl who only had nice things because the government gave them to her.

My attempt to kill the conversation with a kick fell flat. Roseann, who seemed genuinely curious and about as naïve as my sister, asked where we were from. Dave was paying too much attention.

"Far enough that we had stupid bug eyes when we got here." I shot Leah what I hoped was a subtle look to keep her fool mouth shut. "As thorough as the process has been today, I'm glad there weren't photo IDs shot at the door."

"I was so sure they'd take pictures, too." Charlie paused. The edge of her lip slipped into her mouth, like she was biting too hard on her cheek.

"I bet they had to wait. We all looked like we were wearing garbage bags when we showed up." Roseann's concerns did not mirror mine at all.

Leah didn't seem too impressed with her either. Unfortunately, she had used my distraction to start a conversation full of whispers with Dave. Really? Day one and she was making problems for me. Part of the big sister gig meant watching out for her, but c'mon. This trip wasn't on my list of dream vacations and now I'd have to worry about protecting her, too.

I took a deep breath in, fighting the wince at air rushing past my still-razed throat and leaned forward to butt in on their conversation. Only then Dave stood and asked if everyone was done eating. He took our plastic trays, piled them upon his own, and then walked off to turn them into the recycling team. I appreciated his diligence, but hoped his timing was coincidental.

I decided to keep my eyes on him from here on out, just to be sure. Despite his short, staccato replies he talked to my sister more than anyone else in the group. Making friends had always come easily to Leah, though. It was completely plausible she'd have a whole new set of friends by the end of the week and have forgotten about the sulking guy at our lunch table.

Just as Dave returned to the table, Declan appeared at the doorway, flagging everyone to get up and move back to the amphitheater.

"Make sure there are at least three seats between you and your neighbor." I didn't understand the need for the super secrecy in this format. It wasn't like we hadn't already been accepted to the program. They knew what I was good at and their little clipboards likely had all sorts of notes on me.

I wouldn't have been surprised if Declan came by to ask if my elbow hurt during weather pattern shifts after the break three years ago. The way he watched me made it clear he knew a whole lot more about me than I knew about him. Not that it was hard to accomplish; I didn't even know the guy's last name. Weren't military types supposed to have their names stitched on their clothing somewhere? Or was that underwear? I wasn't up for any scenario today that required me seeing what was written in Declan's undies, so I focused on the crisp white paper in front of me.

The starkness of this place jarred me. The paper was so brilliant it reflected back the halogens overhead. Even the fancy paper mom bought to write to Aunt June had a soft yellow tint. How much bleach did they have to use to get the page so white? Seemed like it would have to be enough to offset all the environmental good the air filters did, right? Today wasn't the day to question their whitening techniques, though. They hadn't even let me through the real door yet. The jerks.

Still, I compared my test and answer sheets closely. Flippancy aside, my competitive nature drove me to take these things too seriously. I wanted to win. And a little part of me worried if I was lazy with this test, they would put me on cleaning duty. I really didn't want to scrub toilets.

The latest test covered history. I could argue—but wouldn't aloud —that this test was also about science. Everything covered talked about foreign or extinct plants, the techniques for raising crops and livestock, what happened when the steel mills shut down, why nanotechnologies were limited to governmental facilities, the ways our world changed when we tried to make our own fuels in lieu of fossil ones. In all, it was an epic downer.

It made me so sad to have to answer question after question about the great scientists who tried to save our planet and instead burdened us with a polluted atmosphere that blocked out the sun. There was a section on that, too. Referencing allegorical stories about the sun, testing how much we knew from what always struck me as nothing more than fables.

I hadn't seen a single window in this place yet. Was I expected to earn a view here? If all Cloud Nine's posters at my high school were to be trusted, sunlight was part of the deal. I wasn't so much excited about being blasted with some skull-scouring, bright light, but I wondered what it looked like above the roiling green and grey clouds. Would it be just as dark? I had always imagined the tops of the clouds were softer and warmer. I had no basis for this belief. Just a hunch. From the looks of this level of the station, I would have to wait until my real admittance to Cloud Nine to get a peek outdoors. I am not a patient woman.

My wrist twinged as I continued pressing my tiny bit of lead against the page, marking answer after answer. Nothing became clearer from their questions. To me, everything read as science, but I was sure there was nuance my brain missed. With Leah's complete lack of science skills—I mean, she knew the basic stuff, but hated the thought of a physics course—I wondered how painful these tests were for her. She might be able to tweak them to her own benefit. She did like telling stories, so I mentally crossed my fingers and hoped she was able to parlay that into a job that did not require her to push a broom up and down the corridors.

Not that there is anything wrong with that, but she was such a people person a solitary gig like that would make her batty. Then she'd be chatting up every person she encountered. This would lead to everyone knowing too much and probably her getting in trouble for not staying on task. Hmm. Maybe tomorrow's battery of tests would include something to tell them not to leave her alone. I rebelled under a watchful eye, but Leah thrived when someone set clear expectations and then stayed with her through the process. She's big on teamwork. Probably the reason she had too many friends and not enough confidants.

Despite all the time I spent mentally railing against this whole tests-upon-tests thing, I finished early. It's not like I could get up and leave though. A guard collected my paper and muttered for me to sit quietly. It was the female guard who escorted our little posse through the scalding shower process. My skin was still tender. She didn't look at me when taking the papers from my hand. I liked to think seeing me naked and damn near tarred and feathered was awkward for her. I licked my lips to keep from smiling.

I slid down in my seat until my knees pressed against the chair in front of me and let my head fall back to rest on the cushion behind me. The ceiling had steel beams running parallel across the room. No one had blasted them with white. The flash of silver was the first color I'd seen in the structure. Seeing the cool metal warmed a part of me. This whole place might not be sterile and plastic. At least the ore that created that girder came from the earth. Smelted, sure, but a hint organic.

"Could you stop that?" Declan had mastered putting inflection into a whisper.

His face obstructed my view of the ceiling. "Stop what?" I asked.

He arched a brow and looked at my knees. Were joints suddenly offensive now? My gaze followed his. My right knee battered the back of the seat in front of me. I hadn't realized my twitch was showing. I needed to be doing something or I was going to leak energy all over this place in shakes and snaps. I forced my leg still. Only then did I realize the chair had been making minute squeaks with each move-ment. I doubted Declan had heard it from the front of the room. More likely it was an excuse to hassle me. I wasn't the only one without anything to do. Only three others were still marking their pages.

Declan didn't bother with a polite thank you, but just turned to walk away.

In a stage whisper I called, "You're welcome." His shoulders bunched up. My voice carried well.

It only took another fifteen minutes before Declan called things done for the day. We took a circuitous route through what Declan called the Orientation Level of Cloud Nine.

The long walk to our bunks didn't give me nearly enough informa-tion. We passed closed doors, windows with the blinds shut, and a whole lot of white walls. I did get to peek in one room before anyone noticed I was lagging, but it gave little information, too. It was the world's most disappointing gym. A treadmill, a scale, and a box for doing stair-step exercises. I hoped they had something better when we completed this beginners' crap because I needed more of a workout than hotfooting it on a conveyer belt.

It took us an additional ten minutes to make it over to the dormitory portion of the level. Our bags were lined along one side of the hallway. One of the girls immediately went for her bag, but a guard I didn't recognize stopped her.

There were three rooms for us to sleep in. Leah immediately grabbed my hand as Declan announced the breakdown of the sleeping arrangements: three people in each room, one group of four. He didn't say anything about dividing by gender and I was impressed. Leah would later tell me he was probably forgetful after the long day. His shoulders sagged like he was ready to be done with us, but I'd watched him enough to know that Declan was an attention-to-detail type of guy. They just didn't care if we went co-ed in the rooms.

I, however, did care. I would have been fine sharing a room with a guy or two, but I was less comfortable with Leah doing so. Particularly as Dave looked in her direction. I shot him the look: Move along, buddy. Charlie skirted the edge of the wall and moved closer to me.

"Mind if I bunk with you guys?" While everyone else in the room was loudly hammering out details of who would sleep where, Charlie pitched her voice low. She didn't whisper or sound meek, but like she knew better than to let others know her plans. She could definitely room with us.

"Sure thing." I nudged Leah and let her know we had our third.

Leah did not have the stealth skills Charlie possessed. No. My sister waved her arm in the air. "Sir! Sir! We've got our group."

Declan nodded in her direction but didn't look up. She lowered her arm slowly as the female guard came our way.

"All right, ladies." Ladies? I was wearing combat boots. Where did they find this woman? "You get room 421."

We were allowed to grab our duffle bags from the hallway. I didn't make a big deal of it, but I wanted to be sure my picture frame made it okay. I worried their over-the-top decontamination process might have warped the wood. Then, there was always the possibility they didn't allow organics up here. I snagged the handle and kept the bag close enough to brush my knee.

The guard, I overheard someone call her Deb, escorted us in and then gave us the most pointless tour. The room had three twin-sized beds built into the walls and a small door in the back led to a bathroom with a toilet, sink, and a tiny shower stall.

Not exactly a place we could get lost in.

I threw my bag onto the bed closest to the door. The duffle ate about two-thirds of my future sleep space. I guessed I would curl up at night or have cold toes. The walls didn't impress me with their sound-proofing, but I picked the equivalent of a guard post bed because I wanted to be sure I would know what was happening in the hall.

Leah bounced on the bed next to the bathroom. The look she gave it told me she was sizing it up for toiletry storage purposes, which was about the dumbest concern one could have now. We didn't know what the next few days held, much less what was going to happen to us when we actually made it to Cloud Nine proper. We might hate it. Maybe we'd be locked in windowless rooms for the next three years and slowly go crazy. My sister should have been more concerned about becoming the weird girl who crafted dolls out of human hair than if there would be space for more than one hairbrush.

Whatever. Charlie watched Leah, too. I didn't know if she was as irritated by the excess of levity my sister was giving the situation. I hoped she wasn't as all about Cloud Nine as the others. I'd heard the far table talking at lunch. They were so excited about the possibilities. They were so hopeful about all the good they could do. From the sound of their conversations, you'd think they'd crack the key to climate change the first day.

Doubtful. They all seemed bright enough—except for that Dave kid, who would slow everyone's progress by whining the whole time —but we hadn't even seen the research they've been doing. You can't expect to build on others' work without reviewing it. That's, like, science 101.

Charlie, though, had kept quiet about the possibilities for our future. It was clear to me she was listening to everyone else run their mouths. She took it all in like some epic spy. She knew information was power, too. However, that didn't mean she didn't want to be here. So far I had no indication that anyone other than little ol' me thought this place was a stratospheric sinkhole.

CHAPTER 9
WE DON'T KNOW WHAT THEY CAN DO

We didn't get much time to settle in. They let us dump our bags, and had everyone back out in the hallway within ten minutes.

I glanced down the corridor but didn't see any sign of Declan. Our guard, Deb, was there with two of the others whose names I didn't know. Deb took control quickly, which I gathered was kind of her thing.

"You'll have more time to take things out of your bags and such tonight. You'll only be in these rooms for two nights, so don't get too comfortable, or"—she narrowed her eyes at the girl who tried to snag her bag early—"try to personalize the room by sticking crap on the walls. You'll just have to take it down."

I snorted, but not loudly enough to draw too much attention. Charlie winked at me. Okay, so one person heard it.

"Now, I'm going to show you how to get to the mess hall. Mostly because it's time to eat and I'm starving." Deb feigned a smile, but it was far from real. She'd be great to play poker with. I'd take all her money. Quickly. Rich Ally in two-point-five seconds.

Deb took off to the right and a few steps later took a sharp left turn. I hadn't even realized there was a corner up there. It made me wonder about the real reason the walls were so barren. Maybe this place really was about messing with your mind. Or someone's mind, anyway. I heard they did the same kinds of things in prisons. Lots of turns for no reason, lack of signage and the like. If you made it in and didn't know where you were going, it'd be much harder to make it out. I crossed my fingers that it was a precaution they took only on this level. I didn't want to have to resort to drawing maps in my everyday life. As it was, I was mentally noting how long it took to get to each corner.

We'd made two lefts, a right and another left to make it to the dining hall. This one wasn't the same as the place we had lunch. Instead of the two six-seat round tables, the room held three long ones. Each could probably sit twelve people. Had there ever been enough recruits in a single class to fill this room? I bet it was damn noisy.

It took me a moment to realize there were already a few people seated in the room, in the far corner. Each wore the same charcoal pants the other guards wore, but their tops were more casual. A couple wore tee shirts, and another a pullover jacket. They didn't look up when we entered, or when Deb started talking again.

"This mess hall is not yours." Boy, she had a way with words. Deb pointed to the people in the back. "Anyone who works on this level eats here. That means I eat here, too. I expect you to be respectful. These people are working and don't have time to answer your questions right now."

Yes, because I was so going to run to them and ask how much they loved being here. Idiot. They were quiet at the fringes of the room, but even if they weren't, the way several held hands told me these people had other priorities. Though, I was curious about why others not helping the new folk adjust needed to work on this level. Then I remembered how many shut doors we passed on the way to the dorms. Maybe this floor had multiple purposes.

"Do not horde food. I always feel like I shouldn't have to say this, but if I don't one of you will stockpile stuff for no reason." Deb hated her job. Or us. Maybe both. "There will be plenty to eat every night. It's all pretty good."

She was right about the food being good. Our dinner meal had noodles, which you can get on Ground Level for more money than was sane to spend on a meal. They were soaked in this bright orange sauce and mixed with soft stuff of varying colors. I didn't know what everything in my bowl was, but the taste exploded in my mouth. I scarfed the whole thing too quickly and then had to down an extra glass of water to help my body adjust to all the yum I threw at it.

Eating like this almost made me curious about what the food workers in the procurement department did all day. I hadn't paid much attention to Declan's pitch for them, because chemistry for the win, but I did like the idea of finding out what all these foods were and how you matched them. That's kind of like chemistry. Finding the right pairings to make a whole new flavor. Maybe I was just trying to make everything about me. Mom said I did that sometimes.

A sourness rolled my stomach and it had nothing to do with my overeating. I hoped Mom made it back home without any burns. She was awful about bundling up appropriately. I was still mad at her, but I was rather used to keeping up with everyone and making sure they were safe. One day in and the distance from my routine of flipping locks, checking for tears in clothing and the like was throwing me off my game.

At least they put something on the walls in the mess hall to distract me. There were standard posters for the Clean Air Development Act with happy people looking like they really loved living on a platform twenty miles away from their families. I thought I'd escaped those types of ads when I came here. I didn't think seeing pictures of other people doing their job and looking happier about it would boost morale on the station. Based on the stoic faces of the Cloud Niners in the dining room, I'd say they were not as cheery as those grinning in the posters.

But what did I know? It's not like I was allowed to talk to them.

We walked back to our dorm rooms mostly unescorted. It let me breathe.

Mostly. The air here was different. Lighter. I inhaled and swore I had to force my lungs to hold it down for a moment or it would run away. It wasn't bad, but definitely required more work than I was used to. However, I wasn't about to say anything about it. I didn't want more scrutiny and my gut said it was normal. They warned us they were tweaking the air, upping our oxygen, decreasing the ozone and such. As long as the room didn't start to spin, I was keeping my concerns to myself.

Back in the dorm room, Leah immediately dug through her bag. I had no idea what she was looking for, but her eyes were wide. If something was missing from that bag, I wouldn't have been surprised if she toppled over from the sheer horror. When she pulled out a toothbrush, I had to fight the urge to pull off my boot and fling it at her head.

She darted a look over her shoulder at me. How did she always know when I was contemplating sister abuse? "That dinner made my breath foul."

I just nodded.

"Yours is probably rank, too, you know. Maybe you should do something about it."

It might have been, but I didn't have plans to get close enough to anyone this evening for them to complain about funky breath. Besides, I had never had this taste in my mouth. I wanted to savor it. Was that weird?

Leah brushed her teeth for five minutes. I reminded her two was sufficient, but she ignored me. Once she deemed her breath non-deadly, she headed out into the hallway to mingle.

I did not want to mingle.

Charlie entered the room just as Leah left. "You don't want to meet your fellow recruits?" A wry smile played at the corner of her mouth.

"Will you judge me if I say no?"

"Of course, I'll judge you." She tried to deadpan it, but that smile was already taking over. "Verdict: Smart."

I smiled back at her. "Thanks. I'm just not in the mood to pretend this is summer camp."

"Your sister sure is." Charlie was looking out the door. I peeked around the corner see Leah chatting up two girls we hadn't met. My sister's hands were flying, which meant she was in the middle of telling a story. Hopefully, it was something inane.

"Yes." Leah didn't need my watching right now. There were guards for that. I pushed myself back on my bed until my shoulders hit the wall. "Are you sure you don't want to find out what everyone's plans are?"

"Not any more than I would want to know what their favorite colors are." Charlie mirrored my seating and got comfortable on her bed directly across from mine.

"Are you saying you don't care about my favorite color? But that's vital to my essence." My mock horror carried in our small room, but couldn't drown out the ramble coming from the hallway.

"Pssh. Your favorite color is black." She paused and tilted her head at me. When I nodded in approval, she continued, "I'm more worried about adjusting. And not just to this weird air thing."

I nodded again. "What worries you?" My list was long, but I wasn't ready to share. I suppose it was a dick move to expect her to do what I wouldn't.

"Tests."

That wasn't what I expected.

"Tests? They aren't at the top of my worries. I rather got the impression they're doing them to kill time while we acclimate. Do they really need to check my knowledge of chemical bonding agents when they already have years of test scores from my school to tell them it's kind of my thing?"

The way Charlie looked at me then was unnerving. Almost like she was trying to pry into my brain.

"I think it's more about determining differences between people." She fidgeted. Her eyes kept contact with mine, but her hands plucked at the rough sheets on her bed. "Nuances. I think they do a whole lot more up here than we have any way of imagining, and those tests could put us to work doing something we don't know or are really uncomfortable with."

Hot damn. She was right.

How had I never considered this? Would I have any say over what kind of work I did? What if I thought it was sketchy? I was not going to test anything on rats. Standard protocol or not. Crap. Now I felt like an idiot.

I tried to contain my momentary panic, but a touch spilled into my words. "I hadn't considered that, which is surprising. I thought I'd worked all the angles on this."

Her smile said she saw too much. "I've had months to contemplate how this might go down."

Months? "How did you delay the move so long?"

"Parent issues. My mom kept filing extensions, which was fine by me. I was in no rush to move, but eventually, they gave her a now-or-never talk and the next day, I was on my way here."

"My mom couldn't wait to get my butt up here." Ugh. I sounded almost as sullen as that Dave guy.

"I think mine loved the idea, just not the following through part." Charlie shrugged. "It's easy to say you want this better life for your kid, but a whole lot harder to ship them off for the same reason."

I hadn't thought of my mom as strong in any of this. Charlie's point earned me a pang of guilt deep in my chest. "You're probably right, but did you get to discuss things?"

"Yeah. She talked about it with me and about how I'd be solving the world's problems." Her derisive laugh matched mine.

"My mom used that exact same phrase. Maybe it's in some guidebook they give parents."

"Like the 'So you're launching your child into the stratosphere' pamphlet."

"I'm surprised we haven't been given a heavy orientation guide to read through on our downtime."

"I expect it's still coming." She looked out the doorway again, but her attention snapped back to me immediately. I liked that she was keeping an eye out.

"Agreed. Possibly after we get designations. They probably have eight versions of the thing."

"It's all about bureaucracy." She shook her head for a moment. "And really awkward and painful showers."

I slammed my palm down on the bed. The soft thump did not adequately convey my enthusiasm. "Was that not the most intense detox ever?"

"I've read more books than you can guess about the ways chemicals can latch onto our bodies, but I've never read anything that suggested being coated with sticky stuff and then blasted with scalding water was the way to nullify them."

"What do you think it was? The goo, I mean." There went my mouth, opening before I'd thought things through. I liked feeling as though I could trust Charlie, but simple camaraderie didn't mean she shouldn't have to earn it.

"I honestly don't know." She pursed her lips and held the scrunched face long enough to tempt me to make a joke about it staying that way. "I expect it's something they developed in the CAD program. Though, I have no idea if it's something from here or Chicago or wherever."

That made sense. Mostly. "Why wouldn't they use it everywhere then?"

She sucked in her lips and held her breath, but failed to hold back a snort of laughter.

"Other than the whole naked and burning flesh thing." Wow. Not my best addendum.

Her exhale deflated her like a balloon. Charlie's shoulders fell forward and her chin dropped toward her chest. "It makes us too clean." Her voice was so hushed I itched to close our door all the way to block out the outside clamor. "I think."

That wasn't helpful. I scooted off my bed and walked over to hers. I sat next to her. I wanted to know what she had to say, but I also wanted this to be a private conversation. We needed to be in real whisper distance to make that happen. "What," I said, and then paused, a little scared of the question I wanted to ask. "What do you mean?"

"The air is cleaner here, right? That's the whole reason our moms wanted us to take the shuttle up." She swallowed loud enough for me to hear. "What if what they scrubbed from us this morning is something that you can't escape from down there? No matter where we go at Ground Level—inside, outside—we can't escape certain chemicals."

"That doesn't surprise me, but the fact that they'd believe this bubble capable of keeping out things at that level just feels..." I hesitated. I didn't know if I wanted to say it felt dirty or overly idealistic. I went with, "wrong."

"Maybe." The turn of her shoulders and the way she stared into the distance told me the word didn't match her thoughts.

"The air in here isn't manufactured." As far as I knew. Though, I had to note everything I knew about Cloud Nine came from school projects and textbooks. "The massive filters they use still bring in air from outside. Do you think they are able to do the goo-and-burn cleaning to the air they pull in?"

She finally looked at me. Unshed tears welled over her hazel eyes. "We don't know what they can do up here."

Wasn't that the truth?

CHAPTER 10
THE SAGE INCIDENT

What the hell was that?

I bolted upright in bed and scanned the room.

Leah was sleeping.

Charlie was sleeping.

A hard thump. My head snapped toward the far wall.

Heavy breathing. A muttered, "Oh God, oh God, oh God."

Secure in knowing my sister was safely asleep, I threw the covers back and pulled on the pants I left draped at the foot of the bed.

I only had to take four steps to the door. Opening it increased the volume.

Another thump. And again. How was there no one in the hallway? Weren't there guards watching us to make sure we weren't hoarding food or being jerks or whatever? I stepped onto the cold tile floor and closed my dorm room door behind me. Charlie would keep an eye on Leah if she woke up.

Our room was the furthest to the right, so I started to the left.

Whimpering. Second door.

I probably should have knocked, but then people should just lock their doors if they don't want others to come in. I pushed it open and tried not to gag at the overwhelming scent of rust. One of the girls

Leah was talking with earlier in the night lay at my feet. Black liquid pooled at her shoulder.

Screw her sleeping roommates. Who on Earth slept through this? I slashed my hand to the right and slammed it on the light switch. The bulbs overhead lit immediately and the stark reality of vibrant life, blood, red and sticky, pouring out of the girl became real.

The girl's cries intensified when I turned on the lights. She probably saw just how bad it was.

I dropped to my knees next to her and tried to calm her with nonsense cooing for a moment.

"What's your name?" I asked while tilting her onto her back. She yelped. One of her roommates told us to keep it down. If I didn't have my hands on a bloodied girl, I would have punched her. Hard.

The girl in my hands didn't answer, but returned to whimpering instead. I asked again, and this time she eked out, "Sage."

"It's okay, Sage. I'm going to take care of you." Crap. A deep, jagged wound cut across her shoulder and down onto her upper arm. "Can you tell me what happened?"

"I-I-I don't know." Her sobs were becoming ragged.

I tore away the bottom of my sleep shirt. "Shh. We'll figure it out."

She started to calm a bit, so I kept talking. "I'm going to wrap this tight around the wound. It isn't going to feel great, but it'll stop the blood." So I didn't have stellar bedside manner. Don't judge.

I lifted her shoulder and began winding the fabric around her shoulder and arm. Her wail shook the heavy polycarbonate door behind me.

It only took seconds before one of the guys from the room next door was standing behind me. "Can you shut her up?"

This time, since I had finished wrapping her laceration, I twisted and drove my elbow into his shin. Jerk deserved it.

I didn't look back to see his reaction. I knew how much a strike to the bone hurt, and I had more urgent matters. I pressed the heel of my hand down on Sage's newly bandaged arm and leaned into it. She whined but handled the discomfort better than expected. "Instead of being an insensitive jerk, maybe you could be helpful and call for Declan," I called to the guy hissing behind me.

"I'm here." I looked over my shoulder to see the standard-issue guard pants. A quick glance up confirmed the head honcho had finally made it. Was I seriously the only one who heard this girl get hurt and fall all over the damn place?

"About time." I probably shouldn't have said it, but surprisingly he didn't give me any chastising. Even the guy in charge had to accept sometimes other people were right.

I returned my focus to Sage's arm. I could feel moisture coating my palm. I upped the pressure.

"I'm going to need something else to stop the bleeding. She's already gone through my shirt."

Declan looked at my exposed stomach instead of Sage's arm bleeding out under my hand. I chalked it up to understanding where the bandage came from.

"You," he pointed at one of Sage's roommates. "Bring all the hand towels from the bathroom out here." She didn't move. "Now."

She scurried off. Declan spoke into a handheld comm. I hadn't known they had those here. They were highly restricted at Ground Level, and such a small place shouldn't need them. Still, at the moment, I was grateful.

"Medics are on their way." He kneeled next to me. I noticed the other kids had gathered in the hall. Great. Now that things were under control, everyone was up to rubberneck at the injured girl. People could be so pathetic.

Towels were dropped onto my hands. I caught Declan rolling his eyes. He took the towels away and folded them by thirds lengthwise, then again by thirds the other way. "Hands up." I lifted away from Sage's shoulder. Tears tracked down her cheeks, but her cries had quelled to soft moans.

Declan placed the first folded towel on her shoulder and my hands pressed down on it immediately. I wanted to staunch the blood. If the amount collecting in my pants from sitting beside her was any indication, she couldn't afford to give out any more.

"Do you know what happened to her?" In another situation, I'd be miffed on Sage's behalf. There we were, hovering over her and talking about her like she wasn't there. Only, in a way, she kind of wasn't. Her eyelids fluttered and I worried she might lose consciousness.

I shook my head. "She said she didn't know, but she wasn't exactly with it at the time."

"Did you check her for a concussion?"

"When would I have done that?" I looked up at him, the embers of rage already igniting behind my eyes.

"You said she fell. Did you check for a head wound?" He was slipping his hands beneath Sage's head. I wouldn't be surprised if he found a goose egg. From the look of things, she fell more than once before I found her.

"I checked for the source of all the blood covering the floor. Her head wasn't bleeding, so my attention went to the gaping hole at her shoulder." It was so difficult not to want to pop him one. "It's called triage."

He grunted instead of replying. For the best.

The medics arrived. Finally. It could have been the noise of the nosy onlookers covering their approach or the fact they wore all white—the most effective camouflage in this place—but the two women appeared out of nowhere.

One dropped to her knees next to me and turned to Declan for a rundown. He impressed me by directing her to talk with me. He stepped out into the hall. It might have been his own form of triage. I guessed there was paperwork to fill out if one of the new additions got banged up on day one.

I gave the woman the same rundown I had given Declan, though with much less spite. She was going to do things and based on her labored breathing, I had a good feeling she wasn't used to being on this level with its decreased oxygen. Not her fault she didn't hear Sage flopping about in here.

The medic's hands replaced mine on the rolled-up towel. Her partner encouraged everyone go to back to their rooms so they could maneuver her onto the stretcher and take her to an infirmary. I moved to the hallway, but wanted to make sure Sage was really being taken care of. There was nothing about the medics' behavior to make me think otherwise, but I couldn't override the need to be sure.

Leah peeked out from our doorway to watch me. I was about to tell her to go to bed when I saw a hand touch her shoulder. Charlie must have convinced her because Leah was out of my view a second later. The door didn't close, but I wouldn't have done that either.

"Thanks for taking care of her," the taller medic said. "She's going to be fine. We'll get her stitched up, and hopefully, we'll find out what happened."

"Okay. I didn't see whatever she cut herself on." Cut. Now that was an understatement, but something about the medic's laissez-faire tone had seeped into my brain.

"I'm sure it was a fluke thing. Maybe something broke in her bag on the way here." She said that like it made sense. I didn't bother calling her on it, because if she thought a broken thing in someone's bag could rip deep and jagged into a girl's shoulder then she wasn't exactly the brightest bulb.

Instead, I nodded and tried to keep from giving her a look that told her how much I didn't believe her story.

I guessed it worked, because she said, "Head back to your room. We need the hallway clear to move her out."

Really? It was six feet wide. I was pretty sure they could have walked by me with ease, but like everything else here I had to acknowledge their goofy protocol.

I shuffled off toward my temporary room. I could see Leah lying on her bed, staring at the ceiling. The chances she heard all the gossip from the hallway were high. Seeing as I found the girl, I would have to argue with all the crazy versions of the truth my sister cultivated. I stood at the door pulling in slow deep breaths and wishing the air were heavy enough to galvanize me.

I was about to step in when someone called out from down the hallway. I looked to my left and Declan was poking his head out of a doorway.

CHAPTER 11
MORE RIGHT HOOK THAN CHARM

think I just stared at Declan. Was he really trying to be all covert? His, "Psst. Hey," was not quiet in the least. He was lucky we were the only ones in the area. I checked behind me to make sure the medics weren't moving Sage yet. They weren't.

Declan called for my attention again, and jerked his head back in the international sign for "come here." Part of me rallied to the thought of ignoring him and going to bed. That's what I was supposed to do, right? Curiosity won out. Better to find out what he wanted than spend the night flopping in bed thinking about what I could have learned had I taken the fifteen steps to meet with him.

As soon as I began walking his way, he disappeared into the room. I couldn't even see the door from this angle. The architect who built this place must have been shifty. I'd have to see if that showed up in any library materials.

Declan sat at a basic A-frame desk. It was pushed against a far wall, and he spun his chair around to face me. It didn't look like anyone worked out of this room. It had a couple plastic chairs, like the ones in the dining hall, and a single bed built into the wall. Not too different from the dorm I was supposed to be sleeping in, except it was built for one instead of three.

"Nice work tonight." Declan leaned forward to rest his elbows on his knees like some sort of inspirational soccer coach.

I wasn't buying it. "Thanks." I looked away. I was going to try to keep from calling him out on making me do someone else's job.

"It would be nice if you could help people without knocking around the others though." He sounded amused. I flicked a glance his way. Yep. He was smiling.

"Well, if anyone else had been paying attention, I wouldn't have needed to tend to wounds and handle crowd control at once." I let the disdain drip from every word. "Besides, it's not like I broke anyone's bones. He'll be fine."

"Noted." The cut lines along his cheekbones became deeper. He was clenching his jaw. Good.

After the way he'd watched me like a hawk all day, I didn't get how no one was around to help Sage. "Speaking of which, where was everyone?"

He straightened at that. "What do you mean? It's 2 a.m. Everyone was in bed." He didn't look mussed like he'd been sleeping. Then again, he could probably get ready in three seconds. Super short hair had its benefits.

"You had multiple guards on us while we sat around filling in dots on a page today, but you don't have a single one doing bed check? I call bull."

"Guards?" He let out a quick laugh. I didn't see what was so funny. "We're your safety escort. Police aren't the same thing up here as down on Ground Level."

"Clearly. Do they not have emergency services up here either?"

He ignored me. "Yes, part of my job during the day is to keep everyone in line. It's a big transition to move to Cloud Nine. Adjusting to having peers in control, accepting orders from people your own age or maybe younger than you is weird." He sounded like he'd struggled with it himself, and I wondered who got to give Declan orders.

"Fair enough." I didn't expect any issue there. I treated adults like my equals, too. People had to earn my respect. Their age didn't matter. However, I recognized I was in the minority there. "That still doesn't explain how no one else was around to hear that girl slamming onto the floor."

"You do realize you're the only person who heard her." He scanned my face as though he was going to have to remember my features later. It wasn't as creepy as it sounded. "Even her roommates were still sleeping when you came to her aid." His voice lilted at the end like he wanted confirmation.

"Some jerks put their beauty rest above others' wellbeing. I'm not one of them." I grinned. "It's also why I didn't get elbowed in the shin."

He smiled back at me. It transformed his face. The harsh, brutish qualities melted away and he looked, well, young and like he might have some fight left in him.

"You know, I could make a pitch to take you for my department. You could make things in Security & Order very interesting."

Oh, he had no idea. "Something tells me you would get mad when I punched people."

"There would have to be less punching, but the same amount of thinking on your feet." His smile widened and the guy had dimples. I am not too ashamed to admit my heart did a little flutter before I came to my senses.

"I'd get bored with the lack of cerebral effort and rules against smacking idiots."

"I thought you might say that." He reclined in his chair and crossed his arms over his chest. He had on a basic tee and his biceps strained the fabric.

"There has got to be a gym in this place." Sometimes my brain and my mouth had an instant replay. Also, I was still staring at his arms.

"A perk for the security team. We have to be ready to punch people when necessary, after all." Why was he being playful? This felt too easy.

"Well, research folk might need to punch people, too. Plus, in the event your team is all sleeping, you might need a research backup."

"Look, I know your scores all scream science, but you have all the requisites to work for me." Man, I wanted to know what markers on my file made him think I was the kind to keep people in line. I had a protective streak, but I was certain my file was full of documented acts that suggested my anti-authority stance. Not exactly cop material.

"Again, it's not what I'm after."

"There's a gym." It was good bait. I wished I had been able to work out today. My muscles were so tight from stress.

"You'll let me in the gym, either way."

He stretched his legs out in front of him. His boots were a shiny black. This place was so pristine I doubted they had a chance to get tarnished, but Declan seemed the type to polish them anyway. "I will?"

"You will." I folded my arms across my chest and cocked a hip. I could be all sassy, too.

"Why's that?"

"My charm."

He choked on a laugh. "Charm?"

"Well, it's more right hook than charm, but it's very persuasive." I held my right hand up and pretended to examine my knuckles. It was hard to stop a smile from overtaking my lips.

"You're right, I'll probably let you use the gym anyway, but not because of fear of your punches—I do know how to defend against them. I'm not giving up on bringing you into the security team."

"Why the about-face?" I dropped my hands back to my sides. I didn't get Declan and I was always able to read people. What was his angle? "You didn't think a whole lot of me this morning."

"Wrong." He said it in a way that made me sound like I was the idiot.

I gave him a look that told him exactly what I thought of that answer.

"I had to keep an eye on you. You're faster than anyone else here." He held up a hand to stop me from gloating—and I was going to gloat. "Let me rephrase: on this level. Because of the oxygenation volume and the higher ozone as part of the transition, you're stronger than most here. We're used to cleaner air. It's much harder for me to breathe on this level. It'll be easier tomorrow, but for day one, you had the potential to be dangerous if you got pissed. And don't think I don't know you were pissed all day long."

I liked that he thought of me as dangerous, but it didn't change my distaste for his sudden change of heart. "So now you don't think I'm dangerous?"

"I still think you could be dangerous. Sure. I also think you've shown you care about people and the only people you are a risk to are those trying to stop you from helping others."

"Or people who are being jerks," I reminded him.

"So you didn't think I was a jerk today?" I got the impression he was laughing at me.

"You were too far away to hit."

"Touché."

CHAPTER 12
ALL ABOARD THE GOSSIP TRAIN

There are events you hope change everything. The ones when you expect to wake the next day and have your world altered.

Moving twenty miles up in the air changed my reality, sure. I was silly enough to think last night's bloody debacle would change the tenor of orientation for Cloud Nine. It didn't.

Breakfast was full of gossip. I hate to say my sister led the charge. Leah needled me for information. She asked what I did with my bloody pants. What kind of dumb question was that? I put them in the laundry bag, and as soon as I found out where I could do laundry, I'd wash them. It's not like they were white and I was worried about stains tarnishing my pajamas.

I didn't like the way she talked with the others. They huddled together and didn't bother to dim their voices. Fragments of conversations reached me. Calling Sage a psycho and suggesting she probably got off on slicing herself. Not that any of them had seen anything in the room for her to cut herself with.

The short, squeaky Roseann suggested I pocketed whatever it was. Leah defended me, but not in the way I would have hoped. I wanted to hear her say that was crazy and I wasn't the sort to lie. I would have liked my own sister to know me that well. I sucked at filtering the truth down to being something less than harsh most days.

But that wasn't how Leah came to my aid. No, my baby sister told them I didn't know Sage and I wouldn't go out on a limb for some girl I hadn't even met.

I was no longer convinced we came from the same home.

Charlie was the only person who didn't bother asking me for details about the prior night. She rolled her eyes at the gossip crowd.

"You'd think they'd have bigger concerns," she said.

"I sure do." I pushed my food around my plate. It was crazy delicious again, but hearing my sister completely misjudge my character kind of killed my appetite.

"You and me both." Charlie was siphoning my mood. I felt bad about pulling her down, but also appreciated that she didn't bail just because I was wearing my grumpy pants this morning.

"I can't take another day of paperwork and sitting." I made sure to sit so my back was flush with the chair. If I held awesome posture, I felt like I was working muscles. It made holding still a workout, and thus far less of a waste of time.

"I can handle that." Charlie kicked the empty chair on her right a few times until it was far enough away from the table that she could prop her feet on it. "I'm just ready for answers. Waiting isn't my thing."

My anxiety came with inaction. It wasn't that I didn't care about the big picture; I did. Declan's words rattled in my brain until early in the morning. The possibilities of my future. The reality of living in a place without adults. Accepting that douchebags like the people surrounding my sister would have a say in how things were run. All of it scared me, but right now my problem was waiting to do something. Anything.

Okay, anything but more filling in little ovals on a too-white piece of paper.

Declan hurried everyone to their seats the moment we made it to the auditorium. Charlie and I exchanged a look. One that said we hoped we were about to get answers.

The way the morning flowed gave more peace of mind to Charlie than to me. We weren't rushed to our chairs so anyone could explain what happened to Sage or even give us an update on her. I wasn't quite ballsy enough to ask the question in front of the full room, but I couldn't believe they would just act like there hadn't been a girl slashed up the night before.

It was easier to pretend everything was fine. Ignorance, bliss, and all that crap. But I knew when people were pretending. Everyone in the room was faking it. The people Leah had been talking with this morning were faking concern. The security team leading this place was faking calm. And I was stuck faking apathy.

I had to stuff my anger and resentment down deep. This wasn't the time to explode all over the room and cause a scene. Declan had been right about one thing last night, I was being watched. Until I had more freedom, I had to pick my battles—or at least delay them until opportune moments.

"As of an hour ago, the air solution here has been upped to seventeen percent oxygen, seventy-eight percent nitrogen, and we've finally dropped out all but one percent of the ozone." Declan was pacing at the front of the room and reeling off numbers like he had calculated them himself this morning. Maybe he had. I hadn't given him a chance to detail out all the duties of the Security division. Measuring atmospheric gas levels could be part of the gig. "This puts the air on this level almost the same as what you'll experience when you move to Cloud Nine."

"When will that be?" A scrawny guy with dark hair asked. I was glad someone else was game to call out questions. After all, it sure looked like I was the only one under scrutiny.

"If we get things completed in a timely manner and no one keels over from the changes in the air, I hope to have everyone assigned and moved upstairs by tomorrow evening." Leah and her new buddy Roseann were bopping up and down in their seats.

Charlie nudged me with her elbow. "Assignments tomorrow."

I nodded and whispered back, "Welcome to the World of Tomorrow, tomorrow."

She snickered. Declan gave me a dirty look but in the scheme of things, we were probably the quietest of the bunch.

"In order to make sure everyone can handle the environment on the standard levels, today we have a few more examinations."

The groans in that room might have shaken the walls. Mine was, surprisingly, not the loudest. That may have been because I opted to swear internally.

"Quit complaining," Declan shouted over the din. "We're done with the standardized tests. Today is mostly just physicals and interviews."

I couldn't resist. "No more pencils?"

He glared at me. The guy with the dimples from last night was gone and this version of Declan didn't bother replying to my question.

When Declan stalked toward the lectern, I turned to Charlie. "I'm not that much of an asshole, right?"

"Not more than anyone else." She grinned. "Well, more than me."

"Oh, you're just saying it in your head."

"Yep. That's why people think I'm nice and I don't have people in uniforms staring me down." She glanced over my shoulder, and I peeked. It wasn't just Declan watching me. "It wouldn't kill you to keep your thoughts inside your mind for a little while."

"It might," I muttered, but didn't really mean it. She didn't press the issue.

As the room mellowed, Declan continued, "We're splitting you up today. Four of you will go with Deb and five will go with me. Deb's group will do physicals this morning. I hope you're ready to sweat." He flashed a quick look in my direction. It was so swift, I wasn't even sure it happened. At least he had been paying attention part of the time last night, even if he went back into robot mode in the morning. "My group will do interviews to help match you with the right team for your duty assignment on Cloud Nine. After lunch, the groups will switch. Easy enough, yes?"

Nothing in this place was easy enough. Breathing was harder— though, it was less work now than yesterday. The days were boring. If I was going to be a part of this whole save-the-planet brigade, then they had to let me do something.

Staying still only caused my energy to chafe against my mind. The longer I avoided action, the more my brain plotted all the awful things that could be happening. My worst-case scenarios were not painting a bright picture of future life on Cloud Nine.

I just about climbed over the chair in front of me to get down to join Deb's group. A physical meant at least a little working out, and I needed to expel this energy before I said or did something really dumb.

CHAPTER 13
THE TEST

The real gyms in this place needed to be badass. Epic. The titan of workout facilities.

The tiny room Deb shoved me in was far from a gym, but a whole lot like the one I peeked at the night before. A treadmill was squished on one side of the room. Elbows would need to stay in while running on that thing, lest I jack the wall. There were two black plastic chairs in the room with a tiny table between them. I sat in one and hoped the flimsy thing would hold me.

I tapped the toe of my boot on the tile floor, and the room was empty enough to offer a faint echo. I liked the little rhythm floating back to me. A soft sound can make you feel less alone. I couldn't hear any of the security people helping others, or anyone talking in the hallway. At Ground Level, something was always happening. Even when I was home alone, I had the chug of the generator, the creak of floorboards, and the sounds of life. Here, though, it was like someone had dumped bleach on everything and it couldn't even choke it out.

Cords hung on the wall next to the door. The beige of each tube barely popped against the blank wall, but the black screen of the lifeless monitor was hard to miss.

A girl in a white jacket joined me after what felt like an hour, though the clock indicated nine minutes. She wasn't dressed quite like the medics from last night, but there was no question she was in uniform. Did everyone have special outfits here? I wasn't inherently averse to utilitarian style, but dumping a bunch of kids in a sterile environment and then making them all dress the same creeped me out more than I wanted to admit.

"I'm Jen." She was staring at a clipboard. Was everyone in this place equipped with one? "We have to verify your weight and height real quick and a couple other status things and then we'll get to the more interesting stuff."

Once again, I had forgotten that I was the same age as these people. As soon as Jen opened her mouth, the nerves about the authority element left me. Her tone said she was following a checklist, and a quick peek over the edge of her clipboard confirmed my suspicion.

I gave a thumbs-up to all the numbers they must have gotten from my doctor or my mom. Everything was close enough and I didn't have any desire to traipse around this place hunting down a scale to ensure to-the-pound accuracy.

"Can you go ahead and step onto the treadmill?" She winced when she spoke and a flash of heat crept up the back of my neck. I didn't like that look. "The stupid cords won't reach you unless you're on the thing, and I need baseline numbers."

Oh. I shrugged and stepped onto the black base.

She clamped a heart rate and oxygenation monitor to my index finger and instructed me to hold still. Easy enough.

"Your pulse is a little high. Let's give it a second."

Crap. It spiked when I was anxious. I needed to quit thinking about why they were measuring me. Why did it matter what my heart rate was if I was healthy? I would be dealing with molecules and math. Not exactly strenuous activity for the cardiovascular system.

I fought the instinct to scrub my hands over my face. Jen might be slouching and huffing about having to fill out paperwork on me, but I didn't completely buy it. She would take notes on me, and there was no reason not to think she wouldn't include that this test subject got twitchy at the touch of a simple monitor on her finger. Not the image I wanted to project.

Funny how even when you don't want to be somewhere, it's hard not to care what people think. If anyone asked, I'd say it was about being competitive, but inside I knew it was about survival. I needed to give off an air of control, or others would want to put me under their thumb "for my safety." I didn't need their protection. I was safer overseeing my own affairs, thank you very much.

I was fairly certain my deep breaths were subtle. When we tried the monitor again, the numbers reflected my newly relaxed state.

"Cool." Jen kept her eyes transfixed on the clipboard while she talked. I bet she was an awful liar. "I have all the starter stuff. Now for the workout portion."

She grabbed a couple white circles and peeled a paper backing off them. "They don't hurt, but it's cold when I stick them on." She edged closer. "Can you tug your shirt down a bit? I need to stick these over your heart."

I complied and wished the little pulse meter didn't jump when the electrodes made contact. She wasn't lying about them being cold.

Jen connected thin black leads to the stickers on my chest and hooked them to the monitor on the wall.

"Okay, the starter part here is five minutes of walking. If you feel out of breath, let me know."

I rolled my eyes, which would have been more effective if she'd been looking my way. "Walking for five minutes isn't exactly difficult."

"I've heard that before." Seriously?

"Fine." No point in arguing with the system here. Besides, the sooner I got the walking portion done, the sooner I might get to run. I needed the outlet, and soon. "I'm ready whenever you are."

After five minutes of walking on a treadmill while watching Jen actively avoid looking at me, I was eager for the next round. I could only watch that girl stare at the monitor for so long. I needed to actually exercise or my quest to keep my foot out of my mouth would end swiftly.

"I'm going to increase the speed and the incline." She reached in front of me to up the settings.

"How long until we get to the running?"

She finally looked at me, and I now understood she thought I was a total tool. "Very few people run. Just because you are now surrounded by better air doesn't mean your lungs magically have more capacity. Actually, because you haven't adapted to the higher oxygen levels, you shouldn't be able to perform as well as you could at Ground Level."

There was no point in telling her that I could run a mile back home. It would just make me come off arrogant. I'd rather surprise her with my awesomeness, and then enjoy watching her write it down in silent smug superiority. What? It can feel good to prove people wrong.

After three rounds of increasing incline and speed, Jen was grinding her teeth and I was finally getting a sheen of sweat to break out.

"I need to grab someone real quick," Jen was saying as she bumped up the speed and elevation for my next five-minute round. It felt so good to use my legs. "Will you be okay for a minute?"

I pumped my arms. We were finally at a running pace. "Absolutely." I grinned. This was something I knew. The bliss of endorphins would start filling me soon. Nothing helped a girl accept living in a pod filled with secrets like a huge boost of exercise-induced happy.

My muscles burned in a way that cleared my mind. This was why I worked out. This mind-clearing healthy pain did more than strengthen my body. It could firm my resolve and hold my anger in check far better than being told to think things through.

The downside to my mental tunnel vision mode was I quit paying attention to my surroundings. I hadn't even realized Jen had returned —or brought people with her—until I heard Declan's voice.

"Damn." That single word cut through the air with such force I nearly stopped dead on the treadmill. Declan sounded proud and horrified at the same time. Both reactions made my stomach knot. At least I hadn't eaten much this morning or I might have barfed all over the place.

It took me a second to recover from both the shock of seeing other people in the close-quarters space and from the emotion in Declan's voice. I had moved beyond proving I was healthy and was enjoying the exercise, but clearly, this test meant much more than fitness for life on Cloud Nine.

Jen still avoided my gaze, but her teeth were gnawing at her lip to the point it would soon bleed. She knew something. Crap.

I focused on my breathing; it had gotten easier the longer I ran. Now wasn't the time to let the wonky rules here get the best of me. It was easier to say that since my body was beginning to fatigue.

"Are you just going to stand there gawking at me?" I did my best to sound cocky. It was easier than asking the questions I really wanted answered.

No one said anything. Deb and Jen stood behind Declan like he was the barrier protecting them from raging wildebeests.

The one guy in the room just gaped at me. The women stared at the monitor, but Declan was focused entirely on me. I kept running. I started to reach forward to turn up the pace again, but remembered this was a test. Could I run away from that look?

I might have turned flush if a guy had looked at me that way in pretty much any other situation. Declan was completely focused on my body. I could feel his gaze cutting through my clothes like he was imagining the flex and release of my calves.

"Did you really come in here to watch me run?" My voice shook a little bit, but that was from the exertion, right?

"Kind of." Declan wasn't a Southern boy, but he still managed a drawl.

Deb furrowed her brows, but didn't say anything.

I did. "Excuse me?"

"Can you handle more speed?" When I cocked a brow at him, Declan rephrased, "Are you ready to up the pace?"

"Totally." The three beeps indicating the speed change from the machine didn't echo this time. The cramped room made my statement sound stale, but I was too determined to prove I could beat their pathetic test to consider the scrutiny it signified.

I had to focus to put one foot in front of the other. I sucked down air and let it ease the burn building at my side and spreading across my chest.

"Did you see any indication of issues with the oxygen levels?" Declan was talking with Jen. They hovered in my periphery. I wanted to eavesdrop, but the pace demanded all my focus. As if Death, himself, were chasing me. Fear licked my spine.

"No, she's processing as well as you or I would." Jen paused. I expect she was pulling some sort of face. She seemed the type. "Fine, she's doing better than us."

"Don't be jealous. It's good when people adapt more quickly." He didn't sound so sure.

Jen's voice dropped down to a whisper. I couldn't pick it all out, but I heard the phrase "too strong to be a candidate" and choked. Declan thought my coughing was from the extreme workout session and slowed the treadmill incrementally until it finally came to a stop.

"We have more than enough data, Ally." He offered me a hand and it engulfed my own. Despite how hot I was from running, his hand was still warmer than mine. I didn't mind him steadying me as I stepped off the treadmill. My legs were a little too liquid.

I plopped down in one of the little chairs again and started stretching my hamstrings. Jen was jotting down numbers off the monitor on the wall. I might need to ask Charlie if she knew what they were looking for in there. No one had ever tracked the effects of running on my body. I didn't know what the numbers meant, and I wasn't much for being without the inside knowledge.

CHAPTER 14
NATURAL DISASTER

As soon as Jen completed all the necessary boxes on her checklist, Declan ushered her out of the room. He closed the door and the small room felt positively matchbox-like. Declan's large frame covered the door. I didn't think he was actively blocking me from leaving. It was merely the coincidence of such a small room.

It didn't matter. My self-protection instincts didn't care about the room's nature. My hands balled into fists. I gritted my teeth and clung to the belief that I would leave this room whenever I wanted.

I wasn't so good at covering my emotions when it was just he and I in the room. "You could sit, you know." My words came out sour, but Declan smiled at me anyway. He managed to balance himself on the other child-sized chair in the room. A little part of me had hoped he would crush it. I couldn't believe that it could hold 220 lbs., and there was no question Declan was every bit of that. Muscle is heavy.

"You ran over the allotted time—"

"Are you telling me I missed lunch? Because that's not going to fly." I was starving. Also, it's not like I ran so incredibly long. What? Forty-five minutes?

He just shook his head.

"Can you please just give me an answer about what is going on here? All this watching me silently is creepy enough when it comes from Lab Girl, but from you, it's downright disturbing." It was. One-on-one he came across as genuine last night, and it worried me that he was able to flip sincerity on and off like a light switch.

He wasn't looking at me. "You didn't miss lunch." He shook his head again. That better be a nervous tick or I was going to pop him one the next time he did it. "Typically people last, at most, ten minutes on that thing. No one has ever run before."

"I have." I didn't bother making it boastful. It was a fact. He'd read my file—probably more than once—and I was sure it noted I could run a mile.

"I know." He didn't chastise my smug tone, so I let him keep talking. "But the protocol here is to let you try to run, then have a discussion about if it was better or worse than on Ground Level and general health conditions. We can't exactly do that with you."

"Why not?" His explanation was far from anything decent. Let me run until I'm exhausted then talk to me the same as anyone else. Not exactly thermodynamics.

"Well, because our process tends to take on almost a mentor program where we find someone who matches physicality markers to be the one who helps you transition on Cloud Nine. To build strength and adjust to purer air quality. Eventually, your lungs will turn a bright pink—that typically takes a few years—but before that you'll start to use more of your lung capacity."

No one was going to see my lungs. I cared a lot less about the shade of pink they'd turn and more about what was going on. "Still not seeing the issue or why you looked like a goddamn guppy when you saw me running."

He started to do it again. His mouth opened like no one ever shocked him. I almost rolled my eyes at the action, but he stopped gaping. "No one here can do what you just did."

Make him look like a fish? "Excuse me?"

"Even the healthiest of us can't run that long. There is no one comparable here, and we're stumped because while you were able to run at Ground Level, you certainly wouldn't have jogged for forty-five minutes."

Hell. He had a point. I worked out for an hour every day. Usually muscle stuff like squats and pushups. Not running. At least Cloud Nine might turn me into some superhuman. That could be okay. If it were on my own terms.

"So, what you're saying is I'm more awesome than you?" I smiled. I wanted to diffuse this tension and take the attention off me and my quick adaptation. Maybe it's because I grew up around organic stuff and others hadn't had the chance. I didn't know. But breathing here wasn't too bad for me. I would have to find out if Leah performed similarly. Well, in terms of taking to the air here, because my sister was not much for physical exertion of any sort.

I didn't believe everyone was just in awe of my badass running skills. Deb and Jen had looked frustrated. Not to mention all that talk about not being a candidate or whatever. There was far more happening here than just making sure I wouldn't suffocate when doing my job.

However, I didn't expect Declan to give up the details any time soon. I needed to play this carefully. Crap. Not my strong suit.

"Yes, you're awesome."

"More awesome than you."

He pursed his lips. "Fine. More awesome than me." I beamed at him before I realized I was flirting with the enemy. He added, "In this one regard."

"Qualify it all you want, fella. You're impressed."

"Yes." That one word signified a problem. I didn't want to work for him, and the look he had said he planned to call dibs.

Deflection. I needed to downplay this. If I could pretend it wasn't anything to devote more time to, maybe others would follow suit.

"I'm glad we can agree on that, but I still don't see the big deal. Less work for everyone involved if I don't need the extra assist." I leaned forward to grasp my toes, and then slowly pulled them back toward my body. My calves languished in the stretch. I closed my eyes and pretended people weren't paying too much attention to me.

I didn't want a mentor. I didn't want to talk about how I felt or why this place got under my skin so badly. It was much easier to holler about the idiots in government when they weren't directly overseeing my life. I didn't have anyone to protect me here—I had no illusions of Declan protecting me from any Cloud Nine leaders, himself included —and getting to know someone in charge in a casual setting could spell trouble for me.

I sat back up. I could only hide in my legs for so long. Declan had rested his elbows on his knees and clasped his hands. He didn't avoid my gaze, which made my stomach do flips in the wrong way.

"They're kind of big on protocol here." He swallowed and I watched his Adam's apple bob. "You don't exactly fit into the usual plans."

"Hey, they recruited me." It didn't come out defensive. That would have been better. No, I flung those words loaded with the truth that I didn't want to be here.

Declan was quiet. He kept looking at the door, then away, then back again. I didn't get his angle. So, I just stayed quiet, too. The truth of what I said—and didn't say—covered us like wet gauze. My throat tightened the longer I stayed silent, which made little sense to me but my brain didn't stop the cinching of the invisible garrote.

His gaze darted to the door again, and I finally broke. "Is someone listening to us?"

His sigh filled the room and hung there above us for a second. "Not now."

"But they were?" I loved that this place was full of spies when I didn't need them, but apparently they didn't bother keeping an eye on us when people got hurt.

"No, but people are always listening, always monitoring. You..." He stopped himself, and I didn't know if that was a good thing. Was it for my benefit he was tightening his lips or was it to keep from letting me in too much? "Damn it. You just need to be more careful."

"Of what?" I turned in my chair so I could look directly at him. Our knees nearly touched.

"Ally. Don't." He looked away.

"What is it you're not telling me?" I almost reached out to him. What was wrong with me?

"You just can't say things like that." We had both dropped to a whisper, but it was full of ire and force. The words came out harsh through Declan's hushed tones. "Do not tell people you don't want to be here."

"I didn't say that."

He tilted his head to the side and glared at me. "We both know you believe it, but regardless, you can't tell people you were recruited either."

"Why the hell not?"

"You can't."

"I need a reason. Everyone wanted me here to help with the double displacement testing to help change the air quality." Declan looked shocked. "Oh, you didn't think I'd put it together that after doing an independent study on utilizing displacements to separate out heavier metals I suddenly have to be moved here? Remember, they want me because I'm smart."

"Everyone here is smart."

"Please."

"Different areas of expertise."

"My sister?"

"Has strengths."

"Fine. If we're all special little stars, then why would it be bad for people to know I was asked to come here instead of applying?" I pushed myself back against the chair hard enough it let out a sharp yip as it slid against the floor.

"That's it exactly. Do you want everyone to hate you?"

I frowned. "You're concerned about my social well-being? Please."

"It's tight quarters here. The authorities are your peers. If they're jealous, things won't go well."

I didn't buy it. "There's something you're not telling me."

He ran his hand over the top of his head. The graze didn't affect the styling of his short hair. Every strand still looked perfect. "There are lots of things I'm not telling you."

"We should fix that."

The mirthless laugh he gave made me want to heave. "Not now, Ally."

"You could at least tell me why people who recruited me because I'm special now look all pissed off because—spoiler alert—I am."

"There are..." he paused and licked his lips. He was delaying, probably searching for some perfect words that didn't exist. "Certain expectations. A plan was in place, and people don't like change."

"Change is the whole reason I'm here, though."

"There's a difference between expected change, and rocking the boat. Say you were expecting, and even needing, rain. Instead of a casual rainfall, you get a monsoon. It's more than you can handle because you weren't adequately prepared."

"I'm not causing mass flooding."

"Not everyone sees it that way."

"Do you?"

"I don't think you're a natural disaster."

That was the most messed up compliment I've ever received.

"You're not going to tell me anything else, are you?"

"Not now." He looked at the door again.

"Fine, then I need to shower."

"You remember how to get back to the dorms?" When I nodded, he continued, "You've got about thirty minutes before lunch."

"Then I guess I better hurry."

As I pulled the door open, Declan stopped me. His hand on my shoulder. "Can you please try to watch what you say in the interview this afternoon?"

I wanted to roll my eyes. This was stupid. I didn't need to worry about a sit-down chat this afternoon. But the tightening around his eyes transferred nervousness to my gut. Before I knew it, I found myself agreeing.

Two days in, and this place was already changing me.

CHAPTER 15
ADAPTABILITY

Eight minutes in a scalding shower washed away the sweat, but left an invisible residue of worry.

I came to Cloud Nine knowing they'd want to use me. No one convinces your mom to ship you and your little sister off overnight without a good purpose. I assumed they wanted me to work on air quality research, but now that was changing and I didn't like it.

This place wasn't for me, but it was easier to exist knowing the plan and how they wanted to leverage me. It made it easier to keep my guard up, easier to avoid giving too much information. I had hoped it would also make getting out of this place someday an actual option.

Cloud Nine was a Hey! Look over there! project to make people think the world was getting better. It wasn't. As humans, we'd adapt. We always had. I had grandiose dreams of getting onto the official levels of Cloud Nine so I could prove it, and then turn their research around on them.

I wanted to give them an answer to some of the air quality problems and watch them flounder when they tried to keep me on this station anyway. If we solved the problem, then they had to actually start fixing the issues on Ground Level.

Right now, though, I didn't know if that plan was viable.

Declan said I wasn't what they expected. He'd called me a surprise, but the tone had been clear that I was more of a party crasher than an exclusive guest. While this bolstered my theory about Cloud Nine using me (and everyone else) and expecting certain results, it also said I may have just flipped everything upside down and was about to get completely screwed.

I got dressed while fretting over what I should and shouldn't say in this afternoon's interview. Was it best to be stoic? Probably not. Then they'd want me to be on the zero-emotions Security squad. Pass. I couldn't be overly friendly either because I wasn't much of a liar. Other than Charlie I didn't see anyone here I'd want to be friendly with, per se. Declan was too hot-and-cold for me to want to be open with, even if I kept blurting out too-honest things in front of him. Maybe I needed to slap him into the potentially trustworthy column. I would hold off judgment until he either fessed up about what was happening here, or he gave me a reason to knee him in the groin. Either way, I'd get satisfaction.

Lunch was another food I hadn't had before. Once we were out of this initiation process, I was going to ask someone what it was we were eating. I'd make a mental catalog of all my new favorites. Even that thought, though, didn't perk me up enough to overcome this anxiety gnawing at my insides.

Leah was surrounded by other people whose names I'd already forgotten.

Charlie sat with me. "That much fun, huh?"

"It shows?"

"Oh, it shows."

I shrugged. "How was your morning?"

She mirrored my shrug. "Boring. I felt like I was interviewing for an internship."

"Gross."

"It was awkward. The girl asking me the questions was probably sixteen, and those were so not questions she had written." She smiled at me in a way that said she, too, knew that not everyone on Cloud Nine was a genius. Not that we needed a hub of brilliance, there were so many skills that helped flesh out our world that didn't and shouldn't involve an advanced science background. It's just after Declan's little suggestion that everyone was brought here for his or her smarts, I enjoyed a smidge of confirmation that wasn't necessarily the case.

"Was she from the research department?" I hoped not. If they were bringing in simply anyone for the department, then the progress this place could make would be dismal. Much more work for me.

"Nah." Charlie wound her hair around her index finger, let it go, and started all over again. "She said she was part of Protocols, which I gather is under the Security banner. I would have picked it up even if she hadn't said anything because no one on the research team would stumble over saying the word 'exothermic.'"

We laughed and I felt a little bit like a mean girl. I was laughing at this place's decision to have people from the wrong department interviewing potential researchers about skills. It would be stupid to have me interview someone for a gig in the foods department. I couldn't even identify what I just ate. Skill sets varied, but it made sense to match like with like when it came to pairing potential duty assignments.

We put away our trays. Leah grabbed my arm as everyone was exiting the dining room.

"Can you believe they actually tried to make me run?" She was grinning. So excited. I wished I could have that type of enthusiasm about this. I wasn't good with willful ignorance, though.

"I can believe it." I reminded myself to play along. "How'd you do?"

Her laugh shimmered. How could we have just gone through the same thing and feel so very different? I wished my sister and I were more alike.

"How do you think I did? Barely made it a minute into the jogging portion before I asked to stop." I was shocked until Leah continued, "They made me keep going because I could breathe really well or whatever, but my legs hurt."

Fear ebbed. I wiggled my fingers a bit at my side to release the tension building in my muscles. Leah had adapted to the air like I had. She just had poor muscle tone.

"The more you use them, the less it will hurt." I matched Leah's gait and we walked back down toward the auditorium. Charlie was behind us and most definitely in earshot. It made me wonder who else was listening in.

"Oh, I know. They told me they're going to give me a personal trainer-type thing when we move up to the station."

"I think it's more like a workout buddy."

"Whatever. I'm going to look hot."

How could that be a prime concern right now? She didn't know what she would have to do all day every day, but Leah was still stoked about the change.

I needed to adopt a touch of her thinking. Even if we had to do things we hated, at least I was faster than everyone else. Plus, my sister was right that working out equaled hotness, or at least it gave me a great butt.

CHAPTER 16
INTERVIEW WITH ADAM

was stuck in another boring, too-small room. The possibility that every room in this place had a hospital ambiance was becoming higher by the second. Cold and spotless.

The air vents above me were silver, but with the door closed the lack of space was suffocating. The inability to move, should the need arise, was concerning.

I didn't have too long to work up a complex about it when my interrogator—er—interviewer showed up. He wasn't what I expected. After Charlie's description, I was expecting someone ditzy and young. This guy was neither. He was at least a foot taller than me with wide shoulders, but a lean frame. Declan would still shadow him in bulk.

This guy, though, didn't look young. I wondered how long he'd lived on Cloud Nine. He even had stubble. Like real stubble. A faint haze of reddish hair lined his jaw and it looked, well, good. This wasn't someone using facial hair to pretend they were older. No, this guy wasn't trying hard. It was enough to make me swallow. Twice. Nerves about Cloud Nine and shady dealings temporarily evaporated as I stared much more obviously than I should have.

"Are you Ally Ramsey?" His voice was softer than I expected. Nice.

"Yes." Oh, crap. My voice sounded softer, too. They did not make guys like this back on Ground Level. My body was reacting without my permission.

"I'm Adam. I'm here to talk to you about your background and goals at Cloud Nine." This might not be so bad. I'd focus on the quick questions and not get distracted by the cute guy. I'd be back to brooding in my dorm room before I knew it.

He didn't continue. Odd. I guess he wanted confirmation I was on board with this little chat. "Okay."

He sat across from me. I was on a grey couch, he on the adjacent black chair. Other than an end table, they were the only items in the room. Nothing on the walls to even kill the echo. It made me watch my pitch.

"What did they tell you that you'd be doing on Cloud Nine?"

Was this a trick question? Didn't Declan specifically tell me not to talk about being recruited?

"Have you not read my file?" I tried to make it sound playful. "I got the impression you guys had a chance to see all of that." It might have come out more frustrated.

"The file is all numbers." A non-answer. I no longer liked this guy or his tight tee shirt—I could see his pecs and wow, were they defined —anymore.

"If you've read it, then you know no one talked with me directly beforehand."

"True, but I also have a strong feeling you've surmised the reasoning behind the request you join us." He didn't make it a question.

He watched me closely. Not in the same way Declan did, like he thought I would bolt any moment. No, Adam watched my face and nothing else. He was paying attention. Unnerving.

Especially so, as it's something I did. His eyes flicked down to my mouth when nerves forced me to lick my lips. I caught the subtle way he tilted his head back in an attempt to elicit answers from me. I hated that it worked.

"Research." This had turned into a battle. He was too good for me to divulge much, and something about his mannerisms made me think he was testing me. This wasn't the same experience Charlie had, but then she hadn't scared the pants off the people in the treadmill portion of the day.

"That's a bit of a cheat answer, don't you think?" The very corners of his mouth began to pull up.

"It's a broad answer." I settled back against the sofa cushion and then folded one leg underneath me. Something told me it would be worth getting comfortable.

"It's an obvious answer. I think you're much more detail-oriented than that." His words were those of a disapproving dad, but his voice was much more playful.

"You appear to be pretty detail oriented, too."

He held a fist in the air. "Researchers unite."

So I got a research guy interviewing me and Charlie had a girl who couldn't pronounce half the words in a chemistry textbook. Interesting.

"What area are you in?"

"I do believe I asked you first." He was too charming.

"Fair enough." I was enjoying this far more than expected. I liked things a bit antagonistic. "I'd have even money on my role being related to chemistry, specifically displacing heavy metals from the atmosphere with the lovely byproduct of water creation."

"Guilty." He grinned. "We've made strides in that area, but not quickly enough for Director Abrams. He thinks you'll make the difference there. No pressure."

He laughed, and then glanced at the door like he hoped no one had caught him having fun. I hoped that wasn't a trend with this place.

His attention turned back to me. "Do you like working with reactions like that?"

"Yes, though it's actually more fun for me on paper."

His smile was genuine (and made his eyes cut down to slits). "I understand that."

"Math nerds unite?"

"Something like that." He shifted in his seat like the chair wasn't comfortable or maybe it was this setting. "Your test scores from yesterday showed a nice knowledge of botany."

"Really?" Botany was close to a dead language. I only knew the basics to understand future functionality.

"You sound surprised. Are you not interested in it?"

"Plants don't exist too much these days. It's such an obscure element that it would be hard to have any practical experience there."

"There are greenhouses on Ground Level."

"Yes, and they charge exorbitant amounts of money for foods we used to eat all the time." I probably shouldn't have said that. "Not quite my place."

He sat up straight. Ugh. Definitely shouldn't have said that. How had he pulled this truth from me? His gaze darted to the door and then back to me. It was quick, but I caught it. "What if you could work with plants now, though? Here?"

It felt like a stupid question. How was I supposed to answer that? You needed soil to grow crops. We were miles and miles above the earth. Adam must have guessed from my silence I wasn't going to bite.

"We grow our own food here." He pointed to the ceiling. "The entire top floor is a greenhouse. You've been eating meals that feature peppers and onions and beans. All of it is cultivated here. We're working on ways to make it possible to mass-produce vegetables in small spaces. To make them available across the board again."

"I thought this place was focused on improving the air-quality issue."

"We still are. This is tangential." Adam's hands were up accenting his every word. "While we're working on the greenhouse element and hybridization of plants, we're looking at ways to use the growth of plants to alter the atmospheric blend." He was talking so fast, it was hard to keep up. But I liked him because there was no question this guy loved the science.

All the science students back home hated me. I nabbed national honors and they worried about passing tests. Adam didn't fit the mold. Working with him would make this place that much more bearable.

"You have my attention." I couldn't stop grinning. I probably looked like Leah had at lunch.

"Good, because I'd like to have you on my research team."

"That sounds promising."

"You'd float between both the botanical and chemical projects."

I actually didn't hate this idea.

"Only hitch is that Security & Order is now trying to nab you." He clucked his tongue, but it wasn't directed at me. "They should know it won't pan out, but apparently you're a bit of an ass-kicker."

"Apparently." Adam was only the second person I'd met on Cloud Nine that I wouldn't consider punching.

"So, I have to officially ask you if you have any interest in working with the Security division."

"What would I get to do as part of their team?"

His jaw dropped. I cackled.

"Kidding. I have no interest in going all commando. I'm here for the science." Two half-truths don't make a whole lie, do they? I was here because someone made me come, but I would make the best of it.

"Not funny, Ally."

"It was a little funny." I ran my hand back and forth on the soft fabric of the sofa. I was still impressed that they had such lush materials here.

"Not funny."

My smile was positively flirtatious. I was fine with that, because Adam was flirt-worthy. "The look on your face was pretty funny."

"Are you like this all the time?"

"When I don't have anything else to do? Pretty much."

"So, what you're saying is that I need to make sure you have tons of work?"

I shrugged. "Kind of."

"Will do."

CHAPTER 17
ONE OF YOU IS MORE THAN ENOUGH

The longer Adam and I sat there, the more comfortable I became. Not full drop-your-guard mode comfortable, but the mood lightened.

"Well, since I'm skipping all the irrelevant questions, we have tons of extra time." Adam didn't see this as a problem. I liked that. "Anything you want to know?"

"Tell me there are windows once I get off this level."

He groaned. "Yeah, there are windows. I remember being pissed about that too during my orientation." He slouched down in the chair. "There's actually a lot of windows into hallways, too, though. Makes it feel more open, even if it isn't."

"So you're saying it will be just as claustrophobic up there?"

"Not as bad, but it'll still take an adjustment period."

I shook my head and felt strands of hair escape my ponytail. "That sounds like a phrase people say when things are going to suck."

"You'll get to hang out with me. Not sucky."

I brushed the locks of hair framing my face back with a hand and re-secured them with an elastic. "I accept that."

"Are you excited to see the sun?" It sounded like the kind of thing everyone asks the new kid because it's an easy conversation starter. It bummed me out that his question was out of the new kid stable, but I had asked about windows.

"Not exactly."

He pulled back just a touch. Heh. I'd surprised him there. "Really? I've never met anyone who wasn't thrilled to see the sun."

"Can't the sun screw with your eyes?"

"Sure, if you stare at it." He rolled his eyes as he said it.

I still wasn't buying it. "Just feels dangerous."

"Well, it's a giant ball of burning gas—"

"See? Dangerous." Case rested.

"It's millions of miles away. It will not set you on fire." His face pinched for a moment, like he couldn't decide if he was amused or offended. "I really didn't expect you to be scared of the sun."

I felt my cheeks flush. "I'm not scared."

"We can call it concern, if you'd rather."

I narrowed my eyes and pinned him with a vicious stare. "Don't be a dick."

He laughed. Loudly. This time I looked at the door.

When no one came running, I continued, "I've spent my entire life without seeing the sun, and I liked it. I like the rolling greys and greens of the sky I know. Everything I've read about the sun makes it sound painful or overly romanticized. Neither makes seeing it all that appealing to me."

"I think you'll like it." His voice was soft, or at least far softer than mine—my angry voice carried.

Some of my ire abated. "Why?"

"It's pretty awesome and powerful. Something I have a feeling you'd respect."

He saw too much. It made me want to fidget. Instead, I wrapped my palms around my shin and changed the subject. "How long have you been here?"

"Oh, about thirty minutes."

I didn't even bother rolling my eyes. I just gave him a blank stare.

He sighed. "You're no fun, you know."

"Something like that."

"Fine. I've been on Cloud Nine for almost four years."

"You come with a sibling?"

"Are you looking for a package duo? Because I'm really not comfortable with that."

I wished he was close enough for me to shove.

"I'm sure one of you is more than enough." That came out wrong. Instead of suggesting he was a chore to be around, I was pretty sure it sounded sexual. What's worse is then I started thinking about him that way, and how he probably could overwhelm me. Just the way he twisted words and kept me on my toes mentally had me running through rote doofy girl thoughts. I may have turned the same red of oxidized metal.

I could see Adam biting his lips. Like, literally, he was biting them shut from the inside. Probably to keep from saying something to make it worse.

When he'd finally calmed himself, he said, "Probably true. No siblings came here with me."

"Do you have sisters or brothers?" The way he answered made me think he did. You rarely heard of parents choosing to only send one kid to a Clean Air pod. One golden ticket got everyone in.

"Yeah." That one word held so much weight. It spoke to a fractured family and a broken heart. It made me want to hold Adam and tell him it'd be okay. It even made me thankful for Leah being here because I hated the idea of her not getting to come when she so badly desired it.

I think I whispered an "oh," but I hadn't meant to do so.

"I have a brother and a sister. She was too young to come with me, only six. At sixteen, I was not prepared to watch over a six-year-old even if the EPA officials had allowed it—and they wouldn't. Bryan was twelve and just hated the idea of being here. Didn't want to have to live with his cranky older brother or be away from his friends." That sounded familiar. "Mom didn't make him."

Was it wrong to be jealous? I was pretty sure it wasn't the right reaction, but I couldn't stop the flood of emotion. Adam's mom gave her kids a choice. I'm sure others—like my mom—would argue a kid that age doesn't know what's best for him and she should have taken the opportunity on his behalf. Maybe that's true. At seventeen I sure knew what I wanted, and my mom hadn't even considered it. Hadn't even talked to me.

I wondered what the decision process would have been like if I'd been given a choice.

"Do you wish they were here?" I shouldn't have asked it, but my emotions got the better of me.

"Not really." He covered his face with his hands. "I shouldn't say that, though."

"Why not?"

He dropped his hands to the tops of his thighs; the slap echoed. "We are healthier here, Ally. We eat better, we feel better, and we have access to things not even possible at Ground Level. I should want that for everyone."

"But it's work and being away from friends and parents." And doing who knows what for who knows whom.

"It is, and it's tedious at times." He smiled at me. "Not so much right now, but I work most waking hours. Not exactly ideal for younger kids, and it doesn't make time for me to watch over them."

Would I be able to look out for Leah? "My sister came with me. She's fifteen."

"Would she have come without you?" I was surprised he asked. He'd read my file and probably Leah's, too. He should know that answer, and yet the question felt personal.

He'd been so honest with me, but I still had to hold back. I didn't know this guy. Science bond and lips that looked really soft wouldn't be enough to convince me to open up completely. I hoped he'd earn that trust, though. Partly because I wanted to touch him in a ridiculous way.

"She was very excited about coming here. I'm pretty sure she'd like to throw a Cloud Nine mixer in celebration."

"We do more structured get-togethers than parties. They aren't real big on impromptu parties."

"Aren't the Powers That Be on Cloud Nine teenagers?"

"Yes, and some of them might be amenable to a party. Others are pretty excited about being in power and are quick to report to the real Powers That Be, who are adults living at Ground Level. The folks that fund this project aren't much for hearing about people not working. They've painted Cloud Nine as this beacon of hope and progress, and they have a real fear parents might not want to send their kids there if there was any hint of debauchery."

"Please tell me we're still allowed to have some fun, because you're painting a pretty bleak picture."

"Of course. It just tends to be in groups of four or less."

"Is that a rule?"

He looked away. That said it all. "I'm saying more than I really should. You might be bad for me, Ally. You make me talk too much."

"I think it's a mutual problem."

His sigh was a sweet sound.

"How many people will be in the lab with us?" I asked, simply to change the subject.

"Most of the time it'll be just us and a couple others in the adjacent lab."

That sounded more dangerous than people watching us. Adam had been here long enough he probably wasn't observed all the time. I needed to work on keeping my guard up around him. Why couldn't he look like a gnome? I felt like gnome qualities might help here, because every time he spoke I felt this flutter in my stomach. And before I knew it, I was back to noticing how his tight shirt left little to the imagination.

Upside: Clearly not a uniform.

CHAPTER 18
I GAVE YOU A CHOICE

"You'll get to eat dinner on Cloud Nine proper." The rest of Declan's words were washed out by the giddy chatter of nine excited people.

The air thickened in that moment, like everyone had exhaled at once and saturated the room with relief. The day had been more grueling for some than others, but everyone was exhausted.

Declan would call out the results of the assignment tests, hand each of us a slip with the info of where we'd need to report and other pertinent information, and then we had thirty minutes to go pack our bags. He said they'd meet us in the corridor by our dorms and lead us to the transport up to our new digs.

In the name of making the best of things, I decided permanent housing would be good. Hopefully, Charlie would be rooming nearby. I would need a break from the insanity of Leah. Frequently.

My sister was saying Procurement over and over under her breath with her fingers crossed. Who knew she'd be so excited about a specific job here? Just yesterday she was on the "whatever will work" boat. I guess something interesting happened today that I didn't know about. I hoped it didn't involve the guy from yesterday.

They called the names in alphabetical order. I perked when they called Charlie. "Charlene de la Rosa. Research. Biology and Botany." I let out a happy sigh. Even if she didn't live right by me, we'd see each other in the research department, especially if I had to do some of the botany whatever.

"Allison Ramsey." Declan looked pissed. I couldn't tell if the rage making the vein pop in his neck was directed at me or someone else. "Research. Operations level."

I stepped in front of Declan to get my paperwork, but he didn't release it when I took hold.

He pitched his voice low, keeping this exchange just between us. "I wish you had considered working with me."

"I did consider it, but I'm here for the science."

"You're here because you were forced to be. I gave you a choice."

"Don't—" I didn't get to finish. He let go of the paperwork and I stumbled backward.

I planted my foot to stop from tumbling into the chairs. I gritted my teeth and prepared to launch back at him, but he had already called Leah's name and she was accepting her paperwork far more gracefully. She looped her arm through mine and tugged me toward the door with her.

This wasn't a fight to be had here. I wouldn't get answers from Declan by causing a scene. He only hinted at having my back when we were in private. I wanted to know why he thought he'd given me a choice. Why he thought there was one to be had.

I would get answers from him, though. And soon.

———

"What did you get? No, wait. That's boring. Let's talk about food." Leah drew out the word food like it was taffy and we lived on a boardwalk.

"Food?" I pretended I didn't know what she was talking about. I loved how flustered she got. "I think it'll be a few hours before dinner."

"Ugh. You know I meant me and food."

"You and food? That sounds kind of gross, Leah, but hey I'm not one to judge."

"I don't know why I even bother." She tried to storm off, but I grabbed her arm.

"You know I'm just kidding. Tell me the good news."

"I know you've already figured it out."

"So? Tell me anyway."

"I get to work in the kitchens making all these yummy things."

"So I'm going to have to thank you after dinner every day?"

"Might be lunch." She was close to skipping. I had to double-step it just to keep up with her as we hurried back to our room.

"Do you know how to cook?"

She slowed a bit and the withering stare she gave me was something new altogether.

"Yeah, I know you can make the basic things we eat back home, but what about all this new stuff?"

"They'll teach me. I'll get to find out what everything is and what it tastes like and what happens when you mix it with certain things." She was beaming. "And the best part? I get to taste test, like, everything."

"Okay, I have to admit, that part would be awesome." It was hard enough not to go back for seconds at every meal.

"All of it is awesome." Leah was so happy about the new adventure. I wanted more of it to rub off on me.

I wanted to be grinning about my new gig in the research department. My brain should have been whirring with thoughts about the things I would get to learn and maybe create. I should have been having daydreams about the hypothetical changes I would make, but the image of Declan's face when he handed me the paperwork, the look of utter disappointment, commandeered my brain. I faked the smile on my face for Leah's sake—and maybe a bit for those observing us—but my insides were crumbling into a gooey pit of remorse.

Guilt had plagued me as a kid. It's not that I didn't do what I thought was best. I tried. But you always hurt someone when you made a choice between options A and B. Making choices came easy to me. Living with them was much harder.

"That's one word for it."

"Shouldn't you be giddy about your special science gig? Tina said no one gets assigned to operations out of the gate."

"Who is Tina?" How many people did Leah already know?

"You really need to learn to make friends. Geez. Tina is kind of short with really pretty black hair. I think she's part Navajo."

I had no idea who Tina was; Leah's description didn't change that. Then again, I didn't care who Tina was. This may have been what my sister was getting at, but I had much bigger problems percolating internally than not caring about some random girl.

I pretended to know who she was, lest I had to hear more descriptive factors. "Oh, right. Why would Tina be an expert on jobs on Cloud Nine, again?"

She faked collapsing. Melodramatic much? "You are so lucky to have me."

"That's me: the lucky one."

"Tina researched everything before coming here, and her uncle works for the EPA. She knows stuff and she said that all of the operations staff is promoted from current Cloud Nine staff and has to be approved by the advisory board."

Well, Tina knew the right lingo, but I had a hard time believing anyone who wasn't already within the Cloud Nine program would have a clue about its rules. Also, it didn't feel like enough time would have passed for Adam to get clearance to make me some special case. Unless they had already selected me for operations before I even came to the stupid station.

I really didn't like that thought.

"Well, clearly there are exceptions."

"Clearly." Leah sounded a little put out by it, but she was still bobbing down the hall on the balls of her feet, so I didn't worry too much. "Did the boring interview people give you any hint about it?"

"Not exactly."

"So you just had the same formulaic questions? I wish they could have tailored them a bit more, but this way I got to be surprised when they called out my assignment, right?"

"Did you tell them you wanted to make meals?" I wanted the attention off me. It wasn't that I didn't want to share with Leah. Though, I was a little concerned with her loose lips. There were just too many people around us. I didn't believe anyone here wasn't eavesdropping. If I hadn't been talking with Leah, I would have been snooping on other people's conversations. I'd said it before, I'd say it again: knowledge is power.

"Kind of. I mean, you know, they asked if there was anything in particular I wanted to do. Asked about skills and whatever. I told them I wanted to make stuff. Food is stuff."

Eloquent. So many things are stuff, but now wasn't exactly the time to pick on her. "I'm sure you'll be good at it."

"And I'm sure you'll be good at math and whatever."

"It's chemistry." I switched to a mumble as I continued, "and botany, I guess."

"That's plants, right?"

She knew it was plants. My sister was not an idiot. "Don't mock."

Leah turned the corner before me but called over her shoulder to me, "I thought you didn't get into that stuff."

I waited until I was around the corner, too, and at her side to speak again. We were almost to the room. "It's different here."

"Everything is different here."

Understatement of the decade.

Charlie had arrived at the room a few minutes before us, but Leah was still the first one to have all of her possessions packed.

I was ready to get out of the room, too. Or, more specifically, off this floor. I wanted to be on the real station with access to windows and the ability to move around freely. I hoped to have a less dictated schedule, but based on Adam's reference to working all the time, I wasn't sure how realistic that wish was.

No one was talking about Sage. I figured once we were on the real Cloud Nine, I could find her. I was surprised no one had mentioned her all day, but then maybe Tina had talked about her and I just was oblivious. Not like my day was low-key.

The picture of Sarah and me was still wrapped in my bag. I hadn't unpacked anything that wasn't necessary. I shoved my sleep clothes deep inside the bag and tried to remember where I'd placed the socks I'd been wearing last night. We were lacking in a proper laundry basket. It was something I planned to rectify once we settled in above.

"Did anyone hear anything about Sage today?" I didn't look up from my packing. I didn't need Leah worrying.

"Not really." Leah shrugged. "People thought it was weird. Thought you were either awesome or crazy. I told them both."

"Thanks for that."

"No prob. Besides, everyone had bigger things to deal with today with all the tests determining our future." She said the last word the same way the promotional videos for Cloud Nine said it. A shiver spiraled down my spine.

"I asked about her." Charlie's voice was distant. Hollow.

I turned around and found her packing away, too. I was fairly certain she was employing my technique of pretending to be busy so it didn't show she cared. But it wasn't like I would call her on it. "Is she okay?"

"That security woman Deb—who I'm forever remembering as the bearer of the torture shower—said Sage is fine." No one believed that. The tightening of Charlie's shoulders as she said it told me she was with me there. "Said they moved her up to Cloud Nine proper immediately and she's recovering in the medical unit, which I'm pretty sure is some blend of hospital and doctor's office."

I wanted to make a sick bay joke so badly, but it wasn't the time. "I was thinking of checking on her once we get moved up there." After finding the missing socks and stuffing them in the bag, I zipped it closed and sat next to it on my bed. Leah actively ignored us and kept an eye out our door for the first sign of someone collecting us for the move.

And people said I was the insensitive one.

"I'll go with you," Charlie visibly relaxed. I wasn't the only one bothered by the lack of concern for Sage.

I nodded. "You were assigned to botany, right?"

"I totally forgot about all that for a second there. I had already left when they called your name. Which research side did you get, botany or technology?"

"Ops."

"What?"

"I'll float between both sides and work on the elements that merge the two."

Leah flew to her feet, hands firmly planted on her hips. "How do you know what you're going to do in operations? It's not one of the regular things and they didn't explain the job duties in those template-driven interviews."

"My interview was a bit different from yours, I guess. They did explain what I might potentially do." I tried not to make a big deal of it. Fat chance.

"Ha! I knew it."

"Knew what?" Charlie and I said it at the same time. I appreciated that she was riled by my sister, too, but was still nervous about having a discussion about what Leah thought she knew in front of anyone.

"That they would make some special whatever for you."

"Excuse me?"

"They made this big deal about bringing you here. So why wouldn't they treat you better than everyone else." She stood and slung the strap of her duffle bag over her right shoulder. "And, you know what, Ally? I don't care. You're not going to be the queen of the smarty pants here. She"—Leah pointed at Charlie—"got into your little science coven, too."

She stormed over to the door. I had no idea where all this rage was pouring from, which meant I sat on my bed like an idiot while she vented at a volume sure to carry down the hall.

Leah turned to face me once she reached the door. "You know what else?" I had no damn clue. "They like me here." Everyone liked her. If not for being overwhelmed by her outburst, I would have rolled my eyes in the most melodramatic of ways. As it was, I managed to just gawk at her as she said, "I get to do things you can't do."

Part of me wished I could gather some anger to fire back at her, but the other half was shell-shocked and not wanting what my sister called "special" broadcast to an entire floor. Declan might not be my favorite person currently—or one I particularly understood—but he was right about keeping my recruitment status secret.

Leah, however, did not get that memo. It was for the best that

Declan and Deb showed up in the hallway then and called everyone out for the move upstairs.

Leah was out the door immediately. I moved slowly to grab my grey bag, but my mind was whirring. Where did the venom come from? Had Leah always been this unhappy with me? Would I be able to keep from saying something mean to her just to prove I was right about things later? I might actually try. My skills had never extended to holding my tongue, but from the sound of things I would need to if I didn't want a pillow over my face in the middle of the night.

Someone lightly touched my shoulder. Charlie.

"I think we shouldn't break the news to her that all the cool stuff she gets to play with comes directly from you and me," she whispered in my ear. I pulled back, but when I caught sight of the mischievous smile on her face, laughter tried to bubble up from my chest. I quelled it, but my cheeks pinched tight from the force of my smile.

"Perhaps not," I whispered back as we entered the hall.

CHAPTER 19
THE MOON

The ride up to the real Cloud Nine involved another windowless pod. This time we weren't forced to strap into uncomfortable chairs. That was something. We were, however, a bit cozier with all the baggage. Complaining wouldn't have done much good as the entire journey took less than five seconds.

When I stepped out of the pod, the room wasn't the sickly white I'd been immersed in for the last few days. Instead of the halogen lights, this room was brightened by a soft glow. Big glass panels were set into the walls on the right and left. They were almost black on the left, but on the right, the bold, yellow-ish moon filled my view. Its light warmed the room and made my skin look honeyed.

I'd seen photos of it before. Everyone had. Paintings and pictures and old video reels. Nothing did it justice. Nothing captured its wonder. Nothing had ever made me stop in my tracks literally. The moon did.

Why the hell did everyone want to see the sun when this existed? It was bright, but didn't burn like that vicious ball of gas. I hoped my room had a window that would let me look at the moon all night. I shouldn't have wanted such a thing, because then I might never sleep again.

Watching the clouds from Ground Level used to soothe me. When I'd walk to Sarah's after dark, I'd marveled at the way the black clouds above would occasionally soften to a swirl of charcoal. I'd read about the moon before and knew increased light was touching the clouds on those nights, but it wasn't until now—my skin bathed in that same glow—that I understood.

I turned my forearm back and forth watching the way the shadows were eaten by the luminous orb. If I could, I would have every photo of me taken from now forward done in the moonlight. Everyone else looked so stunning in it, too. Perhaps moonlight was the real-life version of a black-and-white photograph. It smoothed the skin, high-lighted structure, and generally made everyone more beautiful.

I appreciated that the rest of my group was equally in awe. Though, I wished some had chosen to be rooted to the spot like myself instead of clamoring over to the windows. Their noise as they pressed to the glass wasn't particularly loud, but still grated on me. I didn't need a beautiful moment marred by the squeaks of skin against glass. I didn't say anything, though. See, that whole keeping my mouth shut thing was working.

Declan, however, had seen the moon many times before. I wanted to think he was still struck speechless by it—I was sure I would continue to be—but he still only gave us a moment to take it in before urging us all forward.

"All your dorm rooms have windows. You'll be able to look at the moon on your own time."

He didn't bother trying to quell the audible grumbles from the group.

"The sheets with your duty assignments should have a number in the upper right corner. This is your dorm room number. Find that number please." He waited while everyone fumbled with his or her bag. The only person who hadn't stowed his sheet was the sullen Dave kid from day one. The rest of us produced ours.

"What room are you in?" I asked Charlie.

"1007. You?"

I kept my paper out in my right hand. Better to be prepared and all that. "Just three doors down in 1004."

She held out a fist. I bumped it. Sometimes you just have to enjoy the moment. It was easier with Leah actively avoiding me. Charlie and I were at the front of the hall nearest Declan. My sister was at the very back—practically still in the pod. I wasn't stupid enough to think she was scared about being on Cloud Nine. I might have considered it before, but now I knew she was just avoiding me.

If she could keep from telling secrets that weren't hers to share, I wouldn't mind not seeing Leah for a day or two. It might be nice to clear our heads.

Not that it would happen, but it could have been nice.

They segmented us again. Those with rooms in the 900s went to the left and our group with rooms in the 1000s went to the right. Declan led my group, and I wondered if it was because he knew I'd be in that company. It made me feel extremely egotistical to consider it, but he was watching me again with those predatory eyes. Each time we made eye contact, his reaction edged closer to a snarl.

Fine. He didn't like me, but for some reason, I was certain he wanted to know where I was and what I'd be doing. Not exactly an attractive quality.

We made it down a long corridor. What was with this place and long walkways? On the upside, this one had more windows showing the moon on the right.

"We're on level ten of Cloud Nine. This level is strictly for residences." Declan knew how to pitch his voice. He continued leading us down the hall as he talked. "Your duty sheets have the rooms you'll report to for work in addition to your supervisor, for the time being." He looked at me when he said that. Jerk.

"You'll find guidebooks in your rooms with maps of the facility and information on mealtimes and such. Dinner will be in about an hour, and is served on level nine." Declan had slipped into monotonous narrator mode. He didn't care about this, but was simply relaying the same information he'd passed on several times before.

It was so disappointing to see him flip that switch and become the boring guy again. Even when he was angry, he was interesting. I'd much prefer him exaggerated with emotion than in drone mode.

He stopped abruptly. "These should be the lot of rooms for your group."

I hadn't even been watching the room numbers as we'd walked. Sure enough, I saw 1004.

"Please stand in front of your door."

I walked to mine and waited for Leah to join me. She didn't.

They gave her room 1005? Siblings always had to live together if one was under sixteen. Leah was still fifteen. Was this another tweak they had made for me? For her? Was it a mistake? I looked at Declan and his eyes cut across me to Leah and then back. He gave a subtle shake of his head that told me not to say anything. He had to know I'd ask questions later. I bit my cheek to keep from asking them now.

"We use keypads for locks here. Your fingerprints have already been associated with these rooms. Place your right index finger on the pad above the lock."

I did so and a moment later a beep sounded followed by the hiss of the door cracking open. Fancy.

Everyone started to push into his or her new digs. Declan's voice carried over our din. "Do remember that the security team also has authorization to enter your dormitory. For emergencies."

Yeah. Emergencies. They were Johnny on the Spot there, weren't they? I looked back at Declan. He was watching me. Probably knew what I was thinking, too. He nodded at me. To everyone else, it would have seemed like a bland gesture. A tilt of the head indicating he'd seen me. Just being polite, ma'am. They didn't read the tightening of his eyes, the rod forcing his back to straight-edge precision.

That nod said we'd talk later. He had things to say.

I had no idea if those things would be ones I wanted to hear.

CHAPTER 20
TOO MUCH SOCIALIZATION

was apparently the only person who didn't think of the first night on Cloud Nine as the first day of school.

I wasn't sure if this made me the most mature or the biggest downer.

I had hoped to take a few minutes for myself before dinner. Instead, there was some sort of impromptu hallway soiree. Leah assured me that spending time watching the moon or gathering my thoughts instead of socializing would label me an asshole. My sister lacked tact.

So I went.

Little had changed from our preparatory days below. Same group. Same close quarters. But the group chattered like we hadn't spent the last several days together. They exchanged job duties and tried to inflate their importance. I downplayed my own; just saying tech. Leah wasn't having it. She'd spring over my shoulder like some stealth kangaroo and brag that I was in Operations.

Several of the others had already checked the tablets in their rooms for mail from home. I had purposely not done so. Trying to find my place here wasn't going to be any easier if memories of home were wedged in the forefront of my mind.

Leah disagreed, of course. "Did you read Mom's message yet?"

"No." I pitched my voice low.

"She said she was really proud of us." She emphasized the hidden 'both,' but I didn't mind. My sister was holding her own here. For now.

"I'm sure she did."

"She said to think of this like the time we spent the summer out at Aunt Jane's place." She smiled probably remembering the lack of scalding rain in California. "The shuttle to Cloud Nine was way better than having to take eight light rail trains, don't you think?"

"I'm withholding judgment." I wasn't going to say Mom was reminding me that it took me time to adapt to change. My mom knew how to give a subtle elbow to the ribs. She also probably knew that Leah would deliver it.

The longer the hallway session lasted, the more people watched me. My skin crawled under their scrutiny. I was supposed to be watching them. Some were nosy people like my sister, but I saw others with more insightful gazes. I needed my noteworthiness to fade.

Dinner proved to be minutely more interesting, if only by the addition of current Cloud Nine residents. They didn't sit with us. Somehow our group showed up late and there were only three empty tables in the room.

As I gathered my meal—a thick cut of meat took center stage—I surveyed them. There were two guys for every girl. Not the same ratio as down at Ground Level. Something about that turned my stomach. Don't tell Leah, though. I was sure the hookup odds thrilled her.

Most of the current Niners were watching us with far more stealth than my cohorts. People didn't develop that kind of self-preservation skill without having a good cause. For an entire room to be on their subconscious guard, something shady had to be happening on the station.

White walls and spotless floors aside, this place was dirty. At least I came into it expecting to be burned. I thought Charlie did, too, but the rest of them? I let out a deep breath and hoped my fear for them was unfounded.

Adam was in our dining hall. He'd been so eager this afternoon and his eyes lit when he saw me now. My heart sped in response. That worried me. I stumbled into my seat. Would he sit with me?

With one look, Adam made me want to open up. Made me want to be honest. I swallowed so hard my gag reflex cut in. He could get me to be myself here. That made him dangerous.

Relief rippled through me when he turned back to his friends and squished in next to a couple that felt the need to feed each other. Ick. It was bad enough how casual I'd been with him this afternoon—after mere minutes with him—but in a room full of listening ears it could be devastating.

"Who's that?" Charlie's tray clomped down next to mine.

"My boss." I focused on cutting my meat. It fell apart with a fork. Either they had excellent chef skills up here or this meat was a thousand times finer than anything I'd had before. Probably both.

"You already met him?" Her voice lilted at the end.

I shoved a slice of the most succulent beef in my mouth and nodded. Maybe if I kept my mouth full of food, I could keep my feet out of it.

Charlie's small reply of "huh" was directed toward the potatoes she was piling atop her steak. I wasn't the only one wary of this place; I liked that about her. I could use an ally, but it was going to take time before we'd get past things like this. What was I supposed to say here? Even if I wanted to tell her everything—and I didn't—doing it surrounded by fifty strangers wasn't smart.

Maybe she knew that because she changed the subject. "So, your sister was playing social director earlier."

I half smiled. "That's kind of what she does. I bet if there was an assignment here to plan parties, they would have handed over the reins to her without blinking."

"That's kind of terrifying."

"You should have seen her in action back home. Really obscene on party decorations. Tinsel everywhere."

"What do you think they'd do if she tried to put up pink banners in the dorms?"

"Declan's head would explode, and then Leah would scream because blood red just doesn't work with that shade of pink."

The fact that Charlie laughed at gallows humor made me like her more. Sometimes you need to go dark to lighten the mood. Given the fact we were living in a government bubble, it would be just the start of off-kilter jokes.

Others joined us at the table and the conversation switched to a much safer anticipatory tone.

"When do you start work tomorrow?" I asked Charlie.

Tina responded. "Work begins at 7:30 a.m. for every person on Cloud Nine."

I didn't recognize her from Leah's description, but from her know-it-all tone. I didn't know who her source was, but that nose in the air told me she thought she had the inside edge on us all. The slight shake in her hands told me she hadn't completely adjusted to the higher oxygen levels. I managed not to say, "At least I can breathe." I couldn't stop my inner voice from being nasty, but I was working on not saying those things aloud.

Luckily, Charlie was better about saying the cutting things that weren't combative. "Hope that wasn't in the guidebook, because my duty sheet says I report at 8 a.m."

My attempt to conceal a snicker failed miserably. She tried to help me, though. "What time are you supposed to be…" Charlie paused. I didn't want her to point out my special status. Did she see a flash of fear in my eyes? "…wherever it is you report, Ally?"

"My sheet said 8 a.m., but after the first day I'll probably be there by 7."

Tina slid down in her chair and folded her arms over her chest. She didn't argue but held on to the pathetic pout, instead.

"You know what they say about all work and no play," Jorge muttered in a way that made me wonder if he'd ever had a task he enjoyed. I wouldn't be going in early if they stuck me sweeping the floors, but getting the chance to see what kind of tests they're up to in this place? Hell yes, I'd be peeking before everyone else got there for the day.

"For some of us, work is play."

He rolled his eyes. So did Tina. How did these jackasses get invited to this place anyway? The whole Clean Air Development program boasted being the best of the best. Like West Pointe but for science nerds.

"That's because we get to do cool things, God willing." Charlie to the rescue again. The smile I gave her was sincere. Issues of trust aside, a casual friendship would work for now.

I high-fived her, and then reveled in Tina's outright disgust.

General table discussion revealed only Charlie and I were working on the lower levels—me on four, her on three. I pretended this meant higher IQs had further clearance, but it had more to do with who had technology access.

CHAPTER 21
RUNNING MY MOUTH

Moving twenty miles straight up should have made it easy to find solo time. Most of the people I knew lived below the swirl of hazy grey and green clouds underneath my window. Still, there was this social undercurrent I had trouble escaping.

My new abode had a four-foot-wide window set in the far wall. Finally alone, I let the blue-hued light of the brilliant moon calm me. The sky around it was inky. It wasn't like the smudges of soot on a building or the slick, sterile muted rubber of boots. This black had depth. I wanted to climb inside it.

If they made me stay on Cloud Nine indefinitely, I would need to come up with an excuse to investigate that dark sky. Looking out the window at something with actual possibilities, something unknown was new. I liked it.

My duffle bag marred the pristine tile floor. The framed picture of Sarah and me was still swaddled in my clothes. I unwrapped it and placed it on the white plastic bedside table.

The sight soured my stomach. The picture, the wood frame, my friend. None of it fit here. I picked the frame up and held it to my chest. My fingers traced the grain of the wood. My new bed jutted out from the wall, the frame solid plastic. The fabric covering the bed appeared to be the same lush bedding we'd had before. I missed the natural feel of wood beneath my feet. I imagined the cold of the tile seeping in through my boots and a shiver slithered up my spine.

I edged back into the natural light streaming through the window. The dark wood around the pictures of what I'd left behind didn't warm in the moon glow, but it looked more alive. Better than nothing. I flipped the stand out behind it and placed the frame on the desk so it was like Sarah on the right and Mom on the left were looking out into the real sky. I didn't want them to have to live here. I glanced at the thermostat. The digital readout proclaimed 72 degrees Fahrenheit, but it was a liar. I didn't believe even the temperature in this place could be neutral.

"Things are advanced here, but you do have to press a button to change the temperature. Staring at it just makes you look unhinged."

I whirled around to face Declan. My teeth were gritted so tight I was surprised my words resounded clearly. "Ever heard of knocking?"

"I did."

I didn't reply. My feet needed to stay glued to the floor. I needed a few minutes of sanctuary and already I'd lost it. My body vibrated with unspent adrenaline. Declan was smart and didn't move. He watched me as one lion sizing up another. He swallowed.

His stance softened. "I really did. Knock. When you didn't answer, I figured I should come in and check on you."

I glared at him until he averted his gaze. I highly doubted he needed to confirm I was conscious.

"It would have looked weird for me to be loitering outside your room." He muttered the admission, but the bare walls of my room didn't conceal anything. Not even the real emotion he was hiding with faux ambivalence.

Ugh. I wanted to call him a liar. I didn't want to trust anything he had to say. Good Lord, I'd been admonishing electronics moments before. Only, I kind of believed him. So instead of thinking about hitting him, I offered a quick, stiff nod. That was a compromise, right?

"Are you just going to pop in whenever you like?" I shifted my weight to my right foot and tried to look more sassy than violent. I'm not sure I struck the balance well. "I need to know these things. I could have been showering or whatever."

"You weren't showering." His tone was shredded with irritation.

"How did you know that though?"

He tossed his hands up. "I would have heard it."

"Yeah, after you entered my dorm unannounced." I emphasized the after, but he didn't shirk at my admonishment.

"So? I wouldn't have stormed into the bathroom." He gestured to the small door at the back of my room. Lovely, he even knew the layout of my space. "I didn't come here to see you naked."

A flush started to creep up his neck. Now that he'd mentioned me naked, he was picturing me naked. Crap. Now I was blushing, too. We were both picturing me naked and him in the room, and I could not process it. My brain wanted to reboot. I was not going to think about Declan like that. I pulled in a big breath that was more about stabilizing the embarrassment than enjoying a hearty oxygen solution. "Why did you come here? I'm pretty sure using your 'security purposes' access to my room was for something worthwhile. News on Sage?"

He shook his head. "I wish. She's kind of moping, from what I hear." He crossed the room and sat at the foot of my twin bed. "She's not talking to anyone, but they've got her under careful observation."

"She has to be seeing real doctors, though, right?" They wouldn't let teenagers handle something serious, would they?

"Everything in Medical is under the supervision of doctors, Ally." He said this like I was an idiot, but the twist in my gut said our definitions of doctors might vary.

Fine. "You're avoiding the subject."

"No, I was answering your question. Politely, even."

That was debatable. "Well, what's the big rush that has you barging into Chez Ally?"

Declan swiped a hand over his face like it would offer a clean slate for our conversation or pull his thoughts to the surface. "What *don't* we need to talk about?"

I wasn't in the mood for his dramatics. I pulled out the chair tucked beneath my desk. It slid silently over the floor. I positioned it so Declan couldn't avoid my gaze, and sat. "If you're not going to be forthcoming, then I'll just start asking questions."

He looked away again. "That might be easier."

"Why is my sister across the hall instead of in this room?"

"Because that's her assignment."

"If you're going to be a dick, you can just leave."

"I'm not trying to be difficult. I swear. There are just," he paused and stared at my ceiling, "things I can't say."

"Then phrase it carefully. I'm smart, I'm sure I can parse it out."

"Your sister was assigned her own room because you were determined to have your own room."

"Aren't all siblings supposed to live together, though?"

"Until the youngest sibling is aged sixteen."

"Was the exception that Leah will be old enough soon?"

"No."

"Any hints here?"

He fidgeted. His bulk made for fluid movements on a grand scale, but small motions looked awkward and forced. His fingers teased the hem of his shirt. I hadn't realized it wasn't tucked in anymore. It made me feel more comfortable for some stupid reason.

"Okay. Let's try this. Was this choice about her or me?"

"You, but I think you knew that. The Board wouldn't go out of their way for someone to learn how to cook. They would do all sorts of things for someone with impressive research skills and who destroyed their physical challenges. You ran for longer than anyone before. Even those of us who have lived on Cloud Nine for years can't do what you did. It makes those in charge take too much of an interest in you." This wasn't boasting. This wasn't "you're hot stuff." This was a warning. Too. Much. Interest.

God, what had I done?

"I'm already here, though. What's the purpose of the special treatment?" My voice pitched up and my stomach considered following it. I shifted to place my palms beneath my thighs. I needed something to pin me in place. Grounded. I needed to be grounded. I wished that were easier twenty miles up.

"I honestly don't know. I even looked over your file again, but it didn't help." From the twitch of a muscle in the right side of his neck, I believed Declan wasn't used to being out of the loop. "I do think they plan to use you."

I laughed. It was bitter and longer than made either of us comfortable. "They do that with everyone here, though, don't they?"

He looked down at his palms. "Some more than others." His gaze turned toward me. Those brilliant eyes shimmered with something earnest. "I like you, Ally, and you're too good to be chewed up by this place. It's why I gave you a choice. I gave you an out to come and work for me. I could have at least tried to protect you there."

"Protect me from what?"

"I don't know." He rocketed up like he had someplace to go. Instead, he stood there clenching and unclenching his fingers. "I wish I had that answer for you. You knew this place wasn't just some teenage commune when you came here."

"I did." I spoke softly, his ratcheted anger ebbing my own. "I didn't want to come here—"

"Then why not take my offer of working security? Avoid sinking deeper?"

"I like research. The one upside of having to move away from everyone I know and work for some propaganda machine is the chance to get to do some fascinating things. That job is about the only thing I was excited about here."

"I see."

"It wasn't a slight to you that I passed on being your muscle. I just needed this part."

"Did you think that's what they want?"

"Please. I'm not dumb. I know I was recruited specifically to work there. Operations-level gig from the get-go is kind of a red flag, but maybe I'll be able to do something good."

"I don't doubt you could create something brilliant, Ally. I just don't know that they'll use it or you the way you think."

That made two of us.

I pursed my lips. "Would there really be any control for me regardless of my choices, though?" I slouched in the chair. "I'm trying to make the best of a less-than-ideal situation here."

"Less than ideal?" He snorted.

"I was being polite."

"I suppose since it didn't come accompanied by a fist, that's your version of polite."

I gave the door a pointed stare.

"Fine. Sorry." He rolled his eyes, but I accepted his weak apology anyway. He knew more about this place than I did, which made him an asset. He continued, "It's easier to work within the system here. At least if you'd been working for me, I could have helped you. Then you wouldn't be out there drawing attention to yourself."

"I don't think there is any chance of me not drawing attention to myself."

"You could try not to walk around like a bold red flag."

"Have I been throwing people around or running my mouth?"

"Not exactly."

"Then what? Tell me what I'm supposed to do here?" My voice pitched up into squeak territory. "I'm keeping my head down around the others while trying not to be an anti-social asshole—though, let's be clear: those kids suck."

His laugh, though reluctant, rumbled with amusement. That's what I needed. Declan, the pinnacle of understanding. How helpful was this guy if at best he called me out for drawing attention then laughed when I asked for advice? My face tightened as my scowl became darker and darker.

Declan held up a hand like it would block my malevolence. "Yes, most of the new additions are less than thrilling personality-wise. They will fit in swiftly, though." The pointed look he gave me felt like an ice pick to the skull.

I was tempted to rub my forehead to soothe the sting. "You can keep making subtle"—I glared at him to make it clear he was anything but—"comments about how I'm some giant piñata everyone has to stare at or you can tell me what exactly it is I'm doing wrong."

"I didn't say you did anything wrong."

"You sure are implying it."

He groaned. "You stick out."

"So you mentioned. How would you like me to fix that, exactly?"

Declan's hands covered his mouth. I wasn't asking for state secrets —well, maybe a little, I didn't know—but he acted like answering this single question would damn him. Feeling sympathy would have been normal, but I didn't work that way. If he wasn't going to be helpful he could get out of my room and quit ruining my night.

He lowered his fingers until they were just grazing his chin. "I'm not sure." He drew in a deep breath and held it for a moment. When he finally exhaled his eyes were closed. I couldn't tell if it was out of defeat or relief. "You're special, and I don't think you can stop that. Or at least I don't think so anymore."

"Before you thought I could be less special?" That was the most backward compliment I'd ever received, and I wasn't certain it was one.

"Well, I didn't know how stubborn you are." He smiled. I did not. Hmph. "If this has been you keeping a low profile, I doubt I'd be able to do enough to distract others from your actions. If you'd taken a mundane task maybe, maybe, others would have lost interest. Now, there is little chance of that."

"What does that mean?" I didn't do cryptic well. I liked numbers. I wanted things equal. Fair. Balanced. Puzzles like this without some finite answer just pissed me off.

"I-I-I...this is ridiculous." He was refusing to look at me. That was new.

"You bust in my room. Tell me I'm drawing attention. I ask why and now *that's* ridiculous? Are you freaking kidding me?"

I was on my feet. I stormed over to stand next to the door, but didn't open it. I didn't need any of our conversation floating out to nosy neighbors.

"This situation is what's ridiculous." Now he was standing, too.

"If you don't have anything helpful to say, you can leave. Come back when you can make coherent sentences that provide context to your behavior or the actions of others."

"I don't know how to answer your question."

"O-kay. How about a new question? You tell me why it matters if anyone pays attention to me or my sister or you. What difference does it make if I catch anyone's eye?"

"They use you." The words slithered in the air. The foulness of them curled Declan's lips back.

"Additional work? Twisting the tech? What?"

He stared at the ceiling again. Inhale. Exhale. Inhale. Exhale. I swear if he was counting to ten I might lose it. "There is more happening here than just the top-level work."

I shrugged. "You don't build a biodome in the sky and staff it with the smart kids without plans to do something noteworthy."

"It isn't that. Everyone here is involved in the science element." He shook his head. "I wish I could tell you more."

I stepped close to him. He must have showered just before coming here. The crisp smell of soap was strong when I only stood an inch away. "Then tell me."

He had to look downward to meet my gaze. Declan's hand was warm when he wrapped it around mine. "I wish I could. For now, just…" He pulled back. "Be safe. Keep to yourself, if you can."

He walked to the door, his hand hovering over the latch.

"That's it?"

"I'll tell you more when I figure out how." The snick of the door behind him was as much of an answer to my questions as anything else. Loud and without a lot of context.

I wanted Declan to be my answer. Something was happening here. Something more than Science, Ahoy! If it bothered the head of security enough to trust the "special" new girl, then it was going to do more than make me uncomfortable.

Unlike Declan, I had no problems with making objections clearly. I heard his warning, but it didn't do any good until I knew what I was up against.

The people of Cloud Nine had the answers. I had to find a way to unlock them.

CHAPTER 22
SOMEBODY BETTER PUNCH ME

stayed awake most of the night watching the moon. Well, I wasn't exactly watching it as using the bright orb to distract myself from thinking about what on Earth Declan had meant.

I finally passed out around 4 a.m., which meant waking two hours later was more painful than usual. Despite the buzz of anxiety in my abdomen, I was kind of excited. I hadn't lied when I told Declan the one thing making this place bearable was the chance to get in on new research.

My morning routine on Cloud Nine wasn't all that different from back on Ground Level. That helped, I think. The shower was smaller, which meant I earned a wicked bruise on my elbow when swapping out the shampoo bottle for the conditioner. Still, the water was hot and by the time I was done, I felt much more awake.

I didn't bother turning the lights on in my room. There was a hazy glow coming from the window. My moon had disappeared for the day, but I knew the light had to be creeping from the eastern side of the hub.

I crossed the hallway and roused Leah. She wasn't having it. Nothing new there. She blamed going back to bed on a sour stomach, but she'd never been a morning person.

More breakfast for me.

I hadn't noticed it last night, but the mess hall had three big windows on the far wall. I'd been so busy trying to avoid drawing attention—and failing apparently—that I hadn't actually looked around. There were only a handful of people noshing when I arrived. I didn't ask if they were early risers like me or if they had a shift assignment that forced them to be here when the others weren't. No one was chatty. Thankfully.

There was something peaceful about this place when I didn't have to hide. Six people I didn't know were in the room, but most were focused on hustling scrambled eggs to their mouths.

It took the cook a moment to even realize I was standing there.

"Well, you're new." Let's hope his culinary skills were better than his observation ones.

"Uh, yes." Awkward, much?

"New recruits aren't usually in here until just before duty call." The cook was a short guy, maybe five-foot-four. As he pursed his lips at me like I was some experiment, I wondered if he was standing on a box behind the counter.

I shrugged. "Morning person."

He grabbed a plate and added a scoop of scrambled eggs to it. I looked over to the tables to make sure salt and pepper were available. "You're not going to need it, but salt is on the table by the window. So are extra napkins and some jellies."

Jellies? Whatever that was, it sounded disgusting.

"You eat meat?"

Why was it so complicated to get a plate of food? I nodded and it made him frown. Still, he threw a couple meat patties on my plate and then handed it over.

The food was worth the hassle. Off-putting as he was, the cook was right about not needing to add anything to it. I was still getting used to having meat at every meal. Not complaining. It was just strange to have everything so plentiful and for others to treat it as typical. This was holiday-worthy breakfast back on Ground Level.

Was this how things would be now? Too much drama to get anything accomplished, but then feeling sated afterward anyway? My brain did not want to process that. Either it was too much trouble, or it wasn't. Or at least that's how it should have been. The problem here was the things that caused me to groan were essentials—food, shelter, not getting shoved out the door.

After scarfing food down in a manner that would have had my mother a spectacular shade of white, I pulled my duty assignment sheet out of my front pocket. It was folded crisply, but the edges curled now.

I unfurled the page and reread the details. Research Operations was headquartered on the fourth floor. I had clearance to enter there, and then I would work out of office 413B. As I shuffled myself down the barren hallway to the elevator, I hoped the lab was more spacious than what I'd seen of Cloud Nine so far. It wasn't that I couldn't do research in a box. I was sure anyone could adapt, but I didn't function well crammed in small spaces. I rubbed my elbow. Damn thing still stung.

The ride down to the fourth floor took less than three seconds and shifted my breakfast around in my stomach. I made a mental note to keep an eye out for a stair option for the mornings. Puking all over the pristine walls of Cloud Nine was probably frowned upon.

My first step into the research wing of the station was unexpected. After days of narrow hallways and fluorescent lights, I did a double take at the wide-open room greeting me on Level 4.

Sure, all the furniture was still white. What was it with this place and the extreme lack of color? But the space was far from confining. The desks had stacks of papers bound with black plastic. A long, slender table ran below three windows on the far wall to my right. Green stalks and stems shot up from chocolate-y brown silt. I'd never seen dirt that rich in color in person. Even from fifteen feet away, it was bold. Without thinking, I walked toward it, wanting to touch and smell it for myself.

Just as my fingers grazed the soft soil, someone cleared their throat. I whipped my hand back to my side like it was scalded. Guilt heated my cheeks.

"Did you come early just so you could manhandle our plants?" Adam leaned against the doorframe. His casual stance and the charming smirk on his face helped to cool my hand-in-the-cookie-jar embarrassment.

I still slipped the tips of my fingers inside my pockets. "Touching isn't manhandling." I kept my voice light and hoped I hadn't just screwed this up.

"So you were groping the plants? That's weirder."

"You interrupted us before it got too far."

"Well, thank the heavens." He pushed off the wall and sauntered toward me, slow and languid. "You wouldn't have done any harm, though."

"It's not part of a project?"

"Not unless you count boosting morale."

"Then why stop me?"

"To keep you on your toes. I can't have you thinking you run the place on the first day."

"No, I suppose we can't have that." I was grinning despite myself. I turned my attention back to the small patch of grass growing in a five-inch-deep box. "So, boss man, do you mind if I touch it?"

"You've seen grass before."

"Yeah. It's just so alive. My brain is still trying to comprehend such rich soil."

I expected him to laugh at me, in as nice a way as someone can, but he didn't. Adam just nodded like he understood. I let my lungs expand and pulled in the musky scent. It was sad that I had to move miles away from the natural thing to be able to experience what earth was supposed to be like.

It was almost as if the warm soil was attracted to my hand like iron flakes to a magnet. It crumbled softly between my fingers. Keeping a smile off my face was impossible. Back home, the soil had taken on attributes of stone. Here, it was like a fluffy bed for plants. Part of me wished there was enough to lie down in. Then I saw how much of the dark brown bits had made a home on the beds of my fingernails. At least the affection was mutual.

I dusted my fingers over the tops of the blades of grass. They tick-led. "What's the purpose of these?"

"Of grass?"

I shot him a look that reminded him I wasn't an idiot. "No, of having the grass in here. This room isn't a lab and I don't see charts for measuring, well, anything."

"Oh. Yeah, no, these are just decorative."

My brain short-circuited. "Decorative?"

"Most of the people who work in this main room only input data. They never get to spend time with any of the projects. Getting to have something green in the room reminds them they're a part of what we're doing."

It wasn't the green of oxidized copper, but the true green of something new and alive. "And it's pretty."

His smile revealed white teeth. "Indeed."

It put me at ease how casual Adam was with me. I hoped it would last when others arrived. Still, at least his clothes were the same utilitarian style I wore. He had on simple cargo pants in an ashen grey. The short sleeves of his white tee shirt made his arms look bulkier than I'd thought before. Stronger. He let them hang loosely at his sides.

"Ready for the tour?"

"Okay."

I was still brushing my fingers back and forth over the tops of the grass blades as Adam lifted an arm to gesture to the other side of the room in a grand motion. "This is the research bay. Everyone on the research team—both tech and bio—have access to this room. It's mostly people doing paperwork."

I rubbed my fingers against one another, letting the remnants of my flora encounter disappear. "Not where the magic happens, then?"

When he laughed, his eyes cut down a third their size. It made him look younger and even more approachable. Like I needed that. "It's where the magic gets filed."

"That sounds far less fun."

He shrugged. "Well, that is the way of these things." He started walking toward the other side of the room. I hadn't even noticed the windows on the back and left walls that showed more offices.

"It's so open in here."

"That's the idea." He stopped at a silver door in the back corner of the room. He pressed his thumb above the lock. A moment later, the light to the left of his finger lit green and he was able to push the door open. "Though, it's a spacious floor plan with lots of locks." He sighed, and almost to himself added, "Lots and lots of locks."

"I assume I get to go through this door, right?"

"Of course. We wouldn't want you missing out on any of the magic." He winked at me and my stomach did handsprings. My insides needed to calm down immediately.

The next room was smaller, with only three desks on the right and two on the left. A center corridor continued to another door with a tiny red light adjacent to the handle. I better not have to punch in a code to get into the bathroom.

"This is more paperwork folk, but ones with access to documents we don't let outside the lab."

"Why—" I stopped myself from finishing the sentence, but the beginning of the question slipped out. It dangled there between us as Adam unlocked the next door.

He was standing too straight now and his jaw appeared sharper as we passed under the next set of unforgiving overhead lights. "Not everyone needs to know the specifics of what we do, but everyone has a role to play in the research here."

Maybe he wasn't watching me any more closely than he had before, but now when he looked my way, I wanted to squirm. "That makes sense." I guess. Not really. "I had assumed everyone was working on things together."

He relaxed, but I didn't. Not yet. "We have teams, certainly, but you of all people, know the best minds work alone."

Oh, right. I'd told him about my aversion to teamwork. "Sometimes putting three or four other minds together is a good thing. Just don't make me work with them." Could he tell I was forcing the flippancy? It still struck me as wrong that he'd be bothered by my questions.

"Wouldn't dream of it." He paused in the middle of the next room. It was L-shaped and from where we stopped, I couldn't see around the corner. It was bright over there, though. "Some of the work we do here involves touchy issues. Others on Cloud Nine don't need to know the specifics. It's not sketchy." He paused and gave me a knowing look that was more charming than scolding. "It's just confusing if you aren't familiar with the science end of things. Like some of the people in Procurement get squeamish about food engineered instead of grown. Even if the product we make is better than what they might have been able to make happen back home, it still makes them uncomfortable."

That made sense. Mostly because it made me feel a little weird, too. Not so much with vegetables, but I wanted to know, did they engineer the meat, too? That would seriously limit my enjoyment of sausage.

Maybe Adam sensed my conflict. He switched direction and took us away from the bend in the room to a couch nestled between a tall lamp and side table with a very shiny bowl on it.

I sat on the deep blue sofa. It was the first bit of fabric, other than clothing, I'd seen in this place that wasn't white. I sank into the cushion enough that my muscles relaxed a bit, but not so much I'd embarrass myself trying to stand back up.

Adam watched me rub my hands over the cushions. A hint of amusement tinted his features.

"Everything else here is white, you know," I said, not caring that I was petting the furniture.

"Oh, that drove me crazy when I moved here. The biology team developed dyes for Procurement. I think the starkness of the place gets to people."

"If they have dyes then why not use colored fabric elsewhere?"

"Special request kind of deal. If you want, I can ask them to swap out something for you. Maybe a comforter?"

"Oh." I hadn't expected that. "Sure. I mean, yes." My stomach tightened again. Fickle thing.

"What's your favorite color?" I could feel the warmth Adam's skin gave off. He was so close. Too close?

I wanted to focus on something else, but he caught me with those eyes. Without thinking I responded, "Sage green."

The green part was true enough. I found myself falling in love with the naturally occurring colors here, but that sage part? At least I didn't shove my whole foot in my mouth and add "just like your eyes."

If I ever became that doe-eyed, someone better punch me.

"I think we've got that one. Shouldn't be a problem." He didn't scratch out a note or anything. Why should a favor for me be so memorable for him? If he hadn't been looking at me, I would have squirmed.

Instead, I deflected the conversation away from me. "It's comforting to know the muted color scheme I see everyone wearing isn't actually some kind of uniform."

He looked at me closer than I wanted. His eyes narrowed a hint, like whatever he saw required further examination. Investigation. The very thing I didn't want.

"I suppose it does look that way." He tilted his head to the right and his dark hair fell over his eyebrows. It looked like he'd just hopped out of the shower this morning, dried it, and came to meet me. I wasn't even sure he'd combed it. Yet it looked good. At the least, it didn't look forced and I liked that. "I hadn't really thought about it, probably because I've been here so long." He shrugged. A simple gesture made bold by the starkness of the room. Or maybe just from my intense focus on him. "With the locks and the rules and everything else, the matchy-matchy-ness of this place could look a little like a mental institution."

My eyes may have bugged out. "That's not what I was suggesting at all."

"It would be okay if you did." He rested his hand on top of mine. He was warm. My hand turned into some heat vacuum trying to absorb this good moment, his heat, his sincerity. I wanted to collect it all and keep it in a little box to make whatever crap came next easier to endure. It didn't matter if I knew better than to trust him.

"I just meant it looked like we had required outfits."

He relaxed a bit when he saw I wasn't offended, but kept his hand on mine. "You do realize what you're wearing matches the theme, though, right?"

I looked down even though I knew he was right. Why did we do that? The only good reason for confirming I was wearing black cargo pants and a grey shirt was that I needed a moment before responding. I needed an excuse to look away from him.

As if there wasn't enough happening in my life now, I didn't know what to make of this attraction to Adam. I didn't want to like anyone here. I didn't want to trust anyone here. And I sure as hell didn't need the complication of doing both with one person. My stupid heartbeat raced anyway. Traitorous organ.

"True enough." Now I felt the damn thing thumping in my neck. "But I always dress like this."

"Doesn't everyone on Ground Level wear cargo pants?"

"Of course. You need something strong enough to withstand the air and that tucks easily into boots."

"Some things never change."

"Do you miss it?"

"Having to wrap myself up like a burrito just to go get the mail? Not so much."

"Not that part. I hated the goggles, too, but living on the ground, the people, going outside and, I don't know, being autonomous?"

"Are you serious?" It wasn't a joke. He leaned in and waited for me to say something. He could stare all he wanted, but that didn't change my question. Adam finally ended our staring contest by answering, "I think you see Ground Level the way you wish it was. It burns to go outside there, Ally. *Burns.* Pollution has so screwed the place good, healthy food is crazy expensive and because of the damn acid rain, there's no chance of being autonomous. Everyone needs to be huddled in their houses—"

Ranting impressed me. This made me the minority, but it was true. People should feel strongly about something. Anger was a valid emotion and people didn't use it far often enough. Unfortunately for Adam, his fervor only ignited my own. "Oh, right, because being locked in a plastic room next to dozens of identical plastic rooms is totally different."

He guffawed. Full on. "It's cleaner."

"It's boring." I faked dusting off my pants. Adam wouldn't give up, though.

"No parents watching you all the time."

"Don't pretend what happens here isn't monitored." I leaned toward Adam and whispered, "Closely."

"Touché." His eyes narrowed, and I relaxed back on the cushion. He wasn't going to win this, but that didn't stop Adam from pulling out one of the best things about being the Clean Air Development team's lackey: "The food is better."

"You eat what you're served. No choices."

"Wait, you're seriously going to complain about the food?"

"No, I love the food. I would eat more often if they'd let me. Arguing with you is just fun." Probably the most fun I'd had since I came to Cloud Nine.

"No one ever argues with me." He leaned back against the blue couch. He didn't sink in, though, his body instead set in relief to the fabric.

"That's probably because you're their boss."

"Then why are you arguing with me?" His voice took on a singsong quality, and I had to fight from smiling when I heard it.

I did it though. I kept my voice even as I said, "It's in my nature."

He shifted his weight to the right, then the left. I rather liked seeing him look a touch awkward. The power was back in my control.

I finally caved and smiled at him. "I've been being good and not arguing with people here. Don't worry. You're special. Now I only get to argue with people I like."

He grinned bigger than he should have. Crap. I hadn't meant it that way. Or maybe I did somewhere, but not here. They didn't have guys like Adam on Ground Level, and I wasn't ready to deal with fluttery feelings for him. Nerves got the best of me, which didn't happen often, and I blurted, "How long did it take you to get used to the extreme lack of color up here?"

A flash of white. Nope. I wasn't going to allow myself to be sucked in by his smile. "Pretty quickly. This place looks gorgeous in the sun."

Oh, right. "I haven't seen it yet."

He smiled at me and I thought maybe the sun would be like that. I fought the instinct to strike my fist against my head at the idea. "You're in luck, then, because your office gets lots of sunlight."

I straightened and no longer needed the noggin knock to focus. "I scored a sunlit office?"

"Next to mine."

CHAPTER 23
TEAM FRANKENSTEIN

Adam stood and then offered a hand to me. I stood on my own accord. Honestly, did he think I needed the assist? I'm the one who—without thinking about how much attention it would draw—broke their ridiculous run on a treadmill test. I could stand without getting winded.

Adam handled the dismissal well and simply lifted his hand to gesture toward the far corner. The room pivoted there, and from the element hidden by this angle a warm glow trickled in. We had these lights on Ground Level. The label said they were supposed to replicate the sun, but that could have been complete bull. I'd never seen the real thing to compare. Mostly the lights were used to help with growing plants and such, but there was a novelty line that was for your house. Some people actually had these "sun rooms," a whole room that blazed with these bulbs supposedly emanating sunlight. I'd been in one once. My skin kind of hurt, but I didn't feel all glow-y or whatever. And I sure didn't ooh and aah at the thing. They were brown and bulky and never matched the rest of the room.

Whatever was glowing around the corner Adam and I walked toward, it wasn't some overpriced, electrified ball of glass.

We edged around the corner and it was …bright. Overwhelmingly so. This was like every morning my mother had flipped on the lights in my bedroom as a wake-up call. Only multiplied by a hundred. My eyes widened at the light piercing the windows and taking over the hallway, but I wasn't seeing anything. Dark spots popped in front of me. Light brown. Then darker. And darker. Something inside my skull was throbbing.

"You're not supposed to stare." Adam took hold of my shoulders and angled me away from the windows.

The light now heated the right side of my body. It was a soft sensation. Not the searing pain of a scalding shower or the sizzling I'd felt in the fake sunrooms back home. It's not that I didn't know you weren't supposed to stare at the sun. I'd read that. There was probably a giant warning about it in the CAD guidebook lying unread back in my room. The brightness and the heat brought the pain I'd always expected but not anywhere near the levels I'd feared. The shock of it all overtook me. That sounded like an excuse, but seeing as I couldn't even muster a wry retort for Adam, it was real.

Adam didn't mock me for the misstep. It scored him points in my book. Instead, he led me forward to another locked door. He was right: So many locks.

Again, he pressed his finger to the attached scanner and waited for the confirmation of his clearance. When the door popped open, I finally got to see the lab.

The floors and walls were white—no surprise there—but the counters were topped with a beautiful black soapstone. I had been worried we'd be working on treated plastic countertops. The latter were common in basic high school classes. I'd had the benefit of being in one of the districts with a heightened science priority, so we'd had the best equipment for the advanced coursework. Most cities with Clean Air Development stations had science-focused schools. Everyone was striving to be the one to fix the problem and they knew where to find new ideas.

From the time I started elementary school, my mother had pushed the importance of understanding our world. She never hid that the intention there was to one day save it. The sky had turned green long before I was born, but she remembered a time when the rain didn't singe the skin.

We'd taken a trip up to Oak Creek Canyon a couple years after Dad died. I had been in awe of the hints of red amid the tarnished rocks. Mom was on this kick of pushing a "girls have to stick together" agenda, which at 12, I thought was stellar. Only, the trip soured when Mom got caught up in how beautiful the place used to be. She told me her parents were married beneath ponderosa pines in the very spot we visited. I had no idea what those trees had looked like and couldn't understand why the sandstone rocks made her cry.

She'd always been certain I'd be the one to change things, and after that trip, I believed her. I hoped she was right.

"I can kick on the tinting on the windows to dampen the sun, if you want." Adam pulled me from my reminiscing.

"That'd be nice." As much poetry as was written to the sun, I found myself more smitten by the moon. It was cool and soft and didn't scorch your retinas. As far as I knew.

He smiled and tapped a few keys on a control panel laid into the far wall. The holy-crap-why-is-it-so-bright tone of the sun was scaled back as a light gray tint covered the window. Even with the dampened lighting, the room felt cavernous.

I could feel Adam's eyes on me. I liked it more than I cared to think about. "Office first or the five-cent tour of the lab?"

The lab equipment lining the countertops called to me and from the entryway, I could see a large osmosis tank in the back. Decision made. "Tour."

He grinned. "See, I knew you'd fit in here."

"Speaking of which, where is everyone?" The room probably wouldn't feel so massive with people working at the ten stations. The whirring of a centrifuge went a long way to filling quiet space.

"Duty call isn't until 8 a.m." He shrugged. "You got here really early."

"Then why are you here?"

"I always get here early."

"Did you know I would be here early?" The idiocy of my blurted statement made my head hurt.

He smiled and shook his head. "How would I have known that?"

Maybe because we were alike.

As we moved near the wall opposite the windows, I got my first look at a giant osmosis filtration chamber. "That is massive for testing purposes, isn't it?"

"Absolutely." Adam slipped his hands in his pockets and offered no details.

I bit. "What's it for?"

"You're looking at part of the air filtration system for Cloud Nine. All the heavy metals are pulled out before this stage, but it all passes through here."

"Cool. I assumed all the air filters and such would be locked away in some utility area, though."

"Most of it is." He reached out and touched the top of the tank like he was petting an animal. "We have this part here mostly for inspiration, and, I suppose, because if it broke down anyone in this room would be able to help fix it."

The large white tank fit with the room. I was close enough to feel the vibrations from the active filtration happening inside. "How is this your inspiration? We know how it works. Pressure on one side of the membrane, and such."

"Yes, but we can't use this same system to clean the entire atmosphere. And even if we could, the final product would be such a shock to the systems of all those living on Ground Level, it'd cause more harm than good."

"So you need something easy to implement, capable of being mass produced, and that could ease people into the air quality changes."

"Precisely."

"Oh, piece of cake." Filtering pollutants out of the air we could do. With the right filtration system, we could clean the air to an ideal balance. Only, there wasn't quite a way to do that on a global scale. Adam was right; most people, even kids, would react harshly if you just up and started making them inhale higher oxygen levels.

Adam shoved a hand through his hair, his fingers creating deep troughs in the dark locks. "Tell me about it. Got any ideas?"

"Maybe. I need to see what work you and your team have already completed. Let me read what research you've already done. That way I'm not just throwing old ideas at the board."

"And maybe something we've done will spark the great idea from you?"

"Isn't that how all great scientific advances happen? Someone taking another's idea to the next level?"

"Not all of them, but more often than not."

"Well, in that case, allow me to piggyback on your work." I beamed a cheesy grin at him.

"Since you asked so nicely."

We were both on the verge of laughter. A harsh click and a soft whoosh resonated in the hollow room. Adam and I both looked up immediately and sobered a bit as we realized we weren't alone anymore. I didn't intend to, but I took a step backward. It was an open-close motion. Startle me and I go into fight mode. At least I didn't bring my hands up.

On Ground Level, those instinctive moves made people leave my sister and me alone. They stopped people from asking questions about what our family had and why. They meant I was allowed to be alone when I wanted to think. They stopped people on Ground Level. Here, there was only so far they could go.

Declan was right. I drew too much attention, as it was.

Adam didn't react to my pulling away. I don't know why I expected him to, it's not like there was anything wrong with putting distance between us. He waved at the two guys who entered the lab, then a third guy behind him.

"Where's Terri?" He asked the first guy, who had hair cut so short I could only determine its probable color by looking at his eyebrows. Light brown.

"She has paperwork to finish. Said she'd be in the lab in twenty or so."

Adam nodded. "Oh, hey, have you met Ally yet?"

"Not until now. I'm Kevin." He extended a hand toward me. I gave it a firm shake in response and earned a smile in return. "Nice to have you on Team Frankenstein."

Adam deflated. "I told you to quit calling it that."

"Everyone else likes it. Seriously. You need to get the clothes folk to make us Team Frankenstein shirts."

The guy who arrived with Kevin piped in, "I'd wear mine every day."

"You're not helping, Aaron." Adam had lost all of the convivial spirit he'd conjured with me. "They already ask enough questions about what we do. Do you really think it's your best idea to make everyone else think we're putting goddamn bolts in people's necks?"

I couldn't keep my mouth shut. I'd have to work on that. Tomorrow. "Would they honestly think you were using lightning to animate the dead? Because then I've sincerely underestimated the recruiting process here."

Adam whirled on me. His mouth was slightly gaping, but I saw the flash of delight in his eyes before he spoke. "You're not helping."

"It was just a question." When had not smiling become so difficult? I was skating dangerously closer to bubbly than I'd ever cared to be.

He made a distinct brush-off gesture and turned his attention back to Kevin. "Just make sure Terri finds me when she does get in here. I need her involved in preparing for the next round of trials."

Trials? Sure, the process required testing things, but that was the word I expected to hear: "tests." Trials made me think of medicine and makeup and using both on very unlucky animals. My stomach did a whole other kind of flip-flop. The kind where it sank as deep as possible, making me want to bend over, then flew back up in an attempt to escape through my mouth. I maintained a straight face. If I opened my mouth to ask the question, the contents of my stomach would end up on someone's shoes.

"Ally?"

I got the impression Adam had said my name more than once. At least Kevin and the others had already found their way to workstations across the room. I like my moments of weakness to trickle through the grapevine. It's far less interesting if everyone gets to witness it at once.

"Yeah?" I hated that I sounded so dazed. I needed to get control of myself and fast.

"You want to see your office now?"

"Sure." For now, one-word answers would do the trick.

Now wasn't the time to invite concerns from Adam, who hadn't yet earned my trust. At some point, I'd need to find out what he meant by "trials." Maybe it was just that they used different terminology up here. Maybe *trials* applied to plants instead of living things. Who the hell knew?

Adam led me along the far side of the room. I focused on the black countertops and the slight clap of Adam's shoes on the floor. My boots were nice and silent. At least I was winning at the stealth game.

We ended up back by the big windows. My office was around a quick corner. Adam's office had one window open to the lab, and then glass on its front wall facing the giant panes exposed to the overwhelming sun. My alcove was right next to his. We shared a pane of clear plastic. I assumed it was plastic, anyway. I didn't think the Clean Air Development team would be willing to haul glass up here. This place may be fancy with electronics, but glass was exceptionally expensive.

In most ways, my office mirrored his. It faced out to the bright sky, had a big desk, two bookshelves, and a chair that looked like it wouldn't kill my back. Only, his room was brimming with paperwork and books shoved haphazardly onto the shelves. My desk had a simple white tablet, three writing pads, a pencil, and a pen sitting atop its black surface. It was nice to see they'd put the same soapstone in here as they did in the lab. I doubted I'd ever bring that type of work back to this room, but I could appreciate the cohesion.

"What do you think?" Adam folded his arms across his chest and leaned against my doorframe. I'd seen that pose enough now to know it was his go-to move. Was it his way of telling people he was laid back? I had originally found it casual and it put me at ease. Now, I wondered if it was forced. Was he manipulating his body language to trick me somehow?

There were times when I hated being so skeptical. I'd had a nice morning with him, hadn't I? He'd been funny and forthright with me. Mostly. Did one word—*trials*—change everything? I didn't want to think so. Really. My brain and my gut weren't connecting though. Logic can't always override that innate pang deep down.

"I think it looks like no one has ever worked here."

He laughed. I did, too, but mine was fake. Ping! Ping! Ping! My internal alarm kept ringing, and I couldn't find the snooze button.

"You're right, but I'm sure you'll have it looking lived-in, or, well, worked-in soon enough."

"Right you are." How was I going to demand the right to see what the hell they were working on now? Would I get complete access?

He pushed off the doorjamb and tilted his head down a smidge to look directly at me. So genuine. "Just tell me where you want to start."

That was easy. Too easy? Was my internal radar off? "Like I said earlier, I need to know what work you've already done and are currently doing so I can make progress."

"And?" He looked so expectant. Almost hopeful.

"Pick out the most vital projects you're doing now, and send me the thesis on each along with correlated research and test results. We'll go from there." It comforted me that I was telling him what to give me, what to do. Was that a ploy to make me feel powerful in this controlled environment?

"That's a lot of reading."

I shrugged. "I'm fast and I don't sleep a lot."

"You're going to fit in well here, then."

That's what I was afraid of.

CHAPTER 24
LETTERS FROM HOME

Cloud Nine was about as advanced as it got. Bioengineered food. Filtration systems that both removed and replaced particles in the air and water. Salves and serums for just about every skin condition, including simple stuff like healing abrasions quickly.

Why had none of this found its way down to Ground Level? A scraped elbow there meant extra bandages just to walk to school, and if you got caught in the rain, it could burn for hours. I should know. The salve I'd just read about would heal cuts in less than a day.

Who hoarded that kind of base knowledge? I'd spent the last nine hours reading reports on the current and most successful projects from the Research division. I couldn't decide if I was impressed or infuriated. Whoever dictated the protocol around here knew what they were doing. Despite all the advanced technology filling this station—fingerprint locks included—researchers brought in bound paper research reports for me to read. Every forty minutes or so, another person would bring in three or four reams of paper bound with black plastic. They'd give me that sheepish look and plunk them on the corner of my desk or stack them on the shelf to their right.

Everyone was friendly enough. I didn't ask if it was their research I was reading or someone else's. I figured either way I'd come out looking like a jerk. My goal wasn't to call people out for mistakes. I wasn't looking for misplaced commas or noting who wrote funky formulas. I wasn't grading them. I just needed to learn about this place. I didn't know why, but I had to learn this fast. If I didn't get my feet planted in what they already knew, I feared I'd be swept away by lies.

The reports didn't lie. Not outright. The lies were hidden between the facts stacked on my desk. What wasn't there was the bigger problem. Notes of subjects without ever classifying them—plant, animal, or otherwise. The way some projects were considered closed without any indication as to why investigation down that line was stopped.

I'd skimmed enough to notice a habit. If I could detect it in one day's worth of speed-reading, then it wasn't that well concealed. No one carried shame on their shoulders when they brought me these reports. Did everyone know and elect to keep their heads down? Or had no one read enough of these things to get the idea? Either way, my head hurt.

A light, hollow thunk drew my attention. Adam stepped in from the hall. "I'm impressed you're still here."

"Why wouldn't I be?" I felt my brow furrow in the way my mother lamented. Like I cared about wrinkles.

He smiled. The reaction was so expectant. Just what I needed.

"What?"

He flashed his teeth at me in a big grin before answering. "You do realize it's dinner call? Hot food is waiting for you elsewhere."

I tapped the top of my tablet to bring the screen back to life. Sure enough, the digital clock at the top corner said 6:35 p.m. "Huh."

"Did you want to catch a bite to eat?"

I blushed. I didn't even recognize myself when my voice shifted to a soft tone. "I suppose."

"Good. We should hurry, though. They have no shame in serving seconds and we have a few who abuse the privilege."

It wasn't funny, but I laughed anyway.

I pulled my left boot back on—the kind of reading I had been doing required comfort—as I talked with Adam. "Oh, thanks for making sure all the research made it to my office today."

He must have detected my rueful tone. "I should have warned you about our archaic system here."

"Well, at least my bookshelves aren't empty anymore."

"There is that." He sat in a simple black chair while I finished lacing my right boot. "Oh, and the active details on my current project have been sent to your tablet. You'll have to use the fingerprint lock on the lower right to get access to read them."

"I had to walk through how many locked doors to get in here and there are locks on the research, huh?"

"Would you buy: Safety first?"

"Not in the slightest."

"Just keep it to yourself for now. We hate getting anyone's hopes up or having people misinterpret what we're doing because they don't have all the information. That's why everything is on lockdown."

I didn't believe him, but I'd admit it was a good cover story.

———

I'd survived my first day working on Cloud Nine, and it wasn't exactly awful.

The science had been so engrossing—and the sun so irritating—that I had somehow forgotten I was working for the people who let my dad die.

My bedroom was empty and the lack of distractions only let my whirring brain amplify my guilt. Reading a message from my mom didn't help the matter. I wanted to reply to her, but CAD's silly policy about us not communicating with others outside the program for "testing integrity" wouldn't let me.

Charlie's quick rap on my door had me bounding to my feet and over to let her in, in two seconds flat.

"Tomás is already making me crazy. Can I hang with you for a while?" She didn't look too flustered, but I wasn't going to argue.

"Sure. I could use the company."

Charlie snagged my desk chair and settled in with her feet

stretched out in front of her. The relaxed posture made me think she wasn't struggling with a lack of hatred for Cloud Nine. A flash of jealousy pitted my stomach, but when she smiled at me in a conspiratorial way it vanished. Maybe friends made us better people.

"I hear you settled in at Operations today."

I arched an eyebrow.

Charlie looked like she was about to start giggling. "You honestly thought people weren't going to talk about it?"

"There's nothing to talk about. I sat in an office and read a bunch of reports. How is this gossip worthy?"

"Just is." She was quiet for a moment before continuing. "Maybe because everyone had to gather their reports for you?"

I shrugged. "No clue. My day was all reading, no mega breakthroughs and I didn't lock myself out of the office. It was fairly mundane for a first day."

"If you say so." Charlie was smirking.

I found myself smiling at her teasing, but it faded when another thought overshadowed. "Don't suppose you heard anything about Sage?"

Her smile faltered, too. "No one's seen her, but that makes sense if they've got her away at a hospital."

Why did that feel like a fake-out? I mentally shook myself and moved on. "Since you already know what I did today, tell me about your day. Was the botany division everything you hoped it could be?"

"More." A soft pink rose on Charlie's cheeks as she let a grin take over her mouth. "The greenhouse is just about the coolest thing I've ever seen."

"They had a few little plants down on Level 4. I'd never touched that kind of dirt before." I remembered the way it held my skin, and understood Charlie's awe.

"It's the entire top level, Ally. Like the whole thing. Rows and rows of plants, almost all of them ones I've never seen grown even at the super fancy greenhouses."

"Very cool." I tried not to think about the greenhouses back home. The prices for the foods were the equivalent of promising your firstborn child.

Charlie rattled off all the highlights of working with the plants here. Her excitement wasn't as infectious as I'd have liked it to be, but it was nice to see someone else really happy.

"Have you heard from your mom yet?" Charlie's question caught me off guard.

"Twice already."

"Me, too. She's fretting over Tomás, but I'm pretty sure she's worked up about me, too."

"Well, you can't blame her." But I could blame my mom, right? "My mom said she got an update from the EPA saying we'd transitioned successfully into Cloud Nine. So, maybe that will help."

"Is that all she said?" I didn't catch a hint of judgment from Charlie, but my stomach tied at the words anyway.

"No." I tugged on the hem of my shirt like that adjustment was far more important than speaking. "Her first message was to both Leah and I, so that one was much more cheerleader-y."

"Exactly what Leah needed?"

"Pretty much. Not that she needed it to acclimate."

"And the second message?" Charlie's prodding was loosening my tongue instead of erecting my defenses.

I trusted my gut and answered her honestly. "It mostly just made me feel guilty."

"Was she trying to make you feel guilty?"

"I'm not sure. She said the right things to make me feel like a jerk for complaining about coming here." Mom had written that she wished Dad were around to see the scientific advances I'd make while at Cloud Nine. I wasn't willing to share that part with Charlie, but the small admission let my twisted insides relax.

Charlie nodded. "Don't you wish you could just tell her you're fine so she wouldn't worry?"

Yes. I still wasn't happy about her making this decision without me, but now she was on her own in that big, brick house. "If I told her I had a good first day, she'd probably send a doctor over to check my temperature."

Charlie snickered. "So you did have a good day? You probably even liked talking to people."

"Hey now. Let's not go to extremes." I held a hand up like I could stop this train, but there was a lightness bubbling up my chest—the kind I normally felt while goofing off with Sarah back home. "I wouldn't want to be getting a reputation of being a people person."

"Perish the thought." Charlie lowered her voice, like there was actually someone listening in. "But if you decide you do, in fact, not hate everyone else here, you can tell me."

I chucked a pillow at her head.

She caught it. "I'm just saying the Team Frankenstein crew said nice things."

Really? I needed to reinforce my defenses, or this place was going to sneak under my skin without me noticing.

CHAPTER 25
LIQUID NICE?

I poked at the rubbery brown blob on my plate. It didn't jiggle when the fork tines pierced it, but there was still too much movement to make me trust it.

"A few weeks of work and you're going on a hunger strike?" Adam set his tray next to mine, then pulled out a chair to sit at my right.

"What is this?" I poked it again.

"Portobello mushroom." He sliced a chunk of his, keeping the colorful stuffing loaded on top. "Be adventurous. It's delicious." The bite he crammed in his mouth was big enough to make his cheeks bulge while he chewed.

Ravenous as I was, I still took a small bite. The stuffing was creamy and sweet. I recognized the roasted tomatoes and delighted in the way they burst with flavor. The mushroom, though, sent claws raking up my spine. It clung to my tongue in some sort of war. I didn't want to swallow the thing, but I wasn't about to spit it out in front of the others. It was just sticky enough to hold to my taste buds, like it was forcing me to savor it. Rebellious fungi. It took half a glass of water to dislodge it.

"So, you didn't like it?" At least Adam had the good sense not to smile right now.

"Not so much." I scooped a forkful of the cheesy, tomato-y filling. "This part is great though."

I didn't hear Leah set her tray down, but I heard the huff she made when sitting. My sister had never been subtle. It was a family trait.

"You better be coming." I didn't know what Leah was talking about, but her tone rang with accusation.

What had I done now? "To what?"

"Seriously?"

I looked at Adam, but he was every bit as shell-shocked. If we hadn't been in a room full of strangers and if Adam hadn't been seated next to me, I would have called her out on being a self-centered fool. I would have used dirty words. And probably suggested places she could put her high-and-mighty expectant tone.

We weren't alone, though, and I told myself I was trying to keep a low profile. Bleating obscenities at my sister didn't mesh with that plan. Unfortunately.

"I've been up for more than twelve hours, Leah. Most of that was at work. You're going to have to fill me in."

My sister looked downright bewildered. I didn't know if it was because I had brought her fizzy water the last three nights in a row or because she believed I didn't know what she was talking about. She sighed dramatically in case people were watching (they probably were). "Tonight, there's a mixer for all the new people."

I swallowed a big bite of my food to delay my response. "A mixer?" I made sure the second word carried the did you really think I would ever go to something like that? message.

Her nod was more of a rapid bouncing of her head. Was her brain used to the jostling by now?

I glanced at my plate. How much longer would the food ploy work to delay conversation? "That was quick." God, being polite made my side ache.

"That's not the norm," Adam interjected, and I was thankful for it.

"Oh, no, but when I offered to help Lily she couldn't say no." Leah tucked her hair behind her ears, then fluffed it back outward. Was she trying to impress Adam? I hoped not. For more reasons than I was willing to admit.

"Is that a good idea?" She looked paler than usual. "You still haven't beat whatever stomach thing you've got going on."

She stared at the dollops of food on her tray. Last night, she'd argued her nausea was from trying new foods. "I'm fine."

"You don't look fine, and you're not really eating." I reached out to touch her forehead. She hadn't had a fever yet, but something was off. Leah slapped my hand.

"Don't." The bite stung. "I'm fine," she said with more vehemence this time.

"So," Adam said loudly over my huffing. "Lily already wrangled you in, huh?" He was being nice. It looked effortless. Maybe it was in his DNA. Could I clone that?

"I totally offered to help." Leah sat straighter as if this was her taking the high road. Please. "I was kind of the party planning queen at my old school."

"This isn't a school." My voice cut through her joy, and I didn't feel all that guilty about it. I'd been the one checking in on her every night and making sure her stomach settled. None of that counted with her.

"No, I suppose not." She pursed her lips. Mom would have scolded her for the overt pout. I resisted doing so. Leah continued, "Still, you need to make sure you're there. It'll be your chance to meet the regular Niners and be nice to everyone."

Golly gee. My chance to be nice. Where did she come up with this stuff? "I've met people."

"What people?" Leah caught herself and directed her next comment to Adam, "Other than you, of course."

"Of course." His niceness wasn't waning. Seriously. Could I get a bottle of liquid nice? I'd use it only in social settings I couldn't avoid. Like mixers, apparently.

"I met a bunch of people who work in the lab."

"Did you talk to them?" I know we're supposed to say there are no stupid questions. The people who said that never met Leah.

"No, Leah, I stood there and stared at them." I wanted to pour sarcasm over her head. It took her a long time to pick up the concept and she still made a sour face every time I leveraged it. Some of us have wit, others just talk a lot. Guess which one Leah was.

"Fine." She spat the word and I enjoyed the obviousness of our age gap. Just in case Adam was looking at her. Not that he was. "But you should get to know more than the nerds." She looked to Adam again. "Sorry."

She wasn't. My idiot sister didn't even bother trying to hide that she said it knowing she'd offend us both. Classy, Leah. Real classy.

"You might want to stow that line. You forget you now live in the land of the nerds." I kept myself from digging in further and saying explicitly what I was hinting at: She couldn't be here without me, because this was the ultimate advanced placement course.

Her eyes narrowed and her mouth set into a firm line. I liked it better when she was quiet. Even if it was in defiance.

"See, now, Land of the Nerds could work on a shirt." Adam faked a contemplative pose with fingers on his chin. Delight sparkled in his eyes.

"I still like Team Frankenstein."

He nudged me with his elbow. "You would."

"I think you like it more than you want to admit."

"I do, but I'm still not signing off on that."

We continued our conversation as if Leah weren't there. If she wanted to sulk, then fine. She ate her food quietly, watching us like she was waiting for me to apologize. Like that would happen. Holding my tongue practically was an apology. She should have known that.

Adam left the mess hall with me. We stepped onto the elevator just down the hall.

"Which floor?" His fingers hovered over the large buttons on the right panel.

"Four."

He looked over his shoulder at me. He didn't need to say anything. The way his eyebrows tried to disappear into his hairline told me he didn't approve.

I folded my arms in front of my chest in response. My body language hadn't learned to hold back just yet.

"You are not seriously going back down to the lab." His disapproval didn't impress me.

"You're the one who locked down my tablet. If I can't take it to my room to read, then I have to go back to the office."

"You can read it tomorrow." The elevator filled with a low, dull beep.

I reached around him and pressed the button. "I've got time now."

"You have a party to attend in an hour." He hit the "door open" button.

Ugh. Electronics standoffs were not my thing. "Pass."

"You need to attend, Ally." He didn't seem to think much of my response, but I didn't care for his attitude. I guess we were well-matched there.

"Forced socialization isn't really my thing." I stabbed the "door close" button hard with my index finger. I wanted to stamp the ending of this conversation. I didn't need another protector; Declan was plenty.

Adam had the wrong concerns. Me in a room full of strangers was not a good idea. I didn't want to tell them anything about myself, and that would draw more attention. I sucked at small talk and even if there were awesome people here, they wouldn't be so keen on getting to know the girl who refused to tell you what neighborhood she grew up in.

"It isn't anyone's thing." Adam didn't get it.

"You did just meet my sister, right?" The elevator was finally moving.

"It's not forced," he muttered as the doors opened to reveal the lab.

"So then I don't need to go. Glad we cleared that up." I tried to push past him but he cupped his hand around my shoulder; it stilled me.

"You don't have to go, but it would be good for people to get to know you. Might even be fun."

"Noted."

He let out a heavy sigh, and then let me go. "Well, I'll be there and I hope you come."

This morning, that might have stirred fluttery feelings. Tonight, it stifled me. The few moments when I could breathe in this place had been dashed. I didn't like others suggesting they knew what was best for me. That's what got me in this place. It was one thing to endure it from my mother, it was another to have a guy who was supposed to be on my side flip and boss me around. I pressed my finger to the first lock in the lab. Heh. He was actually my boss. Still, that allowed him to give me work tasks, not dictate I play well with others outside of the lab.

And, honestly, avoiding people was playing nice. Reading would take my mind off the weirdness on Cloud Nine. It would keep me from thinking about my sister and how quickly she'd become involved with everyone. It gave me a way to hide.

Or so I thought.

CHAPTER 26
HOW HARD DID I WANT TO HIT HIM?

Six pages. I made it a mere six pages into the brief Adam had loaded onto my tablet when the snick of the nearest door opening distracted me. The comforting quiet now made me paranoid. Had I really heard that or was I bugging out? I set the reader on the desk and stood.

Declan sauntered across the lab toward my office.

"Knock, knock." His announcement was a little slow for my taste.

"You need to work on your stealth skills. I heard you open the door." I dropped back into my chair as Declan entered the office. I didn't offer the open seat to him. I didn't need to. He grasped the back and brought it around to the side of my desk and sat. He was close enough to touch me, but didn't. Smart man.

"The no-sound options for entering this room are almost non-existent, and I wouldn't want to divulge them."

His amused tone relaxed me. Or maybe it was his clean scent enveloping me. "What if I need to make a quiet escape?"

"If you're fleeing from anywhere, I doubt it'll be quiet."

I tried to give him a dirty look, but, well, he was right. "Perhaps." I shifted down in my seat. After the strain of today, talking with Declan felt downright routine. I wrapped my fingers around the edges of my seat and pushed back to get a quick shoulder stretch. "So what do I owe this visit to? I haven't been causing drama today." I quickly reviewed the day in my head. "I don't think so anyway."

"You're going to cause drama if you don't make an appearance upstairs."

"Did you seriously come here to make me go to a party?" I stared at the ceiling. Air from the vent above brushed my cheek. Why did everyone care if I went to this stupid thing? It's not like it was my party.

"I'm not making you do anything."

Damn right he wasn't. I leveled my gaze at him and held it until I thought he might be uncomfortable. It was hard to tell with Declan. If we were friends, I'd ask him to teach me to hide my emotions like that. Then again, maybe I didn't want to know how or why he picked up that skill. I was good at keeping secrets. He was good at making emotions secret. His skill was better suited to life on Cloud Nine. "How did you get in here?"

"Don't change the subject."

"Answer me."

"If I answer, will you talk to me about why you're here?" He rested his forearms on my desk. The move brought him closer to me.

"Yeah, whatever. How'd you get into the lab?"

"I opened the door." Duh.

"Don't make this difficult." What was with this guy and half answers?

He pushed off the desk and leaned back into the hard plastic of his chair until it groaned. "How is that difficult?"

Really? "It's supposed to be secure here." Isn't that what Adam said? The gauntlet of locks should be for something.

"It is. I'm Head of Security, remember? My fingerprint opens all the locks, Ally." He waggled his fingers at me, not bothering to hide his delight in the taunt.

Crap. I forgot about that. Not that I would admit it. "Well, what are you doing here then? Really?"

"Really?" He shook his head. "I'm not as cryptic as you make me out to be, you know."

"We'll have to disagree there."

"Fine." He made it sound like I was being the difficult one. Clearly, we were not in the same conversation. "I'm here to help you."

"Extended olive branch and all that?"

"Do you ever wonder where that phrase came from?" I let go of the seat cushion when he said that, and thought I might just fall off the thing. Declan equaled direct. He was focused. Since when did we turn left on a chicken walk during a conversation? I kind of liked it, but of course, knew better than to trust it.

"Not really. There are so many phrases at this point that have zero relation to our world now. At least I know what an olive is. I'm counting that in the win column."

He nodded. Pensive. It was strange to see his hulking form slump. It wasn't like he was lazy slouching, but this head-to-toe relaxation. Maybe all his muscular effort had moved to his brain. Now there was a thought.

"So, you really came here to tell me to go to a party." I cocked an eyebrow at him. It took me months of practice to perfect the move. Mom and Leah both hated it. Said it made me look defiant. I loved it.

"I came to help you and part of that is getting you upstairs to that ridiculous thing your sister is throwing. Did you know she actually had special food made for this mixer thing? Usually, it's just people hanging out, but I guess she said she'd make the grub."

"Are you trying to lure me there with food?"

"A little." The hint of a blush warmed his neck.

"In all seriousness, though, why does it matter?"

"Why do you think you need to be down here?"

"I'm getting work done."

"Yes, because there is so little time in the day here for reading. I'm sure you spent your whole day unable to do work." The sarcasm poured from his mouth and puddled on the table between us. It was the kind of thing I'd do, so I just stared at him and let the tone linger between us.

"There's a lot for me to get caught up on." That sounded weak, but I tried to look stoic. If my face were made of granite, he'd just have to accept it.

"Excuses." He rolled his eyes. At me. The dick. "You're hiding in here."

"You're the one who said I needed to keep a low profile." Great, now I was accusatory. Good thing he already knew I was a train wreck.

"Yes. There's a difference between staying under the radar and being the weird, anti-social girl who hates people." He was getting too comfortable around me. That had to be it. His honesty chaffed.

"I don't hate people." I folded my arms over my chest, but Declan just stared at me. "Not all people," I amended.

"Either you're going to come off as an elitist research jock or the stratospheric equivalent of the crazy cat lady. I know you're neither."

Did he really know? I was totally that elitist person when I was around my sister. I looked out the window to avoid his gaze. "Why do I care again if people I'm trying to avoid think I'm a whack job?"

"So you admit you're avoiding them?"

Gah. "No. Maybe." I scrubbed my hands across my face. At least I wasn't sweating. "Avoidance is the best way to keep people from asking questions." Truth.

"It keeps them from asking you questions, but it only makes them talk about you."

I tried to shove all the air from my lungs. If I passed out, we wouldn't have to continue this conversation.

"Stop breathing weird." Seriously? He noticed.

"Can't I do anything right?"

He grinned. Playful. "You argue with the best of them."

"That's something." It didn't cheer me up, though.

"I'll make you a deal."

I watched him from the corner of my eye. "What?"

"You make an appearance at your sister's thing." I groaned and Declan held a hand up. "Hear me out. You mingle. Play nice. Make boring talk about what you like about Cloud Nine. Make it up, if you need to."

"And? There better be an excellent quid pro quo here, because making small talk is akin to lighting myself on fire in order of things I want to do."

Under his breath, he said, "So dramatic." Then, louder, like we weren't the only two people on the whole floor, "You do that, and we spar."

A wicked smile nearly broke my face. "How much contact?"

"You're ridiculous." He knew he'd won me over. That was fine. This was a killer deal. I needed a physical outlet for stress and beating up Declan would totally work.

I folded my hands neatly in my lap. "How much?" I was beaming.

"Either light contact without pads or full contact, but I get to put on some protection."

I pursed my lips. It was a tough call. How hard did I want to hit him?

"You don't have to decide now."

"Deal." I licked my lips, loving the temptation. "But it happens tomorrow and no one gets to watch."

"Well, yeah, that would defeat the goal of keeping your low profile."

"And it'd be really embarrassing if word got out that the head of security got his ass handed to him by a girl."

He made a less-than-subtle *hmph*, but at least he didn't roll his eyes or disagree. He was learning. I expected a good workout no matter what, but if he'd argued, there would have been no question I'd annihilate him tomorrow.

CHAPTER 27
PARTY TIME

My sister liked parties.

I supposed someone had to.

It's not that I didn't like people, as Declan suggested. Big groups meant superficiality, and that held zero interest for me. I wasn't good at wearing a mask, but I couldn't be just me around these people. And in a room the size of my house back home, there was no chance any of these people were going to be themselves.

Too many eyes watching. Too many mouths talking. Too many minds judging.

Still. There I was. I didn't change my clothes, though I was certain Leah had. I did, however, brush out my hair and let it stay down. Mom always said it looked prettier that way. I think she meant feminine, but it was a compliment regardless. One I must have taken to heart, if I was doing it when she wasn't around. Funny how little things like that can affect us.

The hum of people talking about nothing and peaks of fake laughter merged into a soft buzz inside the elongated room. Along the far table sat five trays of bite-sized foods. I didn't know what they were, but I planned to find out. There was some music playing in the background, but it wasn't loud enough to beat out the din of seventy people chittering. How Declan thought anyone would miss me among this many people was mystifying, but whatever. I'd punch him for it tomorrow.

I started to beeline it for the food, but caught Charlie waving at me. Contrary to what my sister might think, I did have some social skills. I rerouted myself to meet with her.

"I'm so glad you're here." She held a glass of pink liquid. It didn't look like she'd sipped any of it. "I wasn't sure if you'd come, but I guess since it's your sister's thing..."

She trailed off like it was obvious I was the super supportive sister. A pang of guilt pierced my stomach as I realized I was trying very hard to not be that. I didn't want Leah to like this place. I hated that she did. It was dangerous, and she didn't understand. I wasn't in the mood to lie, though. Plus, I was awful at it. So, I nodded slowly like I was agreeing with her.

"My brother made a big deal out of coming here." I'm such a jerk. I'd been so wrapped up in my own drama I had forgotten she had her own mini-me to keep an eye on. Charlie pointed at him across the room. He was in the middle of a small group, all guys. They were laughing. It was probably fake.

"Looks like he's doing all right."

"Yeah. He was hacking up a lung when we left the dorm earlier. He's fine now, but he was freaking out like he wouldn't have anyone to talk to. Then the second we get here, he ditches me."

"That's better than what Leah would have done if I'd shown up with her."

"Oh yeah?"

"She'd stick to me like glue, which doesn't sound so bad until you remember she's the one throwing this thing. She'd drag me all over and force me to talk to all her awful friends." Damn it, mouth. I had to hope that no one else heard me call Leah's friends—whoever they were—awful. I hadn't talked with many of the people she called her new friends, but what I'd heard of them made me think 'vapid waste of my time.' I wasn't supposed to say that, though.

Charlie snickered. She knew. She probably agreed, but was smart enough to keep her mouth shut on that point. "Luckily, you have me instead."

"You have no idea." I shuffled my feet, unable to find a comfortable stance. Leah should have provided adequate seating. I pointed at the beverage Charlie held, but didn't drink. "What's that and do I want one?"

"Some drink your sister handed me. It's sour. I think it's supposed to be, though." She shrugged and held out her glass. "You're welcome to try it if you want."

I accepted her cup. "Challenge accepted." I took a tentative sip and winced. The sharp flavor sliced through me. I shook my head a moment. "And denied. Please tell me there are other options. I need to rid this from my mouth."

She laughed. "That was my reaction, too. Well, and I wondered what they used to create it." She started walking toward the back corner, and I followed. "All the food is grown here, so I would assume the drinks are natural substances as well. I'm curious what they used, and if I can create a hybrid version of it that doesn't sear my taste buds."

The table in the back had three options for drinks. The first was the light pink abomination. Charlie and I looked at each other and immediately stepped away from that one. The second pitcher was water, as far as I could tell.

"That one." Charlie pointed to our third choice. It was a light brown and big chunks of ice floated at the top of the pitcher. The look I gave her was dubious at best. "Trust me."

"You know what it is or are we being adventurous? Because I am now saving all my bravery for consuming snacks."

"It's tea."

"No way." My grandmother used to make tea when I was little. She had this cache of little tin jars filled with leaves in varying shades of brown and green. She would let me load mine with sweetener. I didn't remember the taste, but I knew she loved it. I hadn't had it since.

Charlie poured herself a glass. She cradled the small cup between both hands, and then carefully sipped. It was then I learned Charlie's lips thinned out when she gave a genuine smile. "Oh, it's tea all right."

I poured myself a cup, too. I wondered if I'd need to dose it with sweetener the way I had as a kid. Charlie hadn't though. I held the cup to my mouth and let the light, musty scent spark my synapses. The last time I'd drank tea, it had been warm and served in a bold pink mug. At the time I was a big fan of pink. I didn't know when I'd lost that.

This tea was cold and its container lacked the flair of old-world pottery. It didn't make it any less delicious. It was mild and a touch bitter and I had to force myself not to gulp the contents of my glass in a single swig. Declan wouldn't disapprove, as it wouldn't make me look special, just like a fool.

"I gather you like it?" Crap. I'd forgotten I was in the middle of a conversation with Charlie.

I had been staring into my cup. "Absolutely. It's been a long time since I've had tea."

She nodded in a clear I've-been-there way. She probably had.

I almost asked about it. The temptation to find out when she'd last had tea and where sat heavy on my tongue. I couldn't do it, though. Maybe that was small talk, but I knew how personal it could be. She would have answered me, I thought, but doing so in a room full of listening ears would have made her uncomfortable. I wouldn't do that to her.

I wanted to say it meant she was my friend. Only, did it? Or did it make me an untrusting tool? I hated the way this place made me constantly question my every action. I was wary on Ground Level. I wouldn't deny it. I didn't work out just for fun. I did it so I could keep prying eyes out of my life. After my dad died, my mom had managed to keep the historic home our family had lived in for years. I'm not sure how she funded it, but it was ours. It was brimming with all the things we weren't supposed to be able to afford and a few things no one was supposed to still have. All of them, remnants of the world before the sky was cast green.

The last thing I needed was anyone piecing together where I lived. I wasn't home anymore. I couldn't protect everyone from the questions of why we were so healthy. I couldn't stop the inquiries about all the organic materials inside our house. Sure, we grew up with the same scratchy linens as everyone else, but our floors were real wood, the molding around the doorframes, too. Oak filled our house. Mom kept the old kitchen table marked with gouges from more than a century of having homework completed and bills paid on its surface.

The food was better on Cloud Nine. There was tea. And I found myself wanting to escape this windowless room so I could see the moon again. Yet, I lived in a place made of plastic. Something told me talking about the irony of living in a station created of oil—one of the things that caused our current predicament—while trying to clear the air of its effects would be a major party foul.

Instead, I did the best I could and tried to stay in the moment. "So, did you already sample the food?"

"No, but I'm surprised you didn't elbow me out of your way to get to it earlier."

Was I that blatant? "I don't know what you're talking about."

"Of course you do. That's okay. I'm loving the food, too."

"Have you had this stuff before?"

"Kind of." Crap. Was I treading on sensitive information? She didn't look tense, but I was quickly learning most people were better at concealing their emotions than I was. "We had the synthetic stuff like most people."

"Oh. Duh." Of course. We'd all had the highly processed versions of real food. I hadn't meant that though, and she had to have known it. I couldn't meet her eyes. I had pried. She deserved secrets, too.

Charlie lowered her voice. "I tested with a greenhouse before getting the approval for Cloud Nine. So, I've sampled the same kinds of fresh vegetables they use up here."

Wow. Something in me unfurled. She trusted me. I would have hugged her, if I were the hugging type and if it wouldn't have been strange in the middle of this setting. "Very cool."

We shuffled along the perimeter of the room. I didn't think we screamed wallflowers, but our curved-in shoulders surely indicated private conversation. "I wasn't sure you'd think so," Charlie admitted.

I furrowed my brow. "Why not?" Clearly, it wasn't a secret I wanted to indulge in organic goodness.

"You're pretty anti-CAD." She didn't look at me when she spoke.

I should have denied it, but I hadn't yet perfected that whole keeping my mouth shut thing. In fact, sometimes I still shoved my foot in it with extreme force. "Is that common knowledge?"

She looked at me like I was an idiot.

Oh. Damn it, I was an idiot. "Really?"

She scrunched her nose like a bunny. It'd have been amusing if she wasn't delivering bad news. "Yeah." She drew out the word like the slow reveal would soften the blow. It didn't. "The general consensus is either you think you're better than everyone or that you hate it here."

"Great." I thought I said it under my breath, but Charlie responded anyway.

"If it makes you feel any better, I think you're justified in both."

"I don't think I'm better than everyone." Or at least I didn't admit that.

We were in a corner now. Plenty of space from the nearest prying ears. "You are better than most people here. I am, too." She shrugged at my widened eyes. "Not quite the caliber I expected. Whatever. Those in the lab seem to be top-notch, though."

"That they do. Once I got into the real lab, I was pleased."

"Same here. It's like our recruitment group was the junior varsity."

Or the dregs. I swished the last sip of tea around the bottom of the glass. "Maybe we just can't see their potential."

She tilted her head to the right. "You don't believe that."

I drank the tea, but even its flavor couldn't dilute the truth. "Not even for a second."

She laughed. "Me, either."

I lowered my voice to a conspiratorial whisper. "Does that mean you hate it here?"

"Not exactly, but something is off. I can feel it."

"I don't trust it." But apparently, I trusted her.

This had better not blow up in my face.

CHAPTER 28
THE WARNINGS MAKE SENSE NOW

Charlie was about to respond—I didn't know if it was to confirm my distrust or to call me out as a paranoid idiot—when one of the guys from my lab, Kevin, bounded up to us. He stopped just inches from my shoulder.

"I knew you were here." His dopey smile stole my attention. "Some of the gang was looking for you."

"The gang, huh?" Charlie was going to rub this in. I could feel it.

"Ally, are you going to introduce me to your friend?" Kevin extended a hand to Charlie like he was some gentleman in a tuxedo. It didn't look as stupid as I thought it would.

I parlayed the mandatory name exchange between the two of them. Charlie was polite, but I doubted she was as impressed with Kevin as he was with her. Then again, I'd never played matchmaker before.

"You know, I haven't exactly seen a horde in Team Frankenstein shirts seeking me out. Are you sure you didn't just want an excuse to say hi?" The look of warning Charlie gave me didn't chafe as much as she intended. Being honest was frowned upon not just at parties but everywhere here. Why was it so wrong to be direct? The dance of politeness watered down conviction. I hated it.

A few weeks with me, and Kevin already had grown accustomed to my brashness. I didn't know if this said more about my personality or his ability to adapt. I chose not to linger on the thought. "The shirts were vetoed, remember?"

"I told him it was a good idea, but I don't think it mattered."

"Maybe it did. He does want to listen to you." Well that sounded jealous. Ugh. How was I going to detour this conversation?

"Well, where is everyone anyway?" I looked around the room, but didn't see anyone I recognized. "If we don't mingle soon, I'll have to devour the appetizers."

"She would." Thanks, Charlie.

"Adam's around here somewhere."

I furrowed my brow at him. "I thought you said everyone was looking for me."

"Right. By everyone I meant Adam." His deadpan delivery made me wonder if he was joking.

"Oh." My lack of eloquence here made them both hide laughs. What was the proper response to that? Was I allowed to ask why he was looking for me? Would it make it look like I cared that he was seeking me out? I had the real concern that hanging out with the boss, the guy denying awesome shirts, would only alienate me from this crowd more. However, I accepted that Kevin was encouraging it. Either he wanted to make Adam happy or it was normal to interact with him socially outside of work. Maybe both?

Charlie let me flounder for what felt like hours. I probably blushed. Gross. The thought brought a flood of heat to my neck. Maybe my friend finally sensed my stress, because she gave me an out. "What she means to say is, lead the way."

We wove through a few groups of people. Kevin said hi to most of them. I nodded at them, pretending their faces looked familiar when they didn't. Being sandwiched between so many strangers and enduring their disingenuous smiles made my skin try to get up and crawl away. It didn't make it far, but the fine hairs covering my arms stood tall. Thankfully they were light, so I didn't think anyone noticed.

Adam grinned when he saw me, and my stomach did that flutter thing again. It was less distracting this time, if only because my body was still on high alert from almost touching three people. Wasn't there more air in this room before? I inhaled slowly through my nose, though my brain yelped for a giant gulp of air. I would fake this.

"We weren't sure if you'd come." Adam moved around our informal circle to stand next to me. I wasn't sure how I felt about it, but the butterflies seemed to like it.

"Of course I came." He's the one who told me how important it was to be here. I didn't have a choice, but I also couldn't sound like a petulant child. "Like I'd pass up the free food."

The small assembly laughed. I recognized everyone in the contingent. Kevin and Charlie, of course. Adam. Next to him was Jennifer. She worked on Level 4, but not in the lab. She was one of the people doing the paper pushing part of research. Boring gig, but she didn't seem to mind. The only person I didn't recognize was a tall guy. He wore black workout pants, which only made me think of sparring with Declan the next day. I wondered what kind of gear would be available. I still had to decide if I wanted to use pads. The thought sent a thrill up my spine. The guy in the gym clothes gave me an odd look. I probably deserved it. It likely looked as though I was staring.

He offered a hand. "Kyle."

My smile was tight, forced, obvious. "Ally."

He stepped back after the necessary handshake was complete.

"Kyle works a floor down from us with the botany team." Adam leaned in close to me, like he was giving me some inside tip. Only it wasn't like he lowered his voice.

"I saw the few plants on our floor earlier. Very cool."

"Those are decorations." Kyle's reaction told me he mentally appended a nasty name for me. I was doing pretty good at this being nice thing, so I didn't know where the hostility was coming from. The guy's chest was puffed up. I started to imagine the ways I could make it deflate, but stopped myself before my mouth would dictate my thoughts. Not the place.

"We'll have to give you a tour of Level 5 soon." Adam redirected the conversation. Thankfully.

"I've still got reading to do, since there are limits on my working hours." I winked at him. Mother of God, I thought, did I just do that?

Now I would have to admit to sharing DNA with Leah because I just winked at a guy. I turned a work conversation into flirting?

Adam slipped his hand around my side to press against the small of my back. I jerked, but managed to stop from leaping forward. The fact that Kyle faced me directly certainly helped keep me stationary.

"I'll work on my slave-driver tendencies." His breath warmed my ear. My toes curled. I didn't want to be this girl.

I wasn't the only one made uncomfortable by Adam's obvious touchy-touchy-ness. Kevin's voice was louder than necessary. "So, your sister throws quite the party. Did she do this a lot back home?"

He was the first person I'd heard call it home, not Ground Level. It made me take a second look at him. I made a mental note to talk with him more. I wouldn't divulge anything, but perhaps he wasn't as ensnared by the initiatives of the CAD program. That would be nice.

"She's been throwing parties as long as I've known her."

"She is your sister, right?" If Kyle inflated his chest or his ego any further, he might explode. I'd watch, but wouldn't be a part of that cleanup crew.

"Yeah. My younger sister." Ugh. Kyle was dense. "Leah used to decorate her whole room to have parties with her dolls." I glanced at Charlie. "My mom often made me attend." I'd been forced to party since I was a child. You'd think someone would get the hint.

"I'm so glad I don't have sisters." Kevin wasn't looking at us when he spoke, but over my shoulder. I turned to follow his gaze. A guard I didn't recognize had entered the room. He had at least four years on me, but I suspected it wasn't his age drawing the others' attention.

The harsh lines around Kevin's eyes didn't bode well for whomever just joined the party. Since I was new, it was safe to ask the obvious question. "Who is that?"

Adam's chin took on a bladed edge as he clenched his jaw. His fingers dug into my back. Not hard enough to hurt, but enough to warn me.

Kyle answered my question, and he sounded too happy to be the one with the knowledge. "Jensen. He works directly for the Clean Air Development board at the EPA. He was one of the original Cloud Nine kids." Kyle sounded proud, a little jealous, and one-hundred percent awestruck. "Now he gets to spot-check the facilities."

Adam whispered so softly I barely made out the words, "He moves from station to station. Gathers updates for the EPA."

"Were you expecting him?" I hoped it looked like I was snuggling into Adam. I hadn't done that before with anyone, at least not in front of people, so I wasn't sure if it looked authentic.

One word. "No."

I swallowed hard and wished for another cup of tea. Something to do with my hands.

Adam's harshness.

Declan's warnings.

This guy had come to meet me, and that certainly wasn't a good thing.

CHAPTER 29
EXIT STRATEGY

The way Adam's arm tensed around me, I was certain Jensen would steam over any second and make someone cry. He didn't even look in our direction, though.

That was worse.

I could deal with a head-on confrontation. I could argue. I could say those witty, caustic things that everyone else thought of three hours later. I could do those things if adrenaline was surging through my veins and making me want to rise onto my toes.

The energy was already seizing control of my brain, readying for a fight. Charlie tapped my hand. I'd balled my fingers into a fist. Letting go of that anticipation wasn't an easy task for me. Ever.

Jensen headed toward the drinks. He was walking away, but I felt watched. The scrutiny made me itchy. If this jerk gave me hives, then I'd really be dying for a fight.

"Why didn't he come over here?" From the tight looks on the others' faces, we were not going to discuss it. So now he was in the room and we were supposed to pretend that wasn't some bad thing. But it was. And I had no business trying to pretend anything.

I shuffled from foot to foot. I could fake you out in a fight. I could make you look left while my hand was coming at your face from the right. I couldn't, however, chitchat like everything was peachy.

"So, Charlie, your brother is Tomás, right?" Kevin was doing the small-talk thing. I wouldn't classify him as good at it, but he was making more of an effort than I had any intention of doing.

"What?" She said, snapping her attention back to Kevin. I wasn't the only one still tracking Jensen out of the corner of my eye. Her reaction calmed me enough to take a breath. Before Kevin could repeat, she realized what he'd asked. "Oh, yeah, he's my little brother."

"He seems like a good kid." Charlie was enough like me that I assumed her mind was wondering how Kevin would know, but she had a better verbal filter than I did.

"He is. Mostly. Just young."

"That's the nature of younger siblings." Adam wore one of his charismatic smiles. How could he ignore the brooding guy across the room? I couldn't.

Jensen was talking with members of the Security department. It looked like light conversation, but if he was actually invested in the content, he'd be looking at them instead of keeping his eyes locked on my head. I wasn't sure that a stare could actually be piercing, but I certainly felt the stab of scrutiny boring into the base of my skull.

Our group continued to talk about nothing important. Why had I agreed to come to this stupid party? Adam nudged my shoulder whenever it was my turn to talk. He looked so pleased with me when I offered anything to the conversation. That look conjured bitterness in the back of my mouth. One sharp enough to make me wish I could spit in the middle of that crowded room. I didn't need his patronizing "help."

The others were talking about my sister. Great. My favorite topic.

"I'm surprised Leah hasn't come by yet," was my contribution. And I kind of was. She wanted everyone to know her. You can't be popular if no one knows you. I'd rather not have everyone curious about what I'm doing, thinking, wearing, or whatever. Still, when she was in hostess mode, Leah turned into a human touch point. A person everyone in attendance had to interact with. Really, she could be quite forceful in her socializing.

"She got assigned to Procurement, right?" Kyle's sneer came through more clearly than he realized. Dick.

Now, I admit, I would have hated to be doing anything other than research on Cloud Nine. For me, what was the point of moving here if you weren't doing something epic? However, that didn't mean the other parts didn't matter. Cooking excited Leah. My shoulders tightened and I stood straighter. That warning hand on my back told me not to say something scathing. I listened. Mostly.

"Yes. Now my baby sister makes food I actually want to scarf down. Win-win, if you ask me." I played it light, but my eyes narrowed. I wanted Kyle to know I'd be happy to follow up our conversation in a way that led to bruises for him.

Even with the underlying "screw off" bit, Adam took the thread and ran with it. He talked about how great the food here was and about all the perks of living here. Basically, he became a one-man propaganda-spewing machine.

I didn't want him touching me anymore.

I scanned the room. Three exits. I knew better than to run to any of them, but the urge burned in my chest.

Then I saw my out. Or at least, what might get me away from Adam's traitorous hands.

Declan's dirty blond hair was unmistakable over the heads of my sister and two girls I didn't know.

Maybe he felt my gaze because he turned toward me. He was still twenty feet away, but I watched his eyes narrow upon seeing Adam at my side.

I widened my eyes and hoped he got the "help me" message. He did. Or I thought so. Declan knocked his head back slowly. I knew the tough guy invitation well. I'd employed it myself.

I parted my lips, but no words came out. I was a crappy liar, and if I told Adam I was heading over to see Declan, he'd try to tag along. I was too much like a possession to him. One he had no right to claim.

I flashed another SOS with my eyes in Declan's direction. I'm pretty sure he laughed. He pointed at Leah and mouthed, "Say you need to talk to her."

Oh. Duh. I started to step forward and Adam's arm slid around to my side. He didn't stop talking, but he didn't appear to like my hint at leaving. I pointed toward Declan, who had ducked down a bit, and it looked like I was gesturing at my sister. Not a lie.

"I'm being summoned." I extracted myself first from Adam, and then from the group. "Back in a bit."

The second I stepped away, I felt better. Two steps more and I could breathe. Five steps and that burning in my chest receded. I walked right past Leah and made sure to avoid eye contact. I didn't actually want to talk to her. Declan took my hand as soon as I was within reach. He pulled me in front of him and right out of Adam's line of sight.

"Thank you so much," I said. Something about standing this close to him calmed me.

"For what?" He wasn't looking at me, but he hadn't let go of my hand either. It wasn't in the possessive, grabby way Adam had held me earlier. Declan was more like a lifeline.

"Saving me from"—I moved my hand in a circle in an exasperated flurry—"this."

"Looked like Adam was taking care of you." Gravel pitted this voice.

I rolled my eyes. "Hardly. The tone over there was not..." I paused, trying to find the right words. We were still surrounded by strangers and I was doing my damnedest to keep my feet on the floor and out of my mouth. "It wasn't enjoyable."

The right side of his mouth ticked up for a moment before he switched back into serious mode. "I don't enjoy his company so much either." Declan let his gaze sweep the room. "You ready to get out of here?"

"I didn't want to come, remember?"

"We can argue the win/loss ratio on your attending the party at another time. Right now, I'd really like to get you out of this room and away from Jensen." He spat the name. History there? When we were alone, I'd ask the questions. Unlike my Research buddies, Declan would tell me something. Not everything, because he was smart enough to protect himself. I saw that now. His secrets drove me batty, but he was playing it smart. I hoped I'd remember that fact when he refused to provide answers later.

"Then we should hurry. He's been tracking me since he got here." I mimicked his hushed voice. I hoped it made a difference. If it didn't, I'm sure Leah would let me know.

"He's looking for you now, edging around the far side of the room." Declan had the height perk. At least my paranoia made it easy for me to plan exit strategies.

"Door at your four o'clock." I glanced over at the unassuming exit. It wasn't the main entrance to the room, but a narrow doorway. No fingerprint lock.

"Leads to the kitchen." He nodded. "That'll work. Just a second." He dropped my hand while he tracked Jensen across the room. "Now."

My attempt at a casual quick walk was awkward, I'm sure. But it wasn't weird enough to have anyone stare at me outright. I slipped through the exit and into a kitchen prep area. The anteroom was about half the size of my bedroom. The walls were bare, like so many here, but tables flanked the sides. Empty dishes were piled on the one nearest me.

I probably shouldn't have stopped moving. Declan crashed into me, knocking me forward. My hand landed next to the other door in the room. Declan's palm covered mine. For a moment it was like someone had thrown a white blanket over my head. I stood there staring at the way his fingers covered my own. He never touched my skin before. The connection I'd set aside at his stubbornness now sparked white and hot until my chest tightened.

His growl vibrated against my ear. "Keep moving."

He wasn't distracted by touching my skin. That bothered me more than I wanted it to.

Ire burned a path up the back of my neck. I hoped it scorched him when he leaned forward again. "Where exactly am I supposed to go? You're the one with the directions here."

"Out the door." He shoved me forward. I stumbled out and he followed closely, nudging me to the left. Moving away from the party made sense.

We didn't talk after that. Declan would grunt and point. Caveman directions at their finest. I'm not sure what it says about me that I preferred it. I had spent days—no, longer than that, *years*—wanting answers about this place. When we stopped our walk-run pace, when we stopped fleeing, when we were somewhere private, Declan was going to give me answers. Some. I'd demand it. The knot in my gut said the truth wouldn't be my liberation, but would simply drive me deeper into the pit.

We made it to the elevator. It moved noiselessly to the fifteenth floor. Declan's pick.

The space was small, but the placard above the buttons clearly said it could hold eighteen people. Declan crowded me. I could smell soap on his skin. A slightly different scent than the one stocked in my shower. Or maybe it was his own flavor turning it sharper. It didn't matter. It overwhelmed me. Every inhale was of Declan. I closed my eyes. When he spoke, his voice vibrated along my collarbone. Or maybe that was the darkness toying with me.

"What did you tell Adam?" Concerned laced the question. While he wasn't accusing me of anything, I recognized that patronizing undercurrent.

My eyes snapped open. I managed not to narrow them at him. "About what?"

"Whatever you've seen down there." He meant in the lab. The research. The knot in my stomach doubled its efforts on winding up my intestines.

"I haven't said a thing to him." I was not an idiot.

Declan's eyes narrowed. "Your notes."

"Why do you assume I've done something here?" My voice started to soar. He held a single finger to his lips in a reminder. I dropped my tone back to a hush. "More importantly, why do you assume I've found something there?"

He shook his head like I was crazy for bringing it up here. He's the one who started the infernal conversation in an elevator. We only had one more floor to go. "Your. Notes." His teeth stayed clamped together as he spoke. "Where?"

"Saved on my tablet. Personal drive on the intranet."

A brief string of expletives flew from his mouth. None landed on me, but I felt their burn nonetheless. "He has access."

"Who?"

He arched his eyebrow.

Oh. Jensen.

The elevator chimed our arrival and the doors glided open. The sudden quiet pressed on me, the hollowness of the moment prepared to swallow me.

My mind spun fast enough, I edged toward dizziness. What had I included in those notes and why would Jensen be monitoring them? I'd jotted down several big questions. Things to ask Adam about, others to investigate. One line stood out in memory though. I hadn't emboldened the text on the screen, but in my mind, it was cranked to the largest font size and underlined twice: <u>Human test subjects???</u>

Declan's hand on my shoulder urged me out of the elevator and down a hallway. Both sides of the corridor here were lined with floor-to-ceiling windows. The moon was as vibrant and alive as I remembered, but I couldn't appreciate it. I didn't even turn to look. I trudged forward, nothing in my way but my darkening thoughts.

I stopped walking when Declan did. No grunts needed. He unlocked and opened a door on the right. I entered first. The room was twice, maybe triple, the size of mine, but still clearly a dormitory. Declan's bonus space was filled with a small, black couch and a coffee table that matched the other black surfaces in the room.

This was my chance to get a glimpse into him, but my mind couldn't absorb the details of his room. I was stuck wondering how Declan had known my notes were the key. Did he know something sinister was going on in Cloud Nine? Of course he did. He'd hinted at it from the beginning. He knew. More than that, he knew more than I did and he still wasn't divulging.

I felt him behind me. Maybe two steps back. It wasn't my fighter's instincts telling me it, either. I pretended otherwise.

The cumulative stress of the night. The frustration since I first stepped foot in this damn station. All of it. Every little hair-pulling stupid moment when I held back and pretended to like people here. Faked like I bought into their 'save the world' crap. I was done acting.

Anger kindled at my core. Adrenaline ignited my nerve endings all at once. My flesh lit.

I narrowed my eyes, tilted my head down, and whirred around

with more speed than I knew I possessed. My fingers curled inward mid-spin and as I faced Declan directly, I took one big step forward. My feet led the motion, but my hand was eager to finish it. My right fist shot directly at Declan's chin.

My anger made me sloppy.

He brought a hand up and deflected my punch. Instead of following through like I would have and clocking my open side, he clasped his fingers around my wrist and stepped forward. He tried to pivot us, but I fought it and instead we toppled to the ground. My butt hit the floor first, thankfully. Declan landed on top of me.

He didn't move. His face was so close to mine, our noses grazed each other.

"You knew." I snarled at him. No other way to put it.

"I'm on your side." He was the picture of serenity. A waveless crystal lake.

I was the dam about to break and flood his alcove. "Bull."

I started to squirm and the rough pile of the rug beneath me scratched at my exposed skin. I wanted to get my foot outside his heel to work my escape. He knew what I was doing and tightened his thighs around me.

He leaned down closer. "I promise. I am on your side." How could he look so genuine?

I started to move my hips, ready to try and buck him off me without a strong trap of his foot. Stupid, but better than nothing.

His lips grazed mine when he pleaded. "Please."

Declan was on top of me. Begging me to trust him. After I'd just tried to punch him in the face.

My lips were on fire where his mouth had touched mine.

Now my bucking plans felt wrong.

I liked his weight on top of me.

His breath—minty—against my skin made my toes curl inside my boots. Every time I'd practiced knocking someone off me like this, I hadn't thought about what parts of theirs were near mine. Now I did.

My heartbeat threatened to choke me.

I blushed the most I have ever blushed in my entire life at that moment. Heat broke out on my neck and I knew it painted my skin a deep rose as it crept up to my face.

Declan smiled like a cat and doubled his efforts pinning my hands. He read me too well. I wanted to smack him for that feline reaction.

He brought his lips next to my ear. The movement brought his neck near my nose. I inhaled deeply and let myself be surrounded by him. His breath tickled when he spoke. "Trust me?"

"Yes." The word was barely audible. How could I have been duped by Adam's charm when my heart raced the moment I was near Declan?

His body relaxed as he released my hands and moved to sit on his heels. Sometimes I couldn't help myself. I agreed to trust him, and I meant it. That didn't mean I wanted him to think I would completely drop my guard around him.

I edged my heel to the outside of his, grabbed his bicep, and flipped him on his back. I didn't linger on top of him, too aware of where our bodies touched and unable to handle more. However, as I scuttled back from between his legs, my hands slid along his thighs out of habit. The thick muscles there were flexed and my body was warmer from having touched them. Sour regret weighed on my tongue. I wished I had truly kissed him.

CHAPTER 30
THE SUBJECTS

I wasn't the only one to be surprised tonight. Declan looked dumbfounded. He gasped suddenly in a way that made me think he had forgotten to breathe for a moment or two. I didn't know if it was the surprise of the flip or my hands on him. It was my doing, one way or another, at least.

"Don't think this counts as our sparring round."

That jarred him back into consciousness. "Wouldn't dream of it."

He posted his fist and popped up from the ground. His right hand went immediately to his thigh. I didn't think I'd hurt him—he had too much hard muscle for that.

I didn't linger and gawk at him. Just a glimpse of him in that softened state was enough to warm my skin again. I didn't much want Declan staring at me while I floundered with emotions. I doubted he'd like it either.

I made my way to that dark couch of his. The cushions were soft, which was a pleasant surprise, and the heavy resin feet looked like they bled into the floor. The look was more organic than anything I'd seen in Cloud Nine—other than that grass, obviously—and the lack of hyper structure comforted me a tad.

I settled and by the time I looked up, Declan was walking over to me. No hint of nervousness and definitely not a rosy tint to his skin. I thought mine had managed to fade as well.

He sat next to me. I reoriented myself on the couch, pulling a leg up and folding it in front of me, so I could have the added space between us. I had big questions. I needed big answers. Unfortunately, my mind wanted to wander. I thought about Declan touching me. Holding me. I didn't want to be that girl.

Perhaps it was for the best that I was worried about the possibility of awful things happening under my nose. It made it easier to quit being a fluttering tool and instead be the one who could keep herself and her sister safe.

I licked my lips. Guess I had to start this off.

"So, you're on my side." I meant it as a statement, but my voice lilted at the end. Maybe I did need to hear it again.

"Yes."

If he was going to revert to one-word answers, I might have to go back to hitting him. "How so?"

"What do you mean, 'how so?'" He actually leaned back. I shouldn't have enjoyed seeing him so affronted by my question, but I did. And he knew it. "Fine. If that's how we're doing this—"

"We were just wrestling." I rolled my eyes in the most affronted fashion. "Did you think the next part would be easier?"

We both laughed. It didn't last long, but it let some of the tension slide out of the room. Every bit counted when it came to us.

"No, I suppose not." Declan cracked his neck. I waited. "Where do you want to start?"

"Why didn't you tell me what was going on here?"

"Because that would make me a moron?"

Antagonistic jerk. "No, it would mean you keeping me from doing stupid things."

"Be honest, Ally. You wouldn't have listened to me. You would do what you wanted to do, regardless."

"You don't know that."

He didn't roll his eyes. I gave him that.

"Okay, still, once I was a little more entrenched you could have let me know that even my notes would be pilfered here."

"What did you think all those hints about how anyone can walk into your room despite the lock keyed to your fingerprint were about?" He gestured wildly, like his words weren't enough.

"Letting me know you could walk in whenever you damn well pleased." My voice kept soaring higher. I caught myself. I had only seen one other door on this floor, but who knew how far my voice would carry or who lived on the other side of this floor? I took a deep breath and held it in while I counted to five. Exhale.

"If one lock can be opened, so can another." He was fighting to stay calm.

"Don't try to be all meditation master here."

"I'm not, but you have to recognize that there are some things that I just can't say plainly." He speared his fingers through his hair. His body was still angling for a fight, even if his brain didn't think it was a good idea. I knew the feeling well. "I have to keep people safe. So, I'm going to need you to work on reading between the lines."

I needed to work on taking criticism. "You know, I've been being told how to behave since I got here without any real reasoning or answers. At your"—I pointed at him with the quickness reserved for throwing sharp elbows—"direction I've kept my head down. I've worked damn hard to keep my foot out of my mouth. I've even played nice with people who are probably as shady as they come. I've done this, and now you're telling me that's not worthy of some direct answers? Screw you."

I didn't remember standing, but there I was, towering over Declan. My jaw clenched tightly after I spat the last two words. Kicking him would have added a little something to my comments, but my body was seized in anger.

He rose to his feet and slowly reached for my shoulders. It was a wise move. If he had moved quickly, I would have knocked him on his ass and stormed out. He would have deserved it, too. His hands were like hot stones searing through my shirt. I started to shake out from under them, but he tightened his hold and bent down enough that his eyes lined up with mine. Why did he have to look so sincere?

I sucked my bottom lip in and gnawed on it, but stayed put. His gaze flicked down to my mouth. Now was not the time to kiss me. He was smart enough to hold back there.

"I'll make you a deal. Tonight only, in this room only, carte blanche. You can ask me whatever, and I'll answer the best I can."

"Is this place sacred or something?"

"I'm the head of security. My room isn't wired for cameras and the only other person who lives on this floor is downstairs playing nice with Jensen. We're good for at least an hour." How would he know? Maybe his floormate would be back up here in a few. He saw my skepticism and pointed to a desk on the far side of the room. "There will be a buzz when the elevators open. Security notice."

I wanted to argue, but I always wanted to argue. So I sucked it down into the place I'd been storing all the "you're an idiot" comments I'd stockpiled over the last few days. I stashed them in my gut somewhere near my right kidney. The twinge of discomfort told me I was running out of space. Either people would have to get smarter or I would have to find a better coping mechanism.

I had so many questions for Declan; I needed more mouths so I could ask them all at once. While my pride urged me to find out if I was right about human testing, it wasn't the most pressing matter. Safety first. "Who is Jensen and why is he here?"

"The second question is a little easier than the first. He's here because of you. Who he is explains why he's a problem." He paused, and I wondered if Declan could see me chewing on the inside of my cheek. I would not interrupt. Recognizing my good-listener status, he continued, "Jensen keeps an eye on the productivity of all the Clean Air stations."

"Does that make him your boss, then?" It wasn't interrupting if it was a relevant question.

"Not exactly. He doesn't oversee security directly, but everything." His words crashed down on me but didn't sink in. "He's more Adam's boss than mine, but he has the power to make things incredibly uncomfortable for anyone within these walls. Myself included."

"How can he be that much of a problem?"

"You know full well the government runs these stations."

"Not exactly a secret."

"You'd be surprised how many people think those on this pod make all the decisions." The sigh he let out was full of pity. I could relate. My sister could easily be one of those people.

"Fair enough."

"Well, Jensen is the person who acts as their eyes and ears."

"He's not all that stealthy for a spy."

"He's not intended as such, I think. I mean, yes, he reports back on everything, but he wants everyone to know he has power."

"What power?" Bravado didn't cover the hitch in my breath. "If he's just the hand of the government, doesn't that make him more a puppet than someone to be feared?"

"He's a dangerous puppet. He has the power of the real leadership behind him. They trust him to make decisions. He's the one who would keep you quiet. He can remove detainees from my cells without talking to me."

"We have cells here?"

"We have a security force. Did you really think we wouldn't have a place to put people if they proved a problem?"

I didn't even want to go there. "But wouldn't he just send them back to their parents?"

"Not always." He looked away for a moment. The hesitation in his eyes encouraged a stake of nerves to burrow into my abdomen. His eyes fixed on mine again, and the stake crumbled. "You remember that girl Sage?"

"The one I had to stop from bleeding all over the place because everyone else was missing or not helpful?"

He narrowed his eyes. "Yes, her."

"I remember."

"She's gone."

"What do you mean? I thought she was in the infirmary. I heard something important got nicked when she cut open her shoulder."

"She was stitched up that same night. Jensen called in and had guards from another location collect her." The way he said 'collect' made my skin crawl.

"Did they send her home? Or even figure out what happened to her?"

"She didn't go home, but I honestly don't know where they took her. It's why I worry so much about you. Ally, you draw so much attention and I can't let them take you. Outside these walls I can't protect you."

"Why would they take her?" I didn't want to know the answer, but had to ask the question anyway.

He just shook his head.

"Why?" I was trying to sound harsh, but it came off hysterical.

"I'd just be guessing..." He wasn't looking at me again. He only did that when he was about to say something I'd hate. Fantastic.

"Then guess."

"People would ask her questions. Ones she either couldn't or shouldn't answer."

"I thought we were done with you giving murky answers."

His exasperated grunt echoed in the room. "That wasn't murky."

"Then pretend I'm dumb."

"You're not dumb."

I wouldn't argue that point. "No, but I appreciate direct answers. It's been a mind-bending kind of a day. I could use some simple, honest answers. Think you could manage that?"

"I'm going to regret this in the morning."

I shrugged. "Maybe. In the meantime, let's live for now."

The palms of his hands rubbed back and forth on the black fabric of the couch. I would have squeezed the cushion, but he didn't. In some ways, Declan was far more controlled than I. "Sage isn't the first person on this station to have an accident that involved a whole lot of blood."

"What do you mean?" The words crept out of my mouth, like if they snuck into the room no one would worry at their arrival.

"It's always with a new recruit. We've had four in the last year." He furrowed his brow. There was more. Damn it. There was more.

"How did she get that cut?"

He stared at the floor. "She did it to herself. They all did. Within twenty-four hours of admission to Cloud Nine, they all cut themselves open." The monotone answer speared through my head.

"No." Now I was shaking my head. "I saw her. There wasn't anything obvious in the room."

"I think she used the edge of her desk." Sure, there had been blood, but she must have fallen. Like he read my mind, "A wound that deep and precise was purposeful."

My brain didn't want to deal with this yet. I flipped myself into clinical mode. Anything to avoid dealing with the emotional knife slicing up my sternum. "What's the common thread? Other than the move to Cloud Nine."

"Well, but that's part of it, isn't it?"

It was, but why would four out of probably forty or fifty people have the reaction? "Something in decontamination?"

"I believe so. Most of the things that happen during the introduction process—"

"Is 'introduction process' the internal code for scald your skin?" I couldn't help myself.

He frowned. "Yeah. Anyway, most of the process involves standard items. The soap, for example, is safe for everyone. The powder part, though, is experimental."

"What do you mean by that?"

"What does the word mean, Ally?"

Clearly, someone didn't like being interrupted, but if I could trust him to give complete answers, it wouldn't have been necessary. I nodded at him, and he continued without whining.

"So much of what happens here is new. Even the foods we eat are ones that aren't readily available on Ground Level. Think about that for a second."

Crap. It's not fun being right sometimes.

"Since Research made a modification to the powder used in decontamination, we've started having new recruits cut themselves. It's not hard for me to draw a correlation there."

It wasn't hard for me, either. Still. "What are the odds they had these issues before coming here, though?"

"The process to get accepted here is rigorous. You're an exception. Everyone else had medical and psychological tests. They want people who can adapt quickly and are healthy enough to handle the sudden change to better air quality, engineered food, and the like."

"Then why did so many of those who came in with me look like they weren't the brightest or the strongest?"

"I've been wondering the same thing." Declan stood and walked over to his desk. He brought a tablet back with him, tapping on the screen while he walked. "There had been one or two less-than-ideal candidates in previous classes, but yours was the first where there was an obvious diversion."

He handed me the screen. The display showed a chart of duty allocations within the station, comparing this year to the previous one. Research held a steady number, as did the team assigned to make dinners and such. However, the number of people in Maintenance skyrocketed. "Is there enough maintenance work for..." I paused and counted. "Forty-six people?"

The number sounded absurd and I started to count again, but Declan stopped me. "We need ten, maybe twelve. It's not that big of a station."

"Then what are they doing?"

"Not maintaining the technology or the building." He wasn't looking at me again.

"Just tell me."

He looked guilty.

"You know more. I can see it. Please tell me."

It was the please that did him in. "You know I monitor the security footage for the station, right?"

"I gathered, yes."

"Every level, every room—aside from bathrooms—are wired. Even the places that aren't supposed to exist."

A blade turned counterclockwise in my gut. "What are you telling me?"

I knew though. I'd known it when I read those research reports. I knew it when Declan told me my notes were the reason Jensen showed up. And I knew it now.

"They're working on the levels below yours." He winced. "As test subjects."

CHAPTER 31
I SAVED YOU

Test subjects.

The phrase banged around inside my skull. I worried my brain might start leaking out my nose from the damage. A headache blossomed at my temples, and for once, I was rendered speechless.

I tried to force my mind back into a scientific zone. It only made my eyes burn. Leah and I were lucky to not be assigned to maintenance detail. That fact kept me from passing out, but didn't provide much solace.

I fisted the edge of the couch and, without thinking, began to pull toward myself. The warmth of Declan's hand on mine stilled me.

"And you wondered why I didn't want to tell you." His half-hearted joke and weak smile came from the right place, but didn't do anything to quell the mish-mash of anger and fear roiling inside me.

Declan pried my fingers from the cushion. He held on to my hand. I liked knowing he was there. It steadied me.

I almost wished for those gooey girl feelings right now. Instead, I tried to count the fiber loops on the rug beneath my feet, as if the menial effort would somehow dampen the acid burning my insides.

"Someone had to approve this." I was grasping for a way to make this okay. Maybe the maintenance group agreed to this. Declan shook his head. I rebutted quickly, "What about the permission forms our parents sign for us to come here?"

"Sorry, Ally, but there's nothing in the paperwork about consent to undergo any sort of drug or chemical trials." His brow furrowed in an attempt to wring out the guilt. "Don't you think I would have looked?"

"What are they testing?" I knew I'd spoken. I'd felt the vibration in my throat, but it didn't sound like me. The words were hollow.

His fingers tightened around my hand. I watched it instead of the floor. I hadn't believed shock could turn a person white. My skin proved otherwise.

His voice was steadier than mine. "I don't know."

My lip started to quiver. I bit it. I didn't sign up for this. I didn't want to be the big damn hero. Martyr wasn't all that appealing either. But here's my design flaw: I couldn't let things go.

It's the reason they wanted me on Cloud Nine. I read and studied more hours than anyone else because I hated not understanding how things worked. I could run longer than others because I practiced every day. Being faster and stronger kept me safe.

I wanted to be safe.

I had been dragged into a hornet's nest. Now I was locked inside with a murderous queen.

"How do you not know? I thought you had eyes on everything, oh Great Overseer." My anger wasn't at him. The fact I kept our hands connected proved that.

He was calmer than I, which stung. "I can see what's happening, but that doesn't actually tell me what the tests are. I just know they're experimenting."

I pulled my hand from his. "For how long?"

"What? I don't know. Kids are in there for about six hours a day. Various rotations."

"No, I mean how long have you watched other people be subjected to some sort of testing."

Declan let out a long breath before he answered. "Maybe a year?"

It was so hard not to slap him, even when I could see the weight of the admission crushing him. It wasn't just his shoulders that slumped, but even his hair had gone limp and his shirt sagged. I may have kept my hands from striking him, but I could leave a verbal welt just as deep. "What is wrong with you? You could watch that and do nothing? I don't know why I thought you'd be someone I could trust."

I was halfway across the room when he caught my arm. I yanked out of his hold, but stopped storming toward the exit.

"I'm keeping people safe." His voice wavered.

"Yeah. I'm sure. Yourself."

"What do you think would happen if I stepped in? I'd get hauled off and there would be no one to look out for everyone else."

"Yep. Good looking out for the people turned into hamsters for testing purposes."

He made a sound in between a yell and a sigh. Whatever it was, it was painful. "I can't save everyone—"

"Have you saved anyone?"

"I saved you."

"No, you dropped hints and I saved myself." I always saved myself.

"You have no idea the things I did to keep you safe."

I didn't, but he wasn't elaborating either. Maybe that was a pride thing, but this wasn't the time for humility. "Then tell me."

"For starters, you were almost taken with Sage that night. You asked questions loudly. I had to make an insane case about how vital you could be to this station."

"I wanted to go home."

"Haven't you been listening? You wouldn't have gone home."

"Okay. Fine. You've had my back. Mostly." He shot me a dirty look and I accepted with vigor. "What about everyone else?"

"I do what I can to help others stay under the radar. I've seen people get moved to the maintenance team and disappear."

"Disappear?"

"Paperwork says they either went home or were relocated. Seeing as I handle that stuff, it's odd I wasn't involved and it always happens in the middle of the night. Do you understand now?"

I understood, but I still wouldn't have behaved the way he did. "Going all ostrich and burying your head on this isn't improving things."

"No, but it keeps more people safe than it hurts."

Debatable. I covered my face with my hands and hoped the momentary confinement would spur a better direction for this conversation. I needed to make a plan.

I hated plans.

The pressure of my palms against my skin was a release as I slid my hands down and off my face. I pretended I took some of the anger seething inside with them. Hokey, yes, but it was all I could come up with.

I could fake being Logical Ally. It might help. "These kids have to know they're being tested on. Why haven't they said anything?"

"What makes you think they know?"

"How could they not?"

Declan was doing that thing again. The thing that made pain burst in the center of my forehead. I scrunched up my face in the hope of relief. It didn't work, so I asked more questions. "How do you know they're being tested on?"

"I saw it." Dumbfounded was not a good look on him. He shifted his weight from right to left and back again. Antsy, too. "I could see the rooms where they were being monitored. One or two people from the Research team would be observing"—he sneered at the word and I couldn't blame him—"and making notes, but they never met with the maintenance kids face to face."

Interesting. That narrowed down the types of things they were testing at the least. At this point, any lead was a win. "What do they have them doing then?"

"Standard technical updates, rewiring computers, programming changes for the tablets." I had forgotten they'd be the ones doing that. On Cloud Nine, your maintenance staff didn't just include the janitor but also the I.T. help desk.

"Do we have so many tablets that we need people working on them every day? They have to be at least a little skeptical."

"The party line is they're working on them for all stations." He shrugged. "I believe that part. There's a weekly shipment out and another back in of various devices needing service."

"That job would eventually still slow down, too, though."

"I think they know that, but most people don't ask the questions you do."

I took a step back. "What's that supposed to mean?"

"You really do make helping you an exercise in frustration." He groaned and then moved closer to me. I didn't back away, but that was probably because I was too busy being insulted. "You draw attention here because you're smart and stubborn. Those things make you great in the research department, but not so great when it comes to keeping your nose out of government secrets."

My vision flared red.

"It's what makes you brilliant." He brushed my hair off my cheek and tucked it behind my ear. I let him. He was having that steadying effect on me again, which was probably a good thing. He continued, "It was meant as a compliment."

"Okay." I licked my lips. When did they become so dry? I took a deep breath and made myself speak slowly. "Okay. We need to decide what to do first." I looked around the room like something there would tell me what to do. Abstract artwork and a whole lot of plastic didn't help my synapses fire.

"What to do?" He made it sound like I'd taken wild pills.

Someone was angling for another punch, but I had moved on to bigger things. Ignoring his comment, I talked while walking back to his couch. "We need to know what things they're testing. Maybe it's just a behavioral study."

We shared a 'fat chance' look.

"Maybe not. Still, maybe I'm freaking out over something small." I sat again, feeling better for my minimizing thoughts.

"Maybe." He sat next to me. "Can you find out what they're testing?"

"I probably already have the information. They've been passing me paperwork, but it takes time to review it all. If you recall, someone made me leave the lab to attend an awful party."

He smiled. "Fair point. The game plan, for now, is to find out what's being tested before we take any action. You get some basic answers and we'll regroup and decide what to do next."

"You sound like you're trying to stop me from causing trouble."

"I am." His smile widened. "I'm also agreeing to help you do whatever is necessary to stop the testing, but I want us to make those decisions together."

He knew how this place worked, had access to everything, and made me feel safe, so my answer was instantaneous: "Done."

Only after I said it did I realize I had put my hand on his thigh. I was comfortable around him the way I was back home with my best friend, until I did something like touch him in a way that let me feel muscles. Then I was conflicted. I might have hated being conflicted even more than I hated planning ahead.

Did I leave it there? I definitely liked touching him. Probably more than I should. But I was also trying to discourage him from thinking of me like some delicate flower. Was he the kind of person who would equate my gushy feelings toward him—ones I was not really admitting —as a reason to get bossy with me? The flip-flop in my stomach did not change things between us. I was leading this show and letting him come along for the ride.

Well, I was leading the getting-answers portion of the event. I had no idea what I was doing when it came to my hand on his body. He placed his own over mine to nullify the question. I was thankful, but didn't say so aloud. I wasn't that much of a pussy.

"The hitch in our plans is our new guest, Jensen."

Oh. Right. Him. In my anger cocoon, I'd forgotten about him. Not smart, Ally.

Declan eased back into the couch. I liked him relaxed even if it made me a little jealous of the way he could just let things go. "If you have to take notes, do it on paper and keep them on your person. Don't even leave them in your dorm room."

"I can do mental notes if I know what I'm looking for, but I think

I'm going to still have to take some notes on other things so it doesn't look weird."

"Good idea." He looked impressed. Nice.

"What should I do about Jensen?"

"Nothing." His hand squeezed mine. "I'll take care of him."

I gave him a half smile. "That sounds nice, but what am I supposed to do when he shows up in my office?"

"Go into it like a fight. Be evasive."

"You make that sound simple. When I try to fight verbally, I end up tasting shoe rubber."

"You were holding your own at the party earlier."

"Banal stuff." I shook my head. "Do I have the wrong impression of this guy? I think he's going to ask me point-blank about the notes."

Declan thought about this for more than a moment. I liked the silence. Or, more aptly, I liked that he was actually listening to me and rearranging his thoughts around my ideas.

"You're right. He's confrontational. He's the type who thinks being a dick makes him hold the power in a conversation." Was there a verbal version of an eye roll?

"Charming." At least Jensen would be direct. I could handle an attack from the front much better than a slow, sneaky one from behind.

"You're going to have to let him think he's in charge."

"Isn't he? I thought he was the one whisking people away to places unknown." Bitter didn't sound right on me.

"You have what he wants. That means you're in charge and he doesn't know it."

Well, I liked that. "Which is better with him: playing dumb or being the sarcasm queen?"

"Playing dumb would be better, but if he's heard anything about you—and I know he has—he won't buy that outright. Downplay your notes and don't worry about hiding your feelings about him being there."

"Is that the nice way of saying I can be a jerk?"

"I didn't call you a jerk."

"You were thinking it."

He elbowed me in the side. I looked up at him and that bright smile. I was saved from sinking into comfort by a soft clicking noise. Declan inclined his head toward his desk where a small yellow light flashed. "We are about to have company. On this floor, at least."

Because if talking about human testing, government conspiracies, and forced heroics couldn't kill a mood, a third wheel would.

CHAPTER 32
NOT COAXED INTO COMPLIANCE

Declan was almost to his door before the first knock echoed through the room. I started to follow him, but he shook his head and pointed to his left. For once, I did as he asked—not that I'd want him to get used to it—and moved out of the visual line of the doorway.

I wasn't exactly hiding. It wasn't like I was breaking a rule by being in Declan's room, but it wouldn't work as a sanctuary if I couldn't keep our meetings quiet.

"Do you know where Ally is?" Adam's smooth voice had my muscles snapping taut with rubber-band-style tension.

"I'm not her keeper." Declan puffed himself up, elbows jutting out when he folded his arms over his chest like my own personal bouncer.

"Her sister saw her with you." Adam made it sound dirty like my friendship with Declan was below my station. Clearly, the guy didn't understand my thoughts on tiered social standings.

Declan twisted his body to maintain his human blockade. If Adam was trying to peek in, it wasn't working.

"You do know how social gatherings work, don't you? I suppose all that time in the lab may have addled your brain, but at parties one tends to talk to multiple people." I couldn't help but smile at

Declan's antagonism. He hadn't done that with me. "Mingling. It's a thing."

"You're not helping her, you know." Who told Adam I needed unsolicited help?

"Is that your job now?" Declan retorted. Condescension slathered their interaction.

I didn't know how much longer I could stand by and let them discuss me. I could hear my sister in my head saying all this male posturing was hot; protective guys were the ones who cared about you the most. I was fairly certain those were the insecure tools, and I could do better. Nothing said sexy to me like trust. Being treated like a person instead of a pet was a relationship requirement.

Neither Declan nor Adam was being all that sexy. I couldn't help myself; a tiny derisive snort escaped me. A muscle in Declan's neck twitched.

It didn't sound like Adam had noticed. "She isn't your concern." His words shook me like thunder in a burn storm. "I've got this covered and you're only going to complicate things."

"Is that why Jensen's here?" Declan was losing his cool.

Bringing up Jensen was a bad idea. Then again, maybe there was enough history among them to make it weird for him not to get worked up over it. Bad idea or not, I needed to hear more. The possibility of a little truth sliding out of Adam's mouth stilled my irritation with him.

"I'll handle Jensen." The dismissal didn't sit well with me. Sure, I didn't like that Adam had this dickish underside, but what rankled was the lack of information.

"Please." I didn't need to see his face to know Declan rolled his eyes. "You'll try to do something, then come running to me at the last minute for help."

"When have I ever come running to you?"

"Oh, I don't know, who cleaned up the Sage incident?"

I perked at that. Tiptoeing a tiny bit closer.

"I didn't ask you to fix anything there."

"You're right. I should have just let the girl bleed out while all the new kids screamed in the hallways. Much better plan." Adam stepped toward Declan, like he was going to try to enter the room. Declan's hand slammed against the doorframe hard enough to shake the wall next to me. "You don't ever ask for my help, but I end up cleaning up after you regardless. Save us both time and just fill me in now."

Adam was silent. I wanted to believe he was considering sharing something we could use.

The throaty rumble of contempt coming from Adam proved how much of a long shot that hope had been. "She isn't going to be impressed by you."

"Excuse me?" I was with Declan. Excuse me?

"Ally chose to work with me. I'll be the one taking care of her. She'll be in line with my team and Jensen will back off." He made it sound like I was a puppy one could charm into sleeping soundly in a kennel with a soft towel and a treat.

I almost slammed my head against the wall. That was it, wasn't it? The hot showers, the plush fabrics, the food that was better than anything I could dream of affording on Ground Level. It was all meant to coax me into being happy here. Into complying.

I needed to punch something. Maybe that cocky Adam square in his arrogant mouth. He was the worst part of this, wasn't he? Pretending he cared and cranking up the charm. Was the friendliness between us artificial, too? Could that be cultured in a lab? The more I thought about it, the angrier I was. Only I was mad at myself. I was good at identifying threats. I recognized people were out to get information and would wield it to their advantage as needed. Yet, I'd actually thought Adam could be a friend.

Maybe he was a product of Cloud Nine, too. Perhaps the longer you lived here, the more you adapted. I didn't want to change. I didn't want to assimilate. I'd keep my foot out of my mouth in the name of self-preservation, but I wanted out.

If there had been an option to open a window and dive toward the moon, I'd have done it. Without a thought to the consequences. Like falling twenty miles to the hard-packed earth and exploding on impact.

Was it wrong that the idea wasn't as horrific as it should have been? Being wary of others' motivations usually led to me being surprised by the good in people. I liked it that way. Humanity should be more caring and thoughtful. That isn't how it was panning out at Cloud Nine. Instead my, 'who to trust' radar had let me down. I needed to become extra vigilant. I probably needed to push Declan and Charlie to arms-length until this Jensen thing was resolved. I wasn't sure if that was realistic just yet.

"Good luck with that," Declan said before shutting the door in Adam's face.

He closed the distance between us with the swiftness of a summer storm. Sudden, overwhelming, and dark.

One can whisper and yell at the same time. And Declan had mastered the hushed tone of secret rage.

"Would it be so goddamn hard to be quiet?"

I understood his anger, respected it more than I should have. "I hoped he'd give us something about Jensen."

"He's not that dumb." But apparently kind of dumb?

"Okay." I didn't know what to do with myself. My ire wasn't directed at Declan and for once, I didn't want to take it out on him. "What's the plan then?"

"Same as before. Gather information and regroup."

Right. Easy peasy. "Will Adam be a problem now?"

"Not any more than he would have been an hour ago." He licked his lips, as though moistening them would make it easier to say whatever he was holding back. And there was no question he was resisting saying something.

"What?" Doing things the slow way rankled me enough. I didn't need Declan going back to covert mode with me.

"You're going to have to pretend to be friends with him." The words ran together, and it took me a minute to parse out what he'd said.

I groaned. "I'm not a good actor."

"We don't know how involved he is."

"We know he expects me to, what was it he said, get 'in line.'" I stared at Declan long enough to make weaker people crumble. Declan didn't wither. "Please, he's invested somehow."

"I don't like him—"

"Obviously."

He pretended I hadn't interrupted. "—but I think you also thought I was siding with them."

"You kind of were."

"Agree to disagree." His tone said we'd have to talk about it again later. Just great. "Regardless, he may be saying things just to get under my skin."

"They got under mine, too," I mumbled. Declan heard, though.

"Pretend it didn't. You can be your normal standoffish self, and still charm him."

"Standoffish?"

"You're missing the point."

"Fine. I'll try and pretend, but know that when this blows up in atom-bomb proportions, I will blame you."

"Wouldn't have expected anything else."

CHAPTER 33
AUTHORIZED PERSONNEL ONLY

never thought I'd be the girl sneaking out of a guy's bedroom.

Then again, in that standard scenario I would have been avoiding disapproving parents and probably would have been wearing my shirt backward. Thankfully, that wasn't my life.

No, instead Declan had ordered me to sneak to the far end of the hallway and use the stairs to escape. He was so certain Adam would be watching within five minutes. Sharing a floor with the guy you hated probably sucked pretty hard, but I wasn't convinced Adam would waste his time in surveillance mode.

Declan disagreed. Adam was searching for me, he argued. He'd come right back here when he didn't spot me elsewhere. Blah, blah, blah.

I was a little over arguing—a possible first—and I needed alone time to think, anyway. That last part made leaving easier. He might have been telling me what to do, but I made my own choices. Besides, his guidance was probably useful. Running down several flights of stairs would be good for me, anyway. I hadn't had a proper workout since moving to this sky-high maze.

I did my best attempt at quiet running—whatever it was worth, the room still echoed with the tap tap tap of my feet against the floor.

Adam didn't pop up in front of me, so I must have done something right. The stairway access door opened with the same soft snick as every other door in this place, and I slipped inside.

The stairwell was the darkest place I'd seen on Cloud Nine. Instead of bright bulbs lining the walls, a solitary fluorescent bulb sputtered at each landing. Shadows could have lived here. Inhaling deeply, I imagined pulling the darkness inside me. I'd keep it for when I'd be in my too-bright office pretending to be impressed by the brilliant sun and the charming guy in the office next to me. Both failed to meet expectations.

While Declan's instructions had been to head down the handful of necessary steps to my room, I wasn't sure that was the best plan. Not that I bothered telling him. Sometimes it's better to take control silently. If Adam really was looking for me, he may have headed back to my room. I didn't want to show up and find him waiting at my door. That would require explanations. My anger would bubble and the whole "be his friend" thing would be shot.

So, of course, I modified the plans. I jogged down the stairs. Level 10 passed quickly. By Level 6, a fine sheen of sweat coated my forehead and the back of my neck. I charged downward. My plan had been to hit the lab. It was a logical place for me to escape to. It held answers and everyone expected me to be there. But once I started running, I couldn't stop. I liked the fire licking my quads and the way my cheeks heated from exertion. The harder I pushed myself, the more I pretended I was actually free from the drama of the Clean Air Development program.

The Level 2 door came up so quickly I had to slam my palms against the door to keep from crashing completely into the metal barrier. I'd hit the end of the road. There was a second door on my left. A small placard above the lock read:

LEVEL 2 MAINTENANCE.
AUTHORIZED PERSONNEL ONLY.

I pressed my index finger to the lock reader and held my breath. The door hissed open before I could exhale.

Well, I'd much rather have to ask for forgiveness than permission.

————

The hallway on the other side was darker than even the stairwell. How much of that was my mind conjuring sinister uses for the tiled corridor, I wasn't certain. It wasn't like the walls were dingy or echoing back pleas for help. It wasn't even cold. But the lighting was dim enough to force my eyes to readjust. That split second was more than long enough for my mind to spin with the possibilities of what I'd find.

Declan had suggested the maintenance staff were the test subjects. Then there would have to be answers here, right? I took a tentative step forward as if the wrong move would result in spotlights and security teams covering me. Nothing happened. My steps were careful and noiseless on the same polished tile that filled the rest of the station.

Seven short strides later the hallway ended. I could go right or left. Both directions had brighter lights than where I currently stood. I didn't know if that was a good sign considering my goals. Screw it. I went left and walked down the hall like I owned the place.

I wasn't good at stealth. Sure, the shoes were quiet, but they carried me and my mouth. Long ago I'd learned confidence was the gateway to being left alone. I might not have been able to fake belonging here due to my poor lying skills and general lack of a poker face, but I could strut like I was in charge of things. That kind of posturing, I could handle. After my last discussion with Declan, I didn't want to consider what that said about me.

My concerns about quiet were pointless, though. This level was like every other one.

Or maybe not.

This level had no windows. Maybe that's why it felt off to me?

That wasn't just it, though. Every other place I'd been on Cloud Nine—even the orientation level—had evenly spaced doors. I had figured the architect thought the science and math kids would like symmetry or something pathetic like that. Now I wondered if it was more about uniformity. It didn't matter now. This floor was different.

Three doors clustered together, then a long gap. Three more doors. Another gap.

I stopped in the middle of a set of doors. My tongue stuck to the roof of my mouth. I started to wish for a bottle of water when another, more concerning thought forced a shiver to spiral down my spine: Was the air different down here?

Now I couldn't stop swallowing. It was all in my head. I wasn't going to go into some sort of dehydration coma in under three minutes. My body was betraying me. I tried to make a fist. My fingers curled in to meet a damp palm. Sweat was fine. A sheen still coated my brow from the jog downstairs. That was different. These were my hands.

This wasn't some basic reaction to increased oxygenation. My vision cut down to small tunnels and dizziness set in. I stumbled into the doorframe, smacking it hard enough to leave a bruise on my shoulder.

This was wrong.

I shouldn't have been freaking out. I knew better. I tried to listen for others on the floor. I needed to be alert, but when I focused the only sound was my pulse throbbing inside my skull.

Too fast.

All of it.

I backed away from the door, retreating until my shoulders hit the opposing wall. Slow-and-steady breathing slowed my pulse. That was something. I listened for a moment. Things were too quiet down here. I peeked at my watch. Well, it was nearly ten in the evening. Normal people wouldn't be working now.

My desire to investigate warred with my need for self-preservation. It wouldn't be smart to walk back over to door 248. Whatever was behind there was not meant for me. Not without proper preparation. I'd need to ask Declan to get the security feed there. Maybe I could get answers without being lightheaded.

To give up now though would be pathetic. I chose to come down here and get answers. This just added more questions. This foray was worth more than that. I dug my nails into my slightly-less-sweaty palm. The pain set my resolve. I took off running down the hallway.

I rounded the first corner and then slowed. More doors in the same pattern. Well, at least they were consistent. When I moved toward door 221, I did it slowly. Lesson learned. My mouth didn't feel like I'd stuffed it with fabric, so either nothing was hinky here or my caution was effective.

The door on the far right wasn't locked. Inside was a barren workroom. Two tables, four stools. Nothing else. If there had been tools on the wall, I'd have thought it normal. Did they have some perverse tool check out program here and everything was locked elsewhere? Doubtful.

There weren't any answers in that room. Basic furniture didn't exactly require additional probing. I tried opening the next two doors. My luck had run out. My fingerprint warranted a red light and no access to either. At least it didn't beep loudly. I rolled my eyes at my optimism. Leah would love that.

Could I blame that on my earlier reaction, too?

I considered it the whole way back to my room. I didn't encounter anyone on Level 2 or on the stairs. Not that anyone else would be inclined to take the stairs here. I decided to do it more often. It wouldn't be the same as jogging laps around the neighborhood on Ground Level—from the black briquette house on Second Avenue to the dark grey stucco of the police station—while the soft green haze of dawn lit the world. But I needed to stay strong here. Climbing stairs would do that. The sneak factor was a bonus.

I'd forgotten about my plan to avoid Adam. That was the reason I went to Level 2, right? Part of the reason.

Unfortunately, he hadn't stopped trying to find me. I popped out of the stairwell door with vigor. Running up several flights of stairs brightened my mood. A hot shower would finish clearing my mind, I'd sleep and figure things out in the morning.

Or I would have if Adam hadn't been sitting in front of my dorm room.

He didn't bother getting up as I approached. Instead, he waited until I was standing next to him to say anything. "You ditched me."

He sounded dejected. Hurt, even. My mind knew better, but my chest still tightened. "I didn't mean to." Well, I had, but if I fidgeted enough when I said it the lie would look more realistic. Just to be safe, I added a little truth, "That room was a little overwhelming for me."

He nodded slowly. How was he so good at pretending?

I reached out to unlock my door, but Adam stood quickly blocking me.

"Look, I'm sorry about bailing. I'll be back to normal after a hot shower and some sleep." I stared at the lock. It was next to his elbow. He edged in front of it.

"I understand. This place can take some getting used to, but I'm on your side."

Please. He was on Team Use Me.

"I appreciate that." I snapped my jaw shut. The last thing I needed to do was spit out more false praise for this guy.

Adam's eyebrows pulled together. I wasn't concealing my irritation well. He couldn't know I was on to him, right? "Why don't I come in and we talk about it?"

I forced the most uncomfortable smile of my life. Tighter than the time my aunt told me she was so proud of me that she trusted me to watch my seven-year-old niece on a night I had big plans with Sarah. "Can we do it tomorrow? I'm exhausted."

My skin crawled when his eyes narrowed. I told myself it was just the reaction of cool air against sweaty skin. Best lie I told all day.

"It is late." Adam paused as if he was actually considering the time. I knew better now. "Where did you go anyway?"

I couldn't remember if he told Declan he'd checked the lab for me or not. I knew he'd come to my room. See, this was the reason lying was difficult. Too many things to keep straight. "I planned to hit the lab, but was too keyed up for reading." I waited for him to look surprised. He did and that smarmy grin crept across his mouth. "I know. Anyway, since no one has shown me a place to exercise here, I decided to run the stairs a bit."

"You were working out?" I liked that I baffled him. The tick of the muscle at his temple suggested he wanted to argue, but the physical signs of my running were plain.

"If you want to be strong, that's what you do."

"Most people here don't really do heavy workouts." Skepticism made his voice waver.

"Most people here can't run a mile without choking themselves." This smile was less forced. Adam had forgotten the whole reason they wanted me here. I didn't mind working for what I wanted. I studied and I trained and kicked anyone who got in my way. He was on the list for a foot to the gut as soon as it was safe.

His laugh sounded real, but what did I know? "Fair enough."

I started toward the lock again. If it whooshed open, he'd have to step away. Only he blocked me again. Even if I didn't think he was sketchy now, his overt power plays would have been a huge turn off. He looked over my shoulder when he spoke again, "I just need to know I didn't do anything to upset you."

If he was really concerned, his stance didn't show it. His shoulders were back, pulling his shirt tighter across his chest. "Nope." I shrugged and hoped he'd move out of my way. He didn't. "I'm pretty direct about things that bother me. Like you making me stay out in the hallway."

He glanced over his shoulder like it was some surprise the way into my room was directly behind him. Jackass. He turned back to face me and gestured over his shoulder at the still-locked door. "Did you want to finish up in there?"

My patience was worn too thin. Today sucked. I wanted to be done and my ability to resist popping Adam in the chin waned with each passing second. "No. I really need to take a shower."

Harsh lines around Adam's mouth made him look older than he was, but they faded quickly. "I understand." He didn't, but he was done tempting fate. "I know Jensen wants to meet you tomorrow."

Crap. I'd forgotten about him. Add one more problem to the giant heap loaded atop my skull. "Sure."

"Can you maybe come early tomorrow?" He paused and smiled, this time a genuine one. "That was a silly question. He's not exactly, um, a friend. I was thinking we could meet with him together."

I didn't believe Adam was on my side, but I did buy that he wanted to protect me from Jensen. If that was because it would serve his interests or because Jensen was such a bad guy wasn't clear. Me alone with

Jensen was probably a bad idea, though. "That's probably smart. Thanks."

I tacked on the word of gratitude and choked back the rush of guilt.

At least snapping out a fist was honest. Saying things I didn't mean? It slicked me in shame.

I would blame Adam for making me scrub my skin more than once that night.

CHAPTER 34

I DON'T WANT TO TAKE ORDERS

Sleep came easier than I predicted. Exhaustion did that to you.

The next morning I was just as beat down as the night before, only my hair was now a swirling nest of knots. The dull ache in my hamstrings reminded me that I should have been using those muscles more frequently. I doubted I could get away with taking the stairs all the time. Being athletic here made me stick out even more. If I was going to get answers about this place, I needed to try to blend in.

I kicked the covers to the foot of the bed and waited for the cool air to bite my skin. Keeping my head down wasn't in my nature. What was the point of pretending you weren't unique? On Ground Level, I ran and studied and said the asinine things that popped into my head without worrying about judgment. That isn't to say people didn't judge. My friend Sarah used to joke that it was justifiable for people to talk behind my back since I wasn't so kind to them if they did it in front of me.

I smiled at the memory and found myself wishing I could talk to her. She had been wrong, though, and I'd told her at the time. I'd much rather someone be honest to my face than save their sincerity for when

I was away. Well, okay, I need them to be honest respectfully. Being a jerk gets one nowhere.

I slammed my head down against the pillow, but it didn't dislodge any good ideas. Going downstairs to the lab and pretending I liked Adam, that Jensen wasn't sketchy, and that I didn't know they were making the lowest levels of the station into petri dishes was asking a lot.

I swung my legs out of bed and stood. The cold tile did more to jolt me awake than the slowly circulating air ever could. I walked to my desk and picked up the picture of Sarah and me. She would have had advice here. It would have been something weak like, "Just pretend everyone is me." That had never worked, but was her go-to suggestion. If it wasn't for Cloud Nine's lockdown policy, I would have called her days ago. I rubbed my thumb against the wood grain of the frame. It was nice to touch something that had grooves.

The posters on Cloud Nine proclaimed living in the future. I hoped not. This future was all hard, solid, and cold surfaces. They may have been porous materials, but the place didn't give me room to breathe. I wouldn't have been surprised if someone needed to monitor the speed at which one compressed her lungs in this place. Cloud Nine wasn't freedom from the past, as the EPA wanted us to believe. It was just a step into a darker future.

That was the way of things, though. We traded one mess for another. Cure a disease, create a plague. I didn't want to be a part of it.

I looked at Sarah standing next to me in the photo. Our squished faces. Happy. In the burning air, with the tasteless food, in the land without sunshine, I'd been happy. Put me on Cloud Nine for a couple weeks and watch me being forced into the liar's corner.

"How did I end up here, Sar?" I asked the picture, wishing she could respond.

I shook my head. "I'm not this person. I don't want to be this person." The words slid between barely parted lips. I needed to hear them aloud. I needed to remind myself who I was. The affirmation probably wouldn't help once I was in the lab staring at Jensen. For now, though, I held on to the knowledge that I wasn't going to be a part of this.

I'd fake it. I'd pretend to be the go-to girl. I'd offer suggestions as to how we could fix the acclimatization process issue. That part, I could do without feeling like a traitor to humanity. I wouldn't give tips on testing techniques though. If they asked, I'd feign ignorance.

They wouldn't ask, though, would they? Adam was smart enough to know I wouldn't take it well. Either he wanted to get caught or he'd underestimated me when he passed over those documents. I'd read between the lines. If only I hadn't been dumb enough to make notes.

I set down the picture frame, pushing it to the back corner of my desk.

"I'm sorry, Sarah." I was. She had such faith in people. She believed the hype about the Clean Air project. Not in the naive way my sister did, but with cautious hope. I nodded like someone was watching. "I'm going to fix this."

As soon as I figured out how.

I didn't feel like eating—another first—but it'd be weird if I didn't have breakfast. The irritating guy who served the extra early risers would miss me. I think he rather enjoyed the challenge of engaging me every morning. I did not glean the same type of joy.

"I've got sausage," he said with an undercurrent of something inappropriate.

"Well, stab it with a fork and hand it over." When I didn't bother veiling my mood, he shut his mouth and passed over a plate loaded with scrambled eggs, which I'd discovered I liked slathered in a bright red chili sauce, and the non-sexual sausage.

I shoved the food around my plate and managed to force myself to swallow some. Even with an extra dose of hot sauce, I didn't taste it. My stomach was triple knotted. I should have been bent over from the tension carving away at my abdomen. Score one for me that I kept a normal posture and didn't give off any overt 'she's going to burn the place down if she can' vibes.

I refused to admit it, but there were times when my anger made me stupid.

Level 4 was quiet when I arrived. Not that I'd expected any different. At most, there had been one additional person other than Adam when I arrived in the mornings. Today I was a full thirty minutes earlier than my standard arrival time. I walked through the multiple access points, thinking for the tenth time that there should be a more direct way into the office.

Adam wasn't in the room next to mine when I arrived. Small favors.

I needed to look over my notes, to know what phrases I used. Lying required almost as much research as adapting the osmosis chamber to handle lighter metals. The thought was unnerving.

The bulky shape in my office concerned me more, though.

My momentary pleasure at Adam's missing-in-action status disappeared. A one-on-one with Jensen wasn't exactly high on my list of acceptable early-morning activities. Unfortunately, showing weakness here wasn't going to be advantageous. I squared my shoulders and continued walking across the lab like I was its queen. I was supposed to be here. They wanted me here, and Jensen would just have to accept they needed me to do the work.

The edges of my mouth turned up slightly. Perhaps I'd tell him I had more important work to do than to explain my notes to him. Sometimes being an asshole could get you out of a tight spot.

My smile faded. All the second-hand impressions I had gotten about this guy said he was an entitled guy. He'd match me on the jerk scale and win. Demure wasn't my thing, but as I stepped toward my door I decided to wing it and hope for the best.

"Took you long enough. I thought you were going to turn around and run back out of the room."

My jaw dropped and I stood there like some dolt, mouth gaping for a full five seconds before I could respond. Even then, I only choked out his name, "Declan."

He nodded toward my desk, "Are you going to sit or what?"

"You scared me half to death." I smacked his shoulder harder than I meant to.

"Seriously?" The pride in his voice cured any guilt over the smack.

I narrowed my eyes. "I thought Jensen had made an early visit." I took my seat and started tapping away on my tablet. Might as well multitask. "I want to see my notes before he gets here to ask me about them."

"Good call." He dropped into the opposing chair. "If only you could have considered being so thorough when sneaking around the station last night."

"What?" My attempt at innocence fell flat. "Fine. I didn't follow your directions. My plan made more sense and now I have better questions. Oh, and I need your help on something."

"You need my—wait, don't distract me. We need to cover this before anyone else gets here."

"Cover what?" I'd just accessed my notes and started skimming. The first page and a half revealed nothing jarring.

"Are you not going to even ask how I know you were on Level 2?" His voice was hushed, like people on other floors would miraculously hear us discussing my evening excursion.

Still, he was right. That burned. I'd been so focused on preparing for Jensen that I hadn't thought about Declan's question.

"You're the one monitoring cameras, so I guess you decided to watch me leave?" I didn't mean for it to come out as a question, but my voice squeaked at the end giving away my guess.

"Yes, I watch the monitors, but I'm not the only one."

"Who else was watching?"

"Last night it was just me. I take the night shift most of the time, but during the day it could be anyone on my staff." His jaw was tight. "Jensen also has access to the main surveillance room. He could enter at any time."

Like I needed that worry knife to the gut right now. "I'll be more careful next time."

"The cameras aren't your problem."

"They aren't? Then screw being extra careful."

"Take this seriously, Ally."

"This *is* serious. Do you know what's happening down there? I couldn't get into some of the rooms, and when I tried something happened. I got dizzy and nauseous. We need to find out what they're doing there."

"Damn it." He shot to his feet. "I can help you, but only if you work with me."

"Why are you mad at me?"

"Because you're putting yourself in danger."

"To save other people."

"You put them in danger when you do stupid, reckless things like that."

"Do I put you in danger?" That had to be why his face was turning red, right?

"Only when I have to go erase all the lock security logs because someone likes to open doors she's not even supposed to know about."

Oh. Oh no.

"I didn't realize..." I let my voice trail off in lieu of sounding sheepish.

"Of course you didn't. You need to discuss things with me beforehand."

"I don't want to take orders, Dec. I'm not one of your subordinates."

"I'm not asking you to do that. I want you to work with me. You and I, we can save people. But it isn't going to work if you keep running off and doing the types of things that draw attention. Give them a reason to ask questions or to doubt your loyalty, and you'll lose your freedom."

"Let's not pretend I have freedom here."

"You have a hell of a lot more than you will if you're caught undermining them."

I didn't have to ask whom he referred to here. My gut told me this went much higher than I wanted to think about. Jensen was only the muscle. If I pissed off the government, they could do a whole lot more than take away fancy food and a room with a view.

The tablet and my notes were forgotten. We needed a better plan than covering our asses. "Okay. I'm in. I'll try to be more..." I paused, searching for the right word. One that wouldn't make me sound patronizing. "Considerate while seeking answers."

"Thank you." He meant it.

"Now, can you see what's inside the rooms down there? I didn't have access to some, and whatever is inside is definitely a problem."

"I can access that, yes, though I don't know that we'll see anything all that helpful."

"Why not?"

"I don't think most of the rooms store anything. The lab geeks"—he averted his eyes when he realized what he'd said—"tend to bring things with them to the rooms."

I chewed on my bottom lip instead of answering immediately. "Okay. See if you can identify what the containers look like. That will help me in figuring out what they're bringing with them and possibly finding which test batches are being used. I have access to all the current projects here." I held up the tablet, still displaying my haphazard notes. "They never specifically say who or what they're testing on, which is why my notes have a lot of question marks in them, but I can read between the lines and narrow our options."

He nodded. "Jensen should be here soon. Adam, too, probably."

"He said he wanted to be here when I met with Jensen."

"When?" Oh, right. He didn't know about the awkward and pushy conversation I'd had with Adam the night before.

"Adam was waiting for me when I got back last night. He was worked up, probably about the Jensen thing."

Declan's brows knitted together, but he didn't say anything. I continued, "I wasn't really ready to be nice to him, but I did my best to postpone talking to him. He made me agree to talk to Jensen with him there."

"Interesting." One word. No tone. That didn't bode well.

"While I think he's involved in the testing stuff, I get the impression he doesn't like Jensen. I figured it was a safe call."

"No, you're right. There's no love for Jensen at Cloud Nine. Even from a troll like Adam."

That was probably the nicest thing Declan had ever said about Adam. Disparaging as it was, it made me feel better about agreeing to Adam's help in dealing with Jensen.

"Adam's going to be here soon. You should probably be gone before that happens." Based on their interaction last night, Adam would have a hard time accepting Declan in my office. I didn't need to start my morning out on an antagonistic note.

There would be plenty of time for that in the rest of the day.

CHAPTER 35
WARNINGS AND WORRIES

t could have been worse.

Yes, the offending "Human test subjects???" line was in my notes.

It wasn't in giant serif font and underlined in a sign of please-be-kidding-me, though. At least I hadn't added that bit of commentary. Other than that single line, my notes were vague—single words and short phrases to jog my memory as to what I'd read.

I doubted Jensen came flying up after seeing "biosynthesis" typed in my notes. It likely didn't mean anything to him. There wasn't enough written down for it to explain how I would merge the pathway for the creation of amino acids with one to help those on Ground Level adjust to better air.

If only I'd been so cryptic with my test subject note. In hindsight, there were so many other things I could have written down, words that would have sparked my brain without sounding the Clean Air fire alarm.

I wanted to believe Jensen wasn't here because of my notes. Then again, I would have been quite happy if they weren't using kids to test chemical compounds. I hadn't gotten a wish granted in months. That wasn't about to change.

It had only been a few minutes since Declan left when the lab door opened. I tapped my screen a couple times to flip it back over to the latest batch of research Adam had shared with me.

I kept my head tilted down like I was reading, but glanced up to see who walked in. I let my abs unclench when I saw Adam striding toward our adjacent offices.

He came directly to mine and slid into the chair Declan had occupied minutes before. I hoped it wasn't still warm. "Feeling better today?"

I almost asked what he was talking about, but caught myself. "A hot shower and a good night's sleep make a difference."

"Glad to hear it." He was watching me. Expectant. What did he want from me? That was as polite as I was getting.

I stayed quiet and relaxed back into my chair. If there was one game I ruled, it was The Quiet Game. I didn't flinch.

He broke first. Naturally. "You're not mad at me, are you?"

Where did that come from? He was more sensitive than I gave him credit for.

"Nah." Yes. "I'm sorry about last night. Big crowds can make me really uncomfortable." Not entirely a lie.

"Right. Right. You told me that last night." Adam was shaking his head, but it was obvious he had wanted to hear my apology again. So sensitive.

"No problem. Are we ready for the Jensen invasion?" I kept my tone light, hopeful he'd adopt it and move on.

His half-hearted smile didn't tell me if he was on board with my plan. "As much as we can be."

Ominous much? "Why don't you like him?" I still hadn't mastered locking down the filter between my brain and mouth.

Adam leaned back into the chair. I guessed my trademark bluntness calmed him. Maybe I'd run my mouth more often to keep him off my back. "You picked up on that, huh?"

"The fact you don't trust me to talk to him alone doesn't look good."

"It's not that I don't trust you. Never that." He held his hands up like he was trying to block a straight punch. He probably didn't realize it. I doubted he'd ever taken a solid one to the chin. "He's tricky and I don't want him to try and use your inexperience on Cloud Nine against you."

"Inexperience?" My eyebrows may have actually disappeared into my hair.

"Poor word choice. I just meant you haven't lived on the station long. I would bet you still haven't even read the guidebook." I shrugged in response and he continued, "He'd love to catch you in a loophole for the sake of causing trouble. I don't want that."

Neither did I.

I tried to make my face as inexpressive as possible. "Okay, but you still didn't tell me why you don't like him." In for a penny…

His face scrunched. I wish I knew if that meant he was going to lie or was merely trying to decide which fragment of truth to tell. He wasn't about to be completely honest with me, but I wouldn't expect better of him.

"Not everything in the CAD program is what it seems." He was hesitating and it made me edge forward on my seat. If Adam was choosing his words carefully, I wanted to extract each and every one of them.

Adam licked his lips. When he started speaking again, his voice was steadier. "I know you came into this place uneasy, and some of that may be justified. I do my best to keep Cloud Nine on the up-and-up. Jensen would be my counterpart. He'd much rather get things done and not worry about the consequences."

If Adam was okay with testing chemical concoctions on people, then I didn't want to know what his definition of wrong was. "Consequences? Like what?"

He dodged my question. "Jensen is focused on results, and getting them as quickly as possible. I want to find answers, too, but we have to get to them methodically and in a way that keeps my staff safe." He smiled at me like I should be touched that he was concerned about my well-being.

What about the health and safety of those who didn't work for him? What about Declan's employees? What about the maintenance staff? What about my sister? Apparently, those people didn't matter to Adam. He didn't even realize what he'd said was wrong.

I wanted to believe Adam came to Cloud Nine idealistic and just bought into more of the government mind-wash once he got here. I didn't know, though. Protecting his own and leaving others out to burn in the wake of his glory sure sounded like more than naiveté. A crumb of morality stood between him and Jensen. I saw it there. Black and coarse and forcing Adam to ethically balance on his toes.

If I didn't know about the testing, I'd try to help him progress back to the side of sanity. But I did know. And that meant I couldn't risk him getting in the way.

A lake of cold regret washed over me. I'd have to use him to stop the atrocities on Level 2. Even if he was one of the bad guys, he deserved to be more than a means to an end. I wanted to be better than this.

How had I become this person in mere weeks?

Now wasn't the time to scrub at my skin, but I still pinched the side of my knee. I couldn't devolve into a sad sack of pity.

"Gotcha." Ugh. This conversation was painful. "What should I expect from Jensen today? Anything I need to do? Be aware of?"

"He just wants to talk to you, himself." Adam's eyes darted to my forehead when he spoke. Only I didn't think it was a complete lie. I wasn't the only one playing the grain-of-truth game.

"Why?"

"Why not?" He shrugged. "He wasn't one hundred percent behind your recruitment, to be honest."

Well, then Jensen and I had something in common. Only my ideas for acceptable means of exit were probably different from his. "So, should I be worried?"

"Of course not. He knows you're bright, and he can't bounce you from the project without a lot of red tape and my involvement." He smiled big and bright just as he had on the first day. "I want you here."

It hurt more than my cheeks to smile back, but I did it.

"But it might be worth making sure you're up to speed on the current projects."

"Does he have a chemistry or physics background?" I hadn't gotten that impression from Declan, but Adam would probably have been Jensen's go-to guy for any Technology team knowledge.

"No." I'd expected a more detailed response. He fidgeted in his chair—tugging at the ends of his shirt sleeves, then pushing them up to mid-forearm, and back down again—but Adam said no more.

"Okay." I drew the word out. It didn't affect his response.

"We'll just chat about the current projects, some of your ideas, and about life on Cloud Nine in general with Jensen and he'll be on his way." There was a difference between being optimistic and being delusional. Adam was clearly the latter.

I, however, was a realist. Jensen came for a purpose. I wasn't about to pretend we'd have noon tea and he'd be on his merry way.

Adam didn't know when Jensen was supposed to arrive, which I figured was some power tactic by Jensen. Better to make us be antsy so he could control the situation.

I could handle that. I'd sparred enough back home to know how to stay loose and agile until just the right moment. Outside of a fight, I wasn't so patient, but this was a fight. I'd wait to get my jab in. Until then, I was going to devour research and try to look like I was far too busy to deal with his petty problems.

———

Most of the current Cloud Nine research projects were focused on biosynthetics. Their delivery system was a huge problem. I hadn't figured out a solution by any means, but realized the issue with their current ideas (mostly pills and modified foods) was that each required people to take some action to interact with the synthetic. Hard to know if everyone on Earth has done that before making changes to the air on a global scale.

I figured the note "mass delivery system needed" wouldn't get me in trouble. Cloud Nine might be the pinnacle of research for my age group, but it was also a breeding ground for self-doubt. Working hard had always been enough for me. Here, though, no one really wanted to let me do my job. They faked allowing my independence with the office and the tablet and the access, but if they were second-guessing my every move, it didn't exist.

A heavy knock against my window drew me from the latest lab report. I inhaled in preparation for unpleasantness, but found Charlie stepping through the door.

"What brings you to my little corner of the laboratory?" My smile was real.

"I do believe you need a break, Miss Ramsey." She was smiling, too. After the last few hours, I'd forgotten what an easy conversation could feel like.

I looked up at the clock. I'd been in the office for more than five hours. "I could go for lunch." As if on cue, my stomach offered an extended grumble.

She laughed. "I've decided it's always a safe bet that you're hungry."

I tapped my tablet screen a few times to lock it—whole lot of good it did—and stood. "Anyone who takes odds on me not wanting a meal is looking to lose money. Take them for all they've got."

She nodded toward Adam's office. We could see him through the glass. The guy was hunched over his desk, brow furrowed and one hand clenched in a fist. Quietly she asked, "Should we invite him?"

"No, he has a lot on his mind." Clearly. I left out that being near him turned my insides into a flaming ball of rage. That was really more a dessert conversation.

The same weaselly guy who worked the breakfast counter was serving lunch. It was rare we saw the kitchen staff pull double shifts. I hadn't paid attention this morning, but his eyes were bloodshot and dark circles underscored his brown eyes. He didn't bother trying to say something provocative this time. Though I didn't know if that was due to his being busy, my tone this morning, or his obviously exhausted state. I kind of hoped it wasn't my fault.

With my plate piled high and Charlie's stacked to a more reasonable level, we snagged seats in the corner. Even with a bustling noontime lunch break, I liked that there was enough space that we could have a private conversation. A modicum of civility went a long way with me these days.

"How are things in the bio world?" I shoveled some bright yellow squash onto my fork. It was childish, but I liked the pretty food the best.

"Oxygenized." She laughed at her own joke. Botany jokes were always dumb. I swallowed my food and nodded in response.

"I've been working more on the botany side this week," Charlie explained. I felt bad that I hadn't even realized she'd been Plant Lady for a week. Being caught up in my own drama wasn't reason enough to be a crappy friend. I'd find a way to make it up to her. "We're trying to get the plants to thrive in nitrogen-depleted soil. Not like, completely without nitrogen, but just not as rich as it's supposed to be."

"Hoping to make it work on Ground Level?" I guessed. It matched the goals in my department, anyway. Made sense for us to be working in tandem.

"Pretty much. Not a ton of success yet. Working on some cross-pollination stuff that might help. I don't know though."

We continued to talk shop for a bit, proving how similar our two teams were. The more I heard about her projects, the more I saw the corollaries to my own. Potential was there for both awesome advances and a whole lot of hurting people. A sharp pain lanced my tongue and the tang of iron filled my mouth. I shouldn't think things like that while eating.

"I haven't seen your brother around lately." I looked around the room to make sure he wasn't sitting nearby. I didn't need to shove my foot in my mouth today. "How's he doing?"

"I think he likes it here less than he thought he would." Her shrug said it all. She and I both came into this place with a sense of wariness. Our siblings? Not so much.

"Has he made friends, at least?"

"Yeah, but he's been feeling crummy for a few days. I think he's got some respiratory thing, which is just what you need on a station with recirculated air."

My stomach clenched so quickly, I bent forward and knocked my elbows against the table. Charlie looked at me like I had lost it. She had no idea. I swallowed the bile sawing its way up my throat, and then forced myself back into a more standard upright position. I shook my head at her look of concern.

"I'm sorry to hear that. I've heard a few other people say they were coming down with something." Great. Now I was lying to her. "What's his duty assignment, again?"

"Maintenance."

I managed not to slam my face into the table. That was the last thing I wanted to hear. I needed to find a way to tell her. Warn her. Something. But this wasn't the place. I tried to cover my worry with banality. "What's he doing for them?"

"Tomás is a whiz with technology. I think he's repairing circuit boards for the whole Clean Air program."

No.

No. No. No. No.

Charlie continued talking, unaware of my internal struggle. That was for the best. I needed to calm myself before telling her that the government was likely using her baby brother as a guinea pig. She wasn't going to take it well. Unlike me, though, she wouldn't punch the messenger. Probably.

"We need some fun, Ally." Wasn't that the truth? Charlie was advocating fun in the middle of my moral meltdown. "I say board games tonight."

"Board games?" It was only the aroma of fresh food that kept my nose from scrunching.

"Yeah. I snagged one from the common room that has random, obscure words and we have to make up definitions for it. Then we all guess what's real and what isn't."

"We'd need more than just you and me to play that."

She rolled her eyes. "I know that. I thought I'd invite a few of the other Research folk." She looked at me closely for a moment. "I won't invite Adam if that helps."

"It does," I said without thinking.

She tilted her head slightly. I was sure I didn't look any different askew. "Everything okay?"

"He's around more than you can imagine. A break would be nice."

She nodded. "Makes sense. He was panicky looking for you last night."

"Oh, I know. He actually sat outside my door and wanted to have this big discussion"—I dropped the word like it carried the weight of all his wrongs—"when all I wanted was some space and a shower."

"I so didn't have him pegged as the needy type. Goes to show…" she trailed off.

"Show what?"

"All it takes is one girl to turn them into fools."

She didn't know the half of it, but I would tell her later. "Understatement of the century."

Leah was entering the mess hall as Charlie and I were dropping off our empty trays. She was beaming, but wasn't bouncing on her heels like normal. I figured work tempered her a smidgen as it did us all.

"You just starting work?" I hoped my tone was playful. My sister had a tendency to misread me as condescending.

"I wish." She sounded more labored than I expected. Now that we moved closer, I saw the signature glow of sweat dotting her temples. "I've been prepping vegetables for tonight's dinner. Chop, chop, chop." She made the motion to go along with each word. I checked her hands for bandages. She wasn't bleeding, which made me proud.

"What are we having?" I must have been rubbing off on Charlie if she was asking about meals before I had the chance.

"Something with zucchini." My sister shrugged.

"Your party was a hit. Nice work." I'd overheard others in the lab talking about it this morning. I really was the only person who didn't find the whole affair delightful. Still, best to be nice to the baby sis.

She was wary. "Uh, thanks."

I nodded. It was awkward for us both.

Leah turned to Charlie. "Did you have a good time at the mixer?" No need to ask me, dear sister. It's not like I was capable of enjoying social events. Why did I bother trying with her?

CHAPTER 36
CAUTION: MAY BITE

Thirty minutes with Charlie improved my mood to the point I'd spaced the whole Jensen dilemma.

There was no mistaking him—or what he represented—when I returned to the lab. Jensen stood in the center of the room, looming over everyone. He stood out as the adult in the room—the years between us stretching long now. He had a full six inches on Kevin, who was the closest. Kevin's eyes were wide in panic, but he hovered on his side of the workbench like he knew it was a bad decision to literally flee from someone like Jensen.

Seeing all that aggression next to lab equipment brought back bad memories: federal agents packing up my father's things. Putting my mementos of him into bags and hauling them out our front door. When I tried to stop one, I had been shoved back into the firm grip of another agent and forced to stand by while pieces of my life were taken away.

I wasn't held back now, but I also couldn't follow my gut and challenge Jensen. He leaned back against the soapstone counter—Kevin's workspace—like he owned the thing. Like the beakers and paperwork lying there were meaningless objects inhibiting his comfort. Kevin wasn't brave enough to say something. Declan wanted me to keep my head down. Adam wanted me to pretend I was the company girl.

What did I want? To be left alone. Not that anyone had asked.

It wasn't an option, so I did the next best thing and spared Kevin from the jackass's attention. "Jensen? Hi, I'm Allison Ramsey. I heard you wanted to chat with me and Adam."

I waved at Adam. He was already on his way out of his office. His eyes were a little wider than I'd have liked. He didn't need to broadcast fear to the whole room.

Jensen grunted. Someone didn't have the verbal skills to get into Cloud Nine.

To Kevin he said, "Think on it. We'll talk more later." It sounded like a threat. Such a charmer this one.

By the time Jensen turned back to me—sour pout marring what was, honestly, a kind of appealing chiseled face—Adam had reached us. It was for the best. In seconds this guy had confirmed all my worst fears about being in an enclosed space with him.

Jensen extended a hand to me, and then tried to feel every bone in mine as he squeezed into the handshake.

"Jensen Rothers." He lifted his chin when he said his name.

I could already picture myself throttling this atrocious ogre. The way my stomach dropped when Jensen glared at me said I'd need the restraint to my temperament Adam's presence provided. I kind of hated that Adam looked like the good guy right now.

Adam and Jensen barely looked at each other as we walked to Adam's office. Maybe they'd be too busy shooting hateful stares at one another to notice me sitting in the same room contemplating all the ways I could take them both down. A girl could dream.

Jensen took the power seat behind Adam's desk. I'd have told the jerk to get his butt out of my chair. It wasn't me, though, and it was becoming clear that Adam didn't much care for confrontation. At least when it came to authority figures. Probably the reason he tested our projects on kids downstairs.

His mom must have never given him the speech about how standing by when others were being mean made you part of the problem. If she had, he might have understood that every day he stood by while these experiments happened, he planted himself deeper and deeper in the evil camp.

Even now he kept his mouth shut.

I took the more inviting of the two remaining chairs. I feigned a look of ease, reclining and resting my ankle on top of the opposite knee.

Jensen watched Adam squirm, a muscle ticking along his jaw. Adam edged his seat closer to the desk. He might have been trying to place himself between Jensen and me. Chivalrous. Almost. He kept adjusting his chair, never finding the right placement.

"If you're done jacking around, can we get started?" I had to admit, I was with Jensen on this one.

Adam blushed and locked his fingers around the edges of the chair. Then he thought better of it and folded them in his lap. All business-like. So much for a worthwhile ally.

Adam managed to reply in an even tone. "Of course."

"So, Ally, what do you think of Cloud Nine?" The hint of a curl at the edge of Jensen's mouth said he knew how loaded that question was.

There was little chance he hadn't heard I was distant and not so much for the group activities. So, I went with the most truth I could muster without suggesting I wanted them to all rot in Hell for being cruel, self-serving cretins. "It's different."

Jensen guffawed. "Care to elaborate?"

I shrugged.

He waited.

I caved. "The station takes a bit of adjusting to. No parents. New friends."

"Your sister is here, though, correct?" He'd read my file. He likely knew why they stuck her across the hall from me instead of making us share a dorm. I hated talking about things he already knew the answers to. If there were ever proof he worked for the bureaucrats, this was it.

"Yes," Adam piped up like he was saving me. "She was assigned to Procurement."

Jensen ignored him. I almost understood the dismissal. "That has to help with the adjustment. Not everyone gets to bring family with them."

"Sure." Getting into my personal relationship with my sister was not going to happen. I didn't discuss her with anyone else, and I wasn't about to break that rule now.

He sucked in his lips. The sunlight from the window behind me did nothing to soften the harsh line of his mouth. He released his lips with a pop. Adam flinched. I arched my eyebrows in defiance and waited.

"We don't have to talk about her." That pivotal power seat move wasn't helping much now, was it buddy? "Have you reviewed all the current research being done at this station?"

"All would be an overstatement, as the Research team has been working diligently." I smiled at Adam like a good employee. I bet Jensen knew it was fake, but it was also expected. "However, I have reviewed the bulk of it. The biosynthetic options are incredibly promising."

"But you don't think they're ready yet?" Disapproval made his voice louder. I glanced to my left and saw a couple people in the lab looking our way. Just great.

"No." I let it hang out there for a moment, letting him get nice and angry, before continuing, "It's an excellent start, but we need a mass delivery system. Relying on people to take the initiative to swallow pills or travel to a clinic for a shot—no matter how helpful—won't be enough. You'll always have people who won't take those steps. If we make the air changes before everyone has adapted, we'd lose lots of people."

"That's been considered." His finality punched through the room. They knew they could kill off millions if a successful biosynthetic wasn't adopted worldwide, and they still wanted to proceed.

I bit my tongue. Literally. My incisor lanced the tip, reopening the wound from lunch, and I let the blood pool behind my teeth. I flicked the wound back and forth. When I flashed a quick smile at Jensen his eyes bugged out and I knew my white teeth were smeared red. "Give me time. I'll come up with something."

Both guys did a double take. I swallowed the blood. Let the pain fuel my anger. When I was certain my teeth were no longer bloody, I inclined my head toward the door. "If you don't need anything else, I should probably get back to work."

They both stared at my mouth as if the blood would reappear. I didn't wait for permission.

Adam and Jensen were still staring at each other when I settled in next door. I pressed my finger against the lock for my tablet, and once the screen came to life I started scrolling through the current biosynthetic delivery system ideas.

I could get them to do this my way.

Or scare them trying.

CHAPTER 37
TIME FOR JOKES

"A bloody grin. Really, Ally?" Declan was working a hole into my floor. His hands flailed about like my choice earlier would lead to the downfall of civilization.

"You did tell me to bite my tongue."

He stopped immediately. When he turned sharply, I brought my hand up to block my side. Just in case. He didn't strike. Instead, he gave me a look of pure incredulity. "Now is not the time for jokes."

"If I don't get my jokes in now, I'll never get the chance. After all, you've determined my not-so-friendly meeting has made me Jensen's sworn enemy. Even his children's children will curse my grave."

"Still not funny." He said that, but a flicker of humor lit in his eyes.

"It did stop him from asking more questions." Which was good, because being near that guy set my teeth on edge.

"For now." Declan took my hand and led me over to the bed. We both sat on its edge. "I thought you were on board for keeping a low profile and gathering intel." Little wrinkles appeared at the center of his forehead. I squeezed my hand under my leg to make sure I wouldn't reach forward to smooth them out. The instinct made my gut twist. I didn't know if I liked it, but I certainly didn't have time for it.

"You weren't there." Accusation was my defense method.

"No, I wasn't." He leaned back and propped himself up on both arms. The movement exposed his belt. I stopped wearing mine days after moving to Cloud Nine. You needed them on Ground Level to keep clothing tight to your skin. Declan had been here for years, but still wore the black fabric band about his waist. The clasp was a shiny matte metal.

The back of my neck warmed. I scratched it. "Look, I'll still get the information. Even from what I read this morning, I know more. They're testing delivery systems for something that would encourage lung cell generation."

He cocked his head. My attempt to state it simply had failed. I tried again. "Basically they want to introduce something that would make people have stronger lungs. Then they could adapt better to cleaner air. That's the idea anyway." When he nodded, and I believed he understood, I continued. "They just need to figure out if people can handle this thing and then how to give it to everyone at once."

"Those are two big problems."

"Tell me about it."

"So you think they're testing reactions to this chemical or whatever?"

"It's a biosynthetic, and yes. They're probably testing delivery methods, too. Though this morning's meeting makes me think they aren't as worried about that end as they should be."

"Did you find anything about the actual tests?"

I smacked at his elbow and he toppled backward. "Was that not enough?"

He pushed himself back upright. "I wasn't being disparaging."

He dusted the front of his shirt, and the mischievous grin on his face proclaimed he'd wanted my attention there. Bigger problems, Chief.

Declan spoke softly. "You're always moving an extra five steps ahead, so I thought it'd be best to ask first before making plans."

That was a compliment. I thought. "Oh."

"Yeah. Oh." His tone was mocking, and it was enough to keep me from wanting to hit him again. Lucky guy.

"Can't you watch to see what they're doing down there right

now?" Anyone with a wall of monitors should be able to do that, right?

"You know I'm the boss, right?"

"Yes." Did he think I was an idiot? "As the boss, I thought you'd have access to everything."

"I do, but it would be odd for me to monitor the live surveillance feeds."

I pressed my tongue flush with the back of my teeth, forgetting about the new wound. I made sure not to wince. "Can you record them?"

"I made sure the backups are stored on my remote server. That way I can review them after hours." Sure. Now he made it sound all casual and easy.

"At the very least we'd know who they're targeting and what the obvious reactions are." I didn't want to know, though. There was no chance we'd watch those tapes and discover everyone was feeling extra chipper. That's not how things worked.

If everyone were doing well, it wouldn't be such a guarded secret. Adam wasn't keeping the human testing from me out of honor to the blind study. Jensen hid it out of project preservation.

They should both fear being found out, because whatever was happening on the lower levels was wrong.

They might not care, but I did.

A knock at my door managed to break my spiraling thoughts. Charlie leaned in the moment I opened the door. "Not interrupting anything?" She waggled her eyebrows in Declan's direction. I looked over my shoulder to see him sprawled out on the bed. I rolled my eyes.

"Not even a little bit." I stepped out of the way and let her enter the room.

"You still in?"

"In for what?" Declan stole the words from my mouth.

"We're having board game night." She sounded so excited. Right. I remembered now.

Sarah and I used to play card games back home. We'd pretend candies were money and bet them in a no-holds-barred game of poker. We did not, however, play board games. Then again, most games required more people to play. I mean, we played poker, which is rough with two people. There was a limit to how hard I'd try to have fun.

The temptation to back out of plans was high. The world would inevitably come crashing down on us soon. I'd like to at least be in a brace position when it happened.

Declan had already hopped up and joined us near the door. "Can I join in, too, or is this a women-only type thing?"

I resisted giving him the crazy eye. I usually saved it for boastful pricks looking for fights. It stopped them nine times out of ten. However, I was tempted to use it to warn him about more pressing matters. He bumped my shoulder with his and grinned. "Ally wouldn't mind a little competition, I'm sure."

I glared then. He deserved it.

"Of course you can come." Charlie clasped her hands together at her chest. Unlike my sister, she wasn't used to being a social director. Color rose on the apples of her cheeks. Declan was making her day. I couldn't take that from her. She continued, "Fair warning though, I'm your real competition."

"What kind of skill will we need for tonight's main event? Money management? Extensive vocabulary? Random trivia?" His dimples were showing.

"No, I'm pretty sure Ally would annihilate us all if vocabulary or negotiation was required." I smiled at that. Damn right. "Tonight we'll be testing your bluffing skills."

Declan laughed harder than he should have. He slapped his thigh and everything. A tear escaped his eye by the time he caught me scowling at him.

"Did I miss something?" Charlie's smile slipped.

"Declan thinks my, shall we say, direct nature will make me very bad at this game." I elbowed the offending guy as he tried to compose himself.

She shook it off. "Oh, I'm sure you'll do fine."

I shrugged. "No, he's right, but I'll at least make things fun."

Charlie reached out and hugged me. I wasn't a hugger by nature, but I accepted her enthusiasm with goodwill.

She let go and pointed at me, then Declan. "Level 10 common room. Five minutes. Be there."

I managed not to laugh and agreed we'd be there in a few minutes.

"I'm going to snag a bottle of water from the pantry on this floor. You want one?" Even with Charlie out of the room, Declan sounded normal.

It would take more than a few smiles and a sneak-attack hug to stop my brain from whirring on about all the things I couldn't fix yet. I wanted to know his secret for turning it off, but asking would require admitting my own flaw. Enough of my mistakes had been exposed this week already. "Sure, I'm going to see if Leah wants to join us."

His lips pressed together into a hard line, but he kept his mouth shut. For once. He waited as I closed my door and stepped across the hall. I shooed him with my hand. "I'll be there in a minute. I'm doing the good sister thing."

I appreciated that he didn't laugh, and instead headed down the hallway without me. He turned to flash a grin at me as he edged past a couple whose make-out session couldn't wait for a dorm room.

I knocked on Leah's door after Declan disappeared into the room storing snacks and beverages. Then I waited.

And waited.

I wondered if my sister had other plans. It wouldn't surprise me, and I'd been so wrapped up in my own things I had zero idea of her comings and goings. I took a step away from the door, readying to leave when she finally opened it.

Her hair was limp, which Leah typically considered a state of national emergency. She blinked at me a few times. The room behind her was dim, only the echo of light emerging from the covered window. She flinched a few times, but finally her pupils constricted enough for her to look at me.

"What?" was all she said.

Normally, I'd chide her for being rude to me. She was never short with anyone else. Not even our mom. But I saw the crumpled clothes she wore and took pity. "Some of us are getting together down in the common room."

"For what?" Something in my stomach twisted at the gravel in her voice.

"Board games." I smiled pretending this was a normal Ally-Leah exchange when it wasn't even close. "I'm told whatever has been chosen is something I'll be awful at. So, I thought you might want to join and watch my public ridicule."

At least one of us was keeping up normal sisterly banter.

She shook her head with fervor. Immediately, she clutched her head. "Nah. I've got a wicked headache."

"Do you want me to grab you some water or medicine or anything?"

"I've got what I need. I just want to lay down."

"Okay. Get some rest. I'll check on you later."

"You don't have to." She offered a weak smile. "I'd be pissed if you woke me up."

"I don't want to risk your wake-up wrath, then." I started to leave, but stopped to add one more thing. "If you do need anything, I am just across the hall. Ask. Okay?"

"Yeah. Okay." She shut the door and I waited until I couldn't hear her feet shuffling against the floor before walking away.

She didn't work in maintenance, but that didn't mean she was safe. Protecting her from leering guys on Ground Level was so much easier than fighting the unknown on Cloud Nine.

I would check on her in the morning. Leah's ire be damned. My stomach roiled. I needed to know her headache was simply from dehydration—which happened to her pretty regularly—and not from outside sources.

As I wouldn't know if it was worth worrying about until morning, I pointed myself in the direction of board games and potential shenanigans.

CHAPTER 38
GAME ON

I straightened my stack of notecards and waited for Charlie to explain why I was holding them. She passed a small pile and a pen to each person clustered in the common room. I shuffled mine to keep my hands busy.

My muscles were tight. Even sitting on the thin carpet with my legs crossed, my posture was the kind of perfection that could be proved with a book balancing on my head. Declan nudged me. He had tossed his cards down to the floor between us. His legs were stretched out in front of him, crossed at the ankles. I wanted his calmness to rub off on me. It hadn't. Then again, he did know everyone in the room.

That was the hitch here. There were a few people in the room I genuinely liked—Declan, Charlie, and Kevin—but I didn't know the rest well enough. Everyone had been on my case about keeping my guard up and not catching attention. How was I supposed to avoid that here?

Declan leaned in and whispered in my ear. "This is going to be fun. There won't be chances to talk about anything you need to be cautious with."

"You don't know that," I said it under my breath, but he was close enough to hear each word.

"If it happens, I'll say something first." He brushed his knuckles against my knee. It tingled. "Tonight you deserve a moment to enjoy yourself. Let me help."

He was right. I nodded and he gave me back a bit of space.

"All right. Everyone has pens and cards, right?" Charlie was practically vibrating with excitement. I was pleased to see her little brother Tomás on the loveseat next to her. His skin had taken on a sallow hue, but he was upright and more awake than my sister. I hoped this meant he was making a recovery. I needed him to be able to come back from those tests. "Okay, so here's how the game works. I'll give a word—it'll be something strange and obscure—then everyone writes down a definition for it on their card."

Tomás jumped in here to clarify, "You write down what you think could be a plausible definition. Don't try to do the real one."

"Yeah. That part's important." Charlie nodded emphatically. "I'll collect everyone's definitions, and then read them all aloud along with the real one. Then we all guess which one was the actual meaning. Your job is to try to come up with something that will make everyone guess yours, even though it's total bull."

Declan was beaming at me. I bit my lip and stared at the ceiling for a moment. To him I said, "Challenge accepted."

Lying for fun—and when everyone else knew you were lying—didn't make me feel nearly as icky as I thought. I still wasn't particularly good at it. Each time Charlie called out a word, my written response was the practical answer.

She called out "Lenticula," and my mind went to "a salad of lentils." No one guessed my answer. More people voted for Declan's "A pre-Easter vampire," which made little sense to me because there was no way that was the answer. It was, however, funnier than I expected from him.

I almost always saw him in protection mode or bouncer stance. I didn't mind the view of clever Dec.

Everyone's answers were wrong. "Overly complicated word to say freckles, if you ask me." I wasn't bitter. Swear.

"That's because you don't have any." Petulance didn't look good on

Tomás. Even from across the room, I could see the dusting of freckles—or should I say lenticula—on the bridge of his nose.

Charlie had them, too. They must have had a fake sunroom back on Ground Level. She backed me up. "I'm with her. Freckles is a much better word."

"I'd rather be fancy." He mocked drinking tea from a tiny cup. "I'm calling them lenticula from now on."

We laughed. Maybe Charlie's baby brother was less petulant than I thought.

The next hour had me laughing so hard that soreness cut across my stomach every time I moved. Who knew word games could be ab exercises? I wasn't the best at the game, but hearing everyone else's answers made up for my lack of ability. When Charlie read out the possible definition of moggan as a "mouse toboggan," Kevin called me out.

"We all know that one's Ally's." Everyone laughed.

"How do you know it's mine?"

"So you admit it?" Kevin was grinning at Declan. What? Did they have some sort of side bet on my reaction?

"How?" I propped a hand on my hip, but the huffy move carried less gravity when done sitting on the floor like a grade-schooler. My inability to keep a straight face didn't help matters.

Declan answered, "You always just put together two words that sound like the one we're trying to define. You'd probably say dally meant Declan and Ally."

"Sitting in a tree?" Tracy threw the barb out there, but it didn't catch flesh. I wasn't the only one who rolled my eyes at her. I didn't know Tracy at all, but had seen her in the dining hall. She worked for Declan's team. He looked more bothered by her comment than I had. The guy whose lap she'd been sitting on was even less pleased.

"Well, it would be cruel if I was good at everything. I mean, I'd hate to have you feel all emasculated, Declan." My cheeks heated.

His eyes flared. "I could take it."

We were talking like others weren't in the room. That had danger written all over it. No matter how much I liked it, I had to stop. I turned back to Charlie so fast my neck jerked. "We know which one is mine, but go ahead and read the rest. I'm dying to know how the guys worked something dirty into the definition."

They had. We were all a bit disappointed to discover a moggan was actually a sock.

"I could make a sock dirty," Tomás said.

His sister leaped off the couch. "You will not."

"He probably already did." Kevin was laughing before the words even made it out of his mouth.

Tomás bent forward. I thought he was laughing at first, but then a deep cough rumbled from him. Once it started, he couldn't stop. Like a big dog who spied a creature across the street, he woofed and hacked. Charlie rubbed his back.

A minute passed and his face shifted to a darker red. Declan suggested everyone head out, and people began gathering their belongings and dispersing. Kevin roomed next door to Tomás and offered to take him back.

"I'll go with." Charlie started to get up, but her brother stopped her.

"I'm fine, sis." His cough said otherwise. "Kevin'll take me back. I just need to take something and lie down."

I hated how familiar that sounded, but what had my teeth gnashing together was the knowledge this was done to him. He was being tested on, probably the rapid air change and biosynthetics.

Educated guesses were all I had to go on so far. The wide-eyed look I gave Declan made it clear we needed to get more information. Quick.

Charlie stayed put while Tomás left under Kevin's aid. I joined her on the short couch.

She reclined into the cushion, stretching her legs out until her toes were pointed in front of her, then sliding down on the seat.

Glances at Declan gave me no clue on how to start. I may not have been a good liar, but I was able to keep secrets. This, however, wasn't one I wanted to keep. Even if I didn't want to scream from the rooftops about what was happening on Cloud Nine, I'd want to tell Charlie.

I needed to tell her. Not just because she'd be helpful in the cause, but also because her family was in danger.

"I don't know what's wrong with him," Charlie spoke through

fingers spread across her face. I wished a simple hand could protect her from this hurt the way her fingers shielded the artificial light above us. "He's been to the infirmary three times. They won't tell us what's wrong. We keep getting sent away with another pack of pills that obviously don't do anything."

"I might have an idea." Was I really going to do this? Declan had pulled a chair over and sat in front of me. He slouched, but both his hands were in fists so tight the knuckles were leached of color.

Charlie pulled her hands off her face, but kept them close by on her chest. "Really?" I couldn't tell if she was hopeful or wary.

I didn't get scared often. Usually, in moments like this, my body clicked over into extreme-focus mode. Only it didn't now. My tongue was too thick for my mouth. I swallowed a couple times. "Maybe." I swallowed once more.

Charlie pushed her hands into the couch and scooted upright. "Why are you being weird?"

I licked my lips. No hesitation. Strike fast, back out of reach. "I think it has to do with where he's working."

Declan stood and I stopped talking at the action. Was I not supposed to say anything? He shook his head. "I'm going to keep an eye at the door. Go ahead."

Declan in guard mode didn't help me relax, but I could handle stress. Plus, he was only ten feet away.

"We all work on Cloud Nine. I know you aren't much for, well, any of it, but c'mon." Charlie didn't understand, and I had to spell it out.

This had better not blow up in my face. "Not everyone here has the same working conditions."

The words seeped too slowly from my mouth and Charlie cut me off.

"Yeah. They don't have windows on Level 2. I know. He complains about it, but I hardly think lack of sunlight is the cause for respiratory distress." Her voice shifted shrill.

Screw it.

"Research is running tests on Level 2." I paused, waiting for another outburst. She only narrowed her eyes. I continued, "Without consent. Air quality tests and, I think, tests on lung modifications via cell generation."

"No."

"That was my reaction, too." I grabbed her hand. "I'm sorry, Charlie."

From the door Declan said, "I didn't want to believe it either. So before you start thinking she's gone conspiracy theory, I've seen the surveillance. They're doing something to the kids working on Level 2, including your brother."

Charlie stared at her knees. I watched her face scrunch up. Tears welled along her lower eyelids, but she didn't let them free. This was why we were friends. Her strength. She would break down, but just like me, she'd do it alone and after she'd dealt with the problem. I would help her there. Her fight was my fight.

I kept talking so she wouldn't feel like the spotlight was on her. "I'm working to find out what exactly they're testing. It's more than one thing, but my discontent hasn't gone unnoticed."

"Understatement." The half-hearted laugh she offered was dipped in sorrow.

"Well, I'm working to avoid Jensen and still get us all the details to stop what they're doing."

"Can you give me the research case file numbers so I can look, too?" I pretended not to notice the undulations in her voice, the strain when she spoke.

"Of course. As much as we want to act immediately, we need to gather enough information to actually know what to do." Since when did I hand out cautionary warnings? Maybe Declan was having an effect on me. "Know your notes on the server will be monitored. Don't write down anything about this. Or use paper."

She finally looked at me, the tears had receded. "That Jensen guy?"

It would be good to have her help. Charlie was smarter than me. "Exactly."

Her heavy sigh brought us back on point. "That's all well and good, but we need to get my brother out of there. Immediately."

"He's sick. Just have him stay in his room." Declan folded his arms over his chest. The action made his shirt look too small for his body.

"Won't they want him to go to the infirmary again?" Her mouth pulled up at the right. "That hasn't worked well for us so far."

"Don't go there again." The command was sharp.

"Why not?" I asked, because Charlie didn't.

Declan glared. "It draws unwanted attention."

It clicked. He wasn't ready to talk about people being stolen away in the night. That was his fear. If we didn't stop Tomás from being a problem, the higher ups would decide to solve the issue. Declan was right; we didn't want that.

"Right." I tried to cover before Charlie dug in too deep. "Does she need to tell anyone about keeping him in the dorm?"

Declan gave her the specifics, but it didn't derail her for long.

"We need to get everyone off that level. I mean, yeah, Tomás is my priority, but—" she shook her head, eyes searching the room for some answer that wasn't there, "this has to stop."

"No argument there." I arched my arms over my head and stretched. This whole conversation had me wound too tightly. "We need to get the information first. Find out who they're testing on and, more importantly, what exactly they're testing."

Charlie did a double take. "Why would the testing material be more important than the people?" The "you idiot" at the end was silent.

"If they're suffering side effects from the tests—like your brother— we're going to need to know what they're testing so we can try to counter it."

She deflated. It was the logical process, but logic didn't always reign in these situations.

"Fine." She spat it, but I could tell she'd accepted the plan for now. She looked at the hulking guy just inside the door. "Why didn't you do something about this sooner?"

"Excuse me?" His hard look would have withered others, but Charlie—even in shock—was stronger than most.

"I find it hard to believe you've only now discovered this stuff was happening. Why didn't you do something sooner?"

His jaw clenched tight. He was about to say something stupid. I did it all the time, so I recognized the signs. I made the preemptive strike. "I already threw that fit."

Charlie cut a slide glance at me, but kept all her weapons—hands, body, feet—pointed directly at Declan.

"Really. Charlie. Trust me on this one." I understood her rage. Mine seethed next to my spine in a constant lava flow. "He needed allies. Without someone on the inside, there wasn't a way to act that wouldn't get more people hurt."

Declan's teeth were still clenched together, but his eyes softened. The deep lines at their corners faded. I took that as a thank you.

"Well, you have help now. How quickly do we move?"

"Get all the information you can tomorrow morning." Declan moved toward us, arms still locked tight, but hips swiveling. A predator. Good. We needed him. "We'll regroup and figure out where the smartest attack is once we know everything."

She nodded once. The motion was quick enough I was sure it hurt. She didn't wince, but left the room quickly after blunt goodbyes.

When she was gone, Declan sat next to me. His weight depressed the couch forcing me to lean into him. I was mentally exhausted, so I stayed there. His arm slipped around my back. My security rope.

"Do you think she's ready for this?" His breath tickled the outside of my ear.

"No." I relaxed into him. "I don't, but I don't think she'd ever be ready to hear it."

"True." His hand moved up a bit, and curled around my side against my ribs. "Should I keep an eye on her, just in case?"

"At this point, we have to keep an eye on everyone."

"I know, but do you worry about her being reckless right now?"

"I worry about her, regardless." Honesty warmed my veins, or maybe it was just being next to Declan.

"Me, too."

CHAPTER 39
TASTELESS

'd seen Tomás's sallow skin and the heaving of his chest in my mind's eye the whole day. I'd gone to the cafeteria in the hope of a reprieve from the endless disappointment and doubt the reports in the lab generated.

A tray clattered next to me. I jerked to flip my elbow up and twisted, slamming the back of my upper arm into Declan's side with enough force to knock him over.

He picked himself up with more grace than I would have managed. "Was that necessary?"

His scowl didn't earn him an apology though.

"Don't startle me." I'd been mentally lost for the last day. I poked my dinner with a fork. It was vibrant with pops of yellow and red, and the meat melted away in my mouth. It tasted like nothingness to me.

Declan took the chair next to me with no sign of fear. I appreciated his bravery, especially as blood began to well beneath the skin on his forearm. I hoped he'd be in a helpful mood when that bruise turned ugly tomorrow.

"What were you so distracted by that you mistook me for someone in need of a proper elbowing?" He took a quick breath, let it out and flashed a quick smile at me. "Nice form, by the way."

More guys should have complimented my combat skills. Or maybe not. The back of my neck heated at the praise.

"Thanks." The word tumbled out awkwardly. I tried to cover it by plowing forward. "My head hurts from trying to pinpoint all the variations of tests happening." I pointed toward my feet instead of saying Level 2. It was probably overkill, we were fifteen feet away from the closest person, but maybe someone could read lips. "Multiple tests are happening at once, so it's difficult to pick which place to move on first."

"Maybe we don't move on one thing at a time."

My shoulders popped up near my ears and eased back slowly. "Easier said than done. We'd need more people."

"True. We need to review our options, then decide where to stri— start first."

I nodded emphatically.

"I have to show you something that will probably give us those answers, if you've read all the research."

I closed my eyes and focused on the air filling my lungs. I wanted answers, but being ready to act on them was a whole other thing.

It had to happen, though, whether I was ready to move. I began to push back from the table, but Declan's hand on my forearm stilled me. I looked over at him, a question in my gaze.

"Stay. Eat. We'll go up in a few minutes."

"I can't eat this." I nudged the tray away.

"If you're not eating, people will know something is off."

"Something is off."

"Stealth. Cunning. Secret missions. That's us now." Kindness and humor warmed his hushed tone. "And those things require you to scarf that food down like it's your last meal."

"It might be." Fear speared my grumble.

His fingers tightened around my arm. A squeeze of comfort. "Not if we're smart. Eat now, we'll plan soon."

Soon. That was what I was worried about. I both dreaded and anticipated the future. I wanted to save people, I wanted to get out of here, but I also wanted to protect myself. Keeping myself safe was much easier than worrying about everyone else. My sister wouldn't ever know it, but I'd knocked out more than one guy I caught trying to trail her home.

Knots of anger in my abdomen weren't new to me, but I'd never had them on this scale. It was one thing to pop a skinny boy who said foul things about your baby sister. It was another to undermine the power of the government, particularly when the consequences of failure would fall on everyone's shoulders, not just my own.

"You're right." I didn't like it and I may not have hidden that well.

He shook his head for a moment then stopped. "Adam's watching us."

"So I should be eating, I suppose." I cut a nice hunk of pork off the chop and plunked it in my mouth.

Declan went raspy. "He's going to have a problem seeing us together."

"Why?"

The visual of incredulous Declan was pretty funny. I expected his hair to turn white. "Seriously? He hates me and is rather taken with you."

Taken? Hardly. "No, he wants to control me."

"That too." He drank half his glass of water in a single motion. "He and I have different ideas of what would keep you safe."

"Forgetting that I'm smart enough to keep myself safe."

"I don't doubt your skills. My plan involves reminding you to use them judiciously. Adam would like to lock you in a room somewhere."

"I'm not a princess. He can't lock me in a tower. Plus, if he tried I'd break his nose. I think he knows that."

Dec laughed. "I'm sure he does. He's used to control, though. Most people on Cloud Nine do as Adam bids."

I rolled my eyes.

"Don't dismiss it. He holds more power than you give him credit for."

"You didn't see him in that meeting with Jensen. The guy nearly wet himself being around that much aggression."

Declan flashed his teeth at me. The act, while filled with humor, was feral. "I don't doubt that, but when Jensen isn't here, Adam gets to play that role."

Merging my idea of Adam—soft, charming, manipulative—into Jensen's role was plausible, but... "I guess so."

"Jensen won't be here for long."

"Are you sure? He didn't get what he wanted out of me."

"He's never going to get what he wants from you."

My turn to become predatory. "No. He wouldn't be pleased if he made a real effort, either."

"Agreed, but you do need to continue to play nicely with them." He thought about that for a minute while I chewed. "As nicely as you can. Maybe without using blood to undermine your words next time?"

"No promises," I mumbled around my dinner.

"I figured as much."

I went to drop off my tray and grab a bottle of water while Declan finished his food. We had agreed to meet in his room in ten minutes.

Declan knew Adam better than I did. It's not that I hadn't felt his eyes on my back earlier. I was good at monitoring my surroundings, but I hadn't expected him to waylay me.

His hand ghosted over my back and settled low. I locked my muscles, fighting the instinct to lay him out for touching me. My problem wasn't so much the flesh-against-fabric action, but the possessive way he'd done it. You earn the right to touch people. Trust and respect gain you access to personal space. I granted it to him before, but things had changed. I now knew he lacked a spine and clearly parts of his conscience.

Only he didn't know I'd changed my mind. He didn't know I saw past the tousled hair and the stories about his family back home. I didn't know if his feelings about them or me were lies. I didn't know if he hated himself for allowing his friends and their family members to be used like rats.

I didn't know these things because he was a liar, and deceitful people didn't earn touch privileges. I pivoted and stepped to the right. It looked like I was moving to face him, but it moved me out of his arms' reach and to where I could watch his eyes for telltale signs of deception.

"Hey." I meant to say more. I wanted to direct this conversation, but I found myself staring at a big cinderblock wall of nothing when it came to small talk topics. The weather, being tired, the banalities of life. Did people really care about those things?

His face lit in a way I was sure his internal fuse box would burst from the surge. "Hey. Did you like the pork chops tonight? They look good."

Adam was good with small talk. Me, less so.

"They were." Or they were supposed to be. I was too wrapped up in trying to figure out how to stop him from going all evil overlord to enjoy them.

"We haven't really had a chance to hang out and talk since that whole Jensen thing." The way his eyes bulged made it clear he was remembering the bloody part of the incident. I relished his reaction more than I should have.

"I know." Not an apology. "I've been doing my best to get as much reading time in as possible. I know Jensen didn't think much of my suggestions, but I have some ideas about ways to slowly introduce changes."

"Really?"

"You don't have to sound so surprised there." I willed my tone to cut deep.

"I just—That was quick."

"All my ideas are in their infancy. You know how it goes, little crumbs of maybes that I need time to develop into tangible options." It was easier to talk when I moved the discussion back to the research. Mostly because it was true. Granted, my motivations had changed. Now I was trying to find a way to ease the changes for people. The concept of the work was still good. Others deserved to breathe air like this. They deserved to see the moon—and the sun, too, I guessed. We needed a way to make that happen that didn't require an "acceptable loss" of life. Contrary to the documentation I read late in the day, there was no acceptable loss to me. None.

He nodded in acquiescence. "Right. If you want to maybe spitball ideas together, I'm free tonight."

I bet he was. He had more freedom on this station than almost anyone. Though, it was lessened with Jensen on the station.

"Is Jensen not here?" He flinched. I shouldn't have said it like that.

"He left about an hour ago." Ice was warmer than Adam at that moment. "He still wants to talk with you again."

"I'm sure he does." Next time, maybe he could bleed a little.

Adam eased closer, lowering his voice in turn. "He wasn't pleased by our conversation."

"I wasn't particularly pleased with it either."

Adam's hand flashed to my wrist, his grip tightening as I attempted to step away. I paused and he yanked me closer. "You need to work with me on this. Let me help you deal with the bureaucrats. Please."

I whipped my hand toward my body and down, forcing his release.

"We're a team, Adam." In the sense that we both worked in the same department, even if we weren't on the same side. "I appreciate your willingness to help with Jensen." Kind of true. Time to go for full honesty. "But if you ever grab me like that again, I will break your arm. Understood?"

He stumbled backward on his heels, his eyes wide. He'd heard me, and it was probably a dangerous move on my part. I didn't care. I agreed to fake being on Team Test on Humans. I agreed to play nicely with those involved. That agreement did not include letting anyone treat me like property. He should have been thanking whatever God he prayed to that I had enough restraint to give him a warning.

Adam didn't understand me, though. The gaze searching my face right now was full of fear. If he'd understood me better, he'd have been afraid long before today. He would have known I only got violent in reaction to a threat. I couldn't say my response was equal, but I could say it was invariably justified.

If he ever restrained me again, I would break something on him. The kind that takes months to heal. The kind that would make him feel as cheap and out of control as he was trying to force me to feel.

I left him standing there like some tragic fish, puckering his lips over and over.

CHAPTER 40
GASPING FOR AIR

I readied myself for Declan to chide me for breaking my "be nice to Adam" promise. I waited until we were ensconced in his room to break the news. He immediately stormed toward the door. "You don't need to wait. I'll break his hand right now."

I followed behind him and pressed my hand against his bicep. It didn't give at my pressure; his fists were ready, too. "That's not necessary."

"The hell it isn't."

I slipped in front of him to block the door. "As much as I'm enjoying your protective side, I handled this."

He threw his head back and kept it there. We stayed in silence while he counted the ceiling tiles or sheep or whatever. Eventually, he brought his gaze back down to meet mine. "I suppose you did."

"What?"

"Handle it." He held out a hand to me, and I accepted the offer.

"Did you just do that because you thought I'd take your hand away in pieces if you touched me without asking?"

"I was being polite."

"You're allowed—even encouraged—to be a little scared of me." I grinned.

He tugged on my arm and I barreled directly into his chest. It didn't give at all, and I liked that. "Does that go both ways?"

"Little bit."

A few strands of hair had fallen from my ponytail. They rested against my cheek. Declan rubbed them between his fingers before tucking them behind my ear.

"He can't treat you like that." His voice was soft, reverent. Anger still danced in his eyes, though.

An electric coil ignited in my stomach, burning away the earlier knots of anger and worry.

"I didn't let him." Now I sounded breathy. I licked my lips, but hadn't meant it as an invitation.

Somehow, though, the moisture turned them into active magnets. The closer my lips were drawn to his, the more the energy covered me. The tiny space between us was charged. It was more than electricity making the muscles in my neck tighten. It was more than adrenaline urging his hand around the back of my head, his fingers spearing into my loosening locks.

My lips tingled even before his touched mine. When the kiss was real, though, the current spiked through my body and to my toes.

My skin was on fire. His body blazed beneath my palms. I slipped my hands up to his shoulders. Despite the fires raging within us, my fingers grasped at him, pulling him closer.

His other hand found my hip, calloused fingers digging in beneath the hem of my shirt. My knees lost all stability as he pressed my body more firmly to his. He deepened the kiss and it was lush and addictive and overwhelming.

His back hit a wall, forcing his hard chest back against my now roaming hands. I hadn't realized we'd moved. His fingers grazed across my ribs. It was too hot in here. Too many clothes in our way. Excitement and fear of letting go warred in my head.

I planted my palms on his chest and shoved, forcing myself back a few steps, and then surprised myself by gasping for air. I needed to practice breathing while doing that. Or not practice. I didn't know.

"We need to stop." I couldn't look at him or I'd find myself back in his arms.

"We needed to do that sooner." He sounded as breathless as I was. Good.

I dared a peek at him. The flush on his cheeks made me smile. "Perhaps, but we have more pressing problems."

When Declan groaned, I realized it was the first time I'd seen him out of control. This was the first time when he wasn't acting like he knew the right moves or the perfect words to say. We were in the same place. It earned him more trust than I could convey aloud.

I walked to the far side of his room using the same deep-breathing technique I used after cardio warm-ups. By the time I made it to the couch, I felt in control.

Then I turned around to find Declan right next to me. His eyes were still smoldering. I held one finger up. "You just stop. I know what you're thinking, but stop."

"Are you sure you know what I'm thinking?" Coy. Charming. Seductive. Exactly what I wanted.

"Yes, and I'm going to remind you people we know are getting sick down on Level 2 and we could be stopping it." I hated being the fun killer.

He tilted his head down and muttered, "You're right."

"Get used to saying that. It happens often."

My playful jab helped. He pulled a leg up on the couch and faced me. "Okay. We save people, and then more of that."

"I can agree to that."

The look in his eyes was all victory dance. Guys.

"Didn't you have something to show me?"

His face fell when I mentioned it, but it didn't have anything to do with the whole not-kissing-anymore thing. The gravity of what was happening, of what we were trying to stop, hit him. He winced like a fist had plowed into his kidney. I resisted my new urge to comfort him with a touch. Bigger problems.

Declan leaned over the arm of the couch to grab a tablet from the side table. He held it so we could both see the screen and began swiping through a list of files. "I started reviewing the videos from yesterday and this morning. I think we can figure out what they're testing on the Maintenance staff, or at least on Tomás."

"You have footage of him?"

"From yesterday." He double-tapped on a file. "This is him working in the morning."

Sure enough, there was Tomás working on circuitry. He was also coughing nearly nonstop.

Declan paused the video and pointed to the clear wastebasket on the floor next to Tomás' feet. "Do you see that?"

"A trash can?" He zoomed in, and then I understood. "Are those all covered in blood?" Horror shook my words. Tissues piled on top of more tissues filled the bin, every one coated with blood.

He had been coughing up blood, and we hadn't known. Did Charlie know?

"Yes." One word. Sharp. I knew how he felt.

I covered my mouth, trying to hold back my disgust. Speaking through my fingers, I asked the important question, "Can we see the people doing this to him?"

Again, one word. This time, though, it resounded with the promise of vengeance. "Yes."

He pulled up another video file. This room was long and narrow. Declan confirmed it was next to Tomás's workroom.

On screen, Adam walked in clutching a small test tube. He spoke with the guy at the desk. I didn't recognize the latter, but I only saw the back of his head. He had short brown hair, which wasn't helpful.

"You need to put cameras where you can see people's faces." I didn't mean to say it out loud.

"Tell me about it. These were placed by Jensen's team, though. They weren't looking to watch the staff so much as confirm they were using the right chemicals."

That made sense. I continued watching the clip. Adam was gesturing toward the one-way mirror. The one I presumed let them see Charlie's little brother hard at work. He set the tube down on the counter, pointed at it, then to a device that looked similar to a centrifuge. He stormed out.

"Watch Lee," Declan ordered. So the mystery minion was named Lee.

"Who is he?" I whispered as if the people on the screen could hear us.

"One of the biology leads. Just watch."

Lee snapped the vial into the machine and pressed a green square button. The liquid disappeared, but nothing else happened. Lee popped the empty container out of the machine and set it on the table, wheeling his chair to the side to pick up a clipboard.

Declan paused the video. "There."

Before I could ask, he zoomed in twice until the test tube was big and centered on the screen. On its side the handwritten note was clear: TEST MATERIAL No. #34957, For Room No. 224.

I stared at the image. I could find out exactly what they were doing. A simple search of the database for the identification number was all it would take.

"This is a huge win," I said, "but…it feels too easy."

"Easy? They have no idea we've seen this, and knowing what they're testing with doesn't make us stop them. It does, however, point us in the right direction."

"A lead is a lead, yes." It wasn't the golden answer I had hoped for.

"Why are you not excited about this?"

"I am, mostly. I'm just worried that knowing what they're testing on him isn't going to be enough. That vial was prepared specifically for Tomás. He was in room 224, right?" When Declan confirmed it, I continued, "What if they're testing variants on every subject? It'd be stupid protocol-wise, but they haven't been doing things by the book here."

"Then we need to find out. At the very least, we can help Charlie's brother, and that's worth something."

I straightened. "You're right. I need to quit focusing on how to take everyone down at once, and go for a brick-by-brick downfall."

Declan acted as though he could actually see the light bulb flickering on above my head. "Welcome to the practical side of things."

"It's where the planners live, isn't it?"

"Unfortunately so." He rested his arm around my shoulders, and leaned in. With the voice of a true conspirator he said, "Don't worry, we'll still let you kick ass and take names."

After agreeing that I'd look into what exactly was in that test tube and that Declan would review the other Level 2 observation-room footage for chances to see what test materials were being used, I had to go tell Charlie.

"Try not to shout it, okay? This is still a top-secret thing." Declan's tease was still a warning. He wasn't fooling anyone.

I took his words to heart nonetheless, and knocked lightly on Charlie's door. It only took her a moment to answer. That wasn't what shocked me so much as her haggard appearance. Her eyes were bloodshot and her hair a loose, shaggy mess. Charlie was the type to craft a perfect coif even to lounge about her dorm.

"You all right?" It wasn't how I planned to open the conversation, but I blurted it regardless.

She rolled her eyes. "Just dandy."

"Can I come in? I have news." I could do subtle.

She bounced on her toes. Okay. Maybe not.

"Really?" Charlie didn't wait for me to reply. "Come on in."

Clothes littered the floor in her dorm, but I wasn't about to judge. I planted myself at the foot of her bed. Nervous energy teemed within the room, making her choice to pace the perimeter less of a surprise.

"How's Tomás doing?"

She stopped walking. "He's resting and coughing and that's about it." Bitterness coated our conversation. "You have news?"

"Yes. Declan and I, well really just Declan, found a video that shows the substance used with your brother."

"What is it? Do we have an antidote? Does he just need time away from there?" The sentences were strung together without so much as a breath between them.

"I only have the material ID number so far. We'll have to search the database for the details of the research program and what exactly it is."

"Why haven't you looked it up yet?"

"I thought you'd want to know right away. Plus, I'm not allowed to take research outside of the lab. Adam's scolded me more than once on showing up down there in the middle of the night. So, I'm going to search first thing in the morning. Unless you want to. I can give you the ID number."

"Oh. Right." Her vitriol faded as she moved to her desk for a pen and paper. "What's the number?"

I gave it to her and she *calmed*. Her reaction put me on edge, but I couldn't place the reasoning. I'd be antsy for answers if my sister were in the same situation.

"I didn't see you at dinner." I wanted to tell her about Adam's bad moves and Declan's subsequent good ones, but it wasn't the time. "Do you need me to get you anything? I could grab snacks or water from down the hall for you."

She brushed it off with placating hand gestures. "Nah. I haven't been sleeping, but now that I know we're close, the exhaustion is hitting me. I might just bunk down and be ready to get answers first thing in the morning."

"Cool. We'll recap tomorrow. Hopefully, I'll have more information and other leads we can take."

"Sounds good." She ushered me out of the room. I didn't think she was suddenly sleepy, but believed accepting truth in privacy was much easier than doing so with someone else sitting on your bed.

But if that were true, why did I feel like I was betraying her by leaving?

CHAPTER 41
FIGHT OR FLIGHT

"We need more space in that kitchen." Leah ranting about her job was something I had never thought I'd experience.

"What makes you think it's tinier than any other kitchen?" It came out more judgmental than I'd intended. It was rare for me to get Leah to head down to breakfast with me, particularly with how crummy she had been feeling. I didn't want to ruin it. Had I?

"It might not be, but we have so many people working there. They've gone to sending us to overflow rooms for food prep."

"Are you in the room by yourself, then?" All the footage we'd reviewed from Level 2 showed solitary test subjects.

"No, it's cramped. That's the point. Three of us jammed in a windowless room chopping vegetables is not my idea of an ideal situation."

Panic tried to choke me, but I swallowed it down. A lack of a view didn't mean she was being locked up for testing. Focus, Ally.

"Do you at least have your own table?" We'd always had the luxury of space back home. Our house was old, but that meant it was far larger than those of our friends. We had our own bedrooms. Leah and I hadn't shared a bathroom even when we were little. It was an adjustment here, but one that I knew made us stick out.

"Yeah, and Melody ends up working with me most days." She rattled on about the room and the food and how Melody was her newest, bestest friend. My sister went through best friends like I went through socks. It's not that she ditched them daily, but the rotation of who was best changed for her. I hated the realization she had just as much trouble trusting others as I did.

"Are you feeling up to working today?"

She shrugged. "What else am I going to do?"

"Drink water. Rest. The normal 'get better' things."

"I can drink water and cut things up. Multitasking is my thing."

"Since when?"

"Since now."

"Okay, but is your headache at least a little better?"

"Some, I guess. It's more a constant ache now than a hammer beating in my skull."

"Well, that's promising." I bumped my hip into hers. She stumbled for a second and I worried it was the wrong move, but she caught herself and snorted.

"Picking on the sick girl. I see how it is."

"Every chance I get." We walked into the mess hall and my stomach growled at the scent of bacon. In the last several days, I had discovered an unhealthy love for the meat. "I'm starving."

"You have been starving for the last five years." She took a tray and handed me one.

"Possibly." I was prepared to razz her about the food back home, but got distracted by the loss of my standard creepy breakfast server. "What happened to the morning guy?"

She wasn't paying attention to me. Her eyes already scanned the room for familiar faces. "Don't know. I didn't see him on the duty roster when I checked last night. Maybe he got transferred."

Panic seized my chest. "That happen much?"

She didn't bother to face me, but her eyes cut toward me. "How would I know?"

"You work with him. Plus, you seem to know everyone here."

She took it as a compliment. I wasn't sure I'd meant it as such. "Well, yeah. I assume a transfer because they'd been moving him around more. Had him doing kitchen prep for dinner with Megan this week."

"Remind me who Megan is." The tension in my chest eased as we fell back into our normal dynamic.

"This is why you should have stayed at the mixer. I would have introduced you to people. Friends are a good thing, Ally."

"I have friends."

She popped a hip out to the side and rested her hand on it. The other hand held up three fingers. She must have been feeling a little better if she could conjure some sass. "Name three."

I almost said Declan's name first, but that would have sparked too much curiosity. "Charlie, Declan, and Kevin."

I stuck my tongue out at her. She did it back. It softened the lump in my chest.

I thought we might see Charlie at breakfast. I was eager to look up the test material and start moving forward. Then again, if it were my brother I'd probably skip breakfast too. Even with the bacon.

———

Declan caught me in the elevator heading down to Level 4. He hit the button next to mine and waited for the door to close.

"What's on Level 5?"

"Boring security stuff." He was in guard mode, which meant no smiling and no touching. I understood how to react to him this way, and I appreciated it. "Can you remember a few numbers?"

My brows knitted together momentarily. "Most likely."

"34997, 34421, and 38002. Got it?"

I said the numbers over and over in my head. Willing them to stick in there the same way 34957 did. "I think so. Same reasoning?"

"Those are the ones I could see from the day before last. I'll review yesterday's material soon." He shuffled closer to me as we neared his floor. His whisper sounded stern. "Dinner with me tonight?"

"To review things? Okay."

"Well, to eat. Then we'll review."

I blushed a little, hated myself for it, and then agreed.

Declan stepped off the elevator at Level 5, and two seconds later I did the same at 4. The front rooms were empty of people like usual. I took a moment to pet the blades of grass jutting from the soil in the window boxes. Touching them reminded me of the reason this research was important. I didn't need to stop helping altogether; I needed to force them to make changes in a safe and smart way.

Why didn't everyone think like me? It would render this whole problem moot.

Tucked away in his office, Adam was typing furiously. He was working very hard to avoid having to talk to me. I was okay with that. However, for the sake of keeping from burning bridges I might need— Declan would be so proud—I did tap on the glass between our offices and wave before sitting down at my desk.

His weak wave in return was what I wanted. I didn't need him to come into my office with his fake apologies. Being left alone was precisely what I wanted.

I logged into my tablet and scanned the requisite memos. Propriety made me double-check the calendar to make sure no one would be bothering me in the next couple hours. When it all looked clear, I flipped over to the research files and searched for "No. 34957."

My mouth went dry as the search took more than half a second. The possibility of "no matches" coming up had my pulse throbbing audibly in my ears. My worry was unnecessary. The file had last been checked out by Lee, the lab tech from the video clip. If that wasn't a sign I was on the right track, I was doing this whole investigation thing wrong.

Thirty minutes of reading gave me lots of information on the test material, but little on the test subjects. The plural kept popping up with generalized lists of responses, reactions, and nulls. This concoction, which was an aerosol delivery meant to force lung cell generation, was being used in a larger test than just Tomás. It was the kind of double-edged answer I both wanted and feared.

According to the document, Tomás wasn't the only one hacking up blood. And, in true scientific form, they'd been collecting the tissues afterward. I felt so sorry for that lab tech, who probably didn't know why she was being forced to analyze tissues. Some of the new cell generation was coming up right along with that blood. The body knew they didn't belong.

The test had been ongoing with this chemical blend for the last six weeks. They'd started the second round upon Tomás's arrival, and he wasn't the only one. Toward the end of Lee's notes I found this: "Subjects from reception date 11.1.89 are less receptive to higher doses. Continue trials at 2x volume per Adam with expectations to see rejection transition to adjustment or fail."

They knew he might die. Adam knew he might die, and encouraged continued testing knowing death was a possibility. What else could fail mean here? I slammed the heels of my boots into my desk hard enough to feel the inertia zing up my shins.

Adam was at the window between our offices in a flash. The sound was muffled, but I knew he was asking if I was okay. I held up both hands in placating surrender. "Accident," I hollered back. It wasn't even a lie. I didn't mean to lose my cool with him next door.

Fight or flight had always landed in the former for me, but at that moment I wanted to run. I couldn't leave though. My throat snapped shut, my teeth gritted together and I fought back the fear. Even if I could abandon the research—and I couldn't—Adam would wonder why I stormed out. He'd ask questions. It'd raise eyebrows. It'd do all the things I was supposed to be avoiding.

Answers. Staying in this room would get me answers. Air trickled into my lungs slowly, but the thought galvanized me.

I opened the file search window and started looking for the next case log from the list of numbers Declan gave me. The first two from his list showed the tiny variations in the material used with Tomás. Different test groups with different dosage levels. Still airborne releases, still causing coughing and restlessness to varying degrees.

Not one of the "test subjects"—I was already sick of that phrase— had accepted the cell generation well. Possibly because there was no easing them into it. My ideas needed to wait, though, because if Adam kept cranking up the dosage on these people, more were going to end up spewing blood and soon.

My stomach pitched. I stuck my head between my knees and willed my body to still, swallowing back bile. I worked through every muscle group, beginning down at my toes, and focused on making them release.

I made it to my hips when Adam stepped into my office. He was winded, which was weird since he had come from next door. I looked up and he was clutching the back of the chair near the door. "You okay?"

"Breakfast isn't agreeing with me." *Because I ate it and then read about how you're a despicable human being.*

He nodded, but was looking down the hall. "I have to run. I'll likely be gone the rest of the day. Do you need anything?" His weight shifted from one foot to the other the whole time he talked. Not like a fighter staying light to dodge out of the way of a striking blow, but like he was in serious discomfort. Was it wrong to hope all his time around those chemicals earned him a little pain?

"No."

He made for the lab immediately, and I slid down my chair. I inhaled the clean air and held it in my lungs. I counted the seconds before the burn would take over. Twenty-six was when it started to become uncomfortable. I waited a few more seconds before releasing the deoxygenated air. That edge cut through the brain fog and let me focus on the important thing: Problem A just walked out the door leaving me alone to find answers to Problem B.

CHAPTER 42
I'M GOING TO KICK YOU

The query of the final test material ID I had didn't bring me to the same type of testing. The structure of the document was different, too. The lead tech on this trial was named Terri. I didn't know her. Terri worked in botany. I read it three times to make sure I hadn't mistaken the word. Why was the botany department so involved with human trials?

The answer shouldn't have been such a kick to the gut. I was good at expecting people to be liars at this point. It didn't shock me when people looked out for themselves first. It did however catch me off guard to see that they were still looking at small-scale delivery methods for the biosynthetics. Jensen acted like they had accepted the loss ratio of going with the air deployment, but I was looking at the report. Instead of distributing via air, this trial proposed using engineered foods, mostly produce, to introduce the synthetic building blocks for lung cell growth.

Ideally, this would give people the choice. They could choose to buy the foods or not. Only if we started clearing the air, those people would die. The food distribution method didn't make sense for so many reasons. I had trouble believing Adam signed off on it, because the undertaking of getting modified foods out to every person in the world was so massive. It had to be expensive to go this route—unless they weren't planning on using it for everyone. Breath caught in my throat as the thought sliced my brain.

The test was new; it started the day we moved to Cloud Nine proper. The research documentation I'd reviewed last week showed food modification as a project from more than a year ago. Terri's notes here suggested this method of delivery would decrease rejection of the new cells. Her reasoning was distinctly hand-wavy.

This first round of testing had to do with food handling. Sweat dampened my forehead. The experiment gauged enzyme absorption through the skin. The idea being she could then determine proper levels in conjunction with eating the foods. I tried to shove my hair back, forgetting it was already clasped there with an elastic band. Instead, I ran my hand up and down my throat, urging my pulse to calm.

The other chair in my office collided with my desk hard enough to make it vibrate. I stood with enough force to send my own seat toppling over behind me.

Declan filled the vacated space on the other side of my desk, his arm still extended toward the discarded furniture.

Sweat gathered at his temples. A storm raged in his eyes. I didn't know the source, but I would filet whoever caused such pain.

I spared a quick glance toward the windows. Kevin arched a brow of concern. I placated him with a quick smile. He bought it and refocused on his work.

"You've been here all day?" Declan seethed.

My face pulled together as if I could actually hide my worry. "Of course. The answers are..." My hands shook and I took a breath to still them. "Detestable."

"You didn't even leave to go to the bathroom?"

Gripping the edge of the desk was all I could do to steady myself. "No. Why?" My words were hard, even when my gut had gone to jelly.

He righted the chair on his side of the room and promptly fell into it. "Thank God."

"Tell me why you just scared me like that." Snarling didn't look good on me, but I backed it with a kick to the wastepaper basket. It flew over the desk and barely missed Declan. He didn't flinch, which only irritated me further.

"I was making sure you were safe." He popped his foot up on the desk. Faux casualty I could see though; his neck was still red and his jaw locked.

"From what?" I threw my hands in the air because I was too far away to jam them into his throat.

He tilted his head and stared at me for a moment before finally responding. "You know from who. I needed to make sure you were on camera in this room all morning."

"Why would that be important?" The words were pulled from my mouth in a honey drizzle.

"Something happened."

"I got that part. I thought you were done being difficult."

"Could you maybe sit down?"

"No, I'm not going to sit down. If you don't answer my question soon, I'm going to kick you in the groin. You will cry. I will laugh. Then I will get answers. Is that what you're after here?"

He groaned. "Don't kick me."

I edged around my desk. I needed to be within throttling distance. "Tell me what has happened."

"Charlie did something monumentally stupid."

My knees softened and my butt caught the edge of my desk. "How stupid?"

"She took all the testing materials marked with the number for her brother's trial and poured them down a drain."

"What?" I needed to work on volume control, because Kevin and Holly in the lab looked my way with sincere flashes of concern. I fought back the nerves making me want to act. I shook my head to my friends. I'm good. In a lower, but not calmer voice I asked, "What happened?"

"Lee caught her." He shook his head as if it would clear the image.

"The guy-running-the-tests Lee?"

His head barely moved, but I knew it was an affirmation. "She was next to the sink having just poured the last tube down. I guess she had some benign concoction she was going to replace it with, but didn't get the chance."

"What did he do?"

"What do you think he did, Ally?" He sounded more disgusted with himself than with my question. "He called security and Adam."

No no no. "He ran out of here looking like he was about to be sick."

"Wouldn't surprise me. The Powers That Be are livid."

I had to fix this. "Where's Charlie now? What can we do for her?"

"Do?" His mirthless laugh was an icy shower. My stomach clenched, but he didn't stop there. "She's already gone."

I choked. "Gone?"

"Adam called Jensen immediately like the bratty child he is."

"I thought Jensen had already left?"

"He's on Ground Level. Still nearby." Declan's chair whined as he pulled on the edge. The noise stilled him. "He ordered my team to bring Charlie to Ground Level detention. Deb's escorting her—female guard for female prisoner—and Adam's running along, too, so he can suck up."

"What are they going to do to her?"

"I don't know," he whispered.

"When will she be back?"

He looked up at me then and I sank into the deep wells. He bit his lip, let go, and said, "I'm sorry."

"Sorry?" Breaking down in this room was not an option. The windows. The lab. The too-bright sun. I clenched my fists and wished slamming them on the desk wouldn't draw so much attention.

"We should go get lunch." He was already standing.

My body rumbled with fury. "Lunch?"

He lowered his voice. "We need an excuse to get you out of this lab. We need privacy. So," he spoke loudly now, "come have lunch with me."

Lifting my hands from my sides took more effort than I'd ever admit aloud. Declan reached for me and didn't comment on the violent way my hands shook. He took one in his own. His tight muscles countered my shaky ones. At least one of us was staying solid at the moment.

I needed to pull it together because if I didn't, the chance of me setting Adam's office on fire was high.

Declan held my hand as we walked through the lab. Eyes pierced my back, but I refused to look back. The steady grip Declan had on me was all that stopped me from exploding in profanity and fists.

Whispers whirled behind us as we made it to the hallway. The doors closed to my silent thank you, cutting off the "I told you they were together."

One side of Declan's mouth turned up. "No one thinks you're involved with Charlie's actions now."

"No," I huffed. "I suppose not."

Dec pushed open the stairwell door, holding it for me. Once inside we stood on the landing waiting for the other to speak first.

Wrangling my emotions became more complicated by the second. "No cameras in here?" Short sentences I could handle, though.

"Nope. They'll have seen us come in here, but not what's happening inside." The insinuation lingered.

"Safe to talk?" My whisper echoed.

"Yes." He leaned back against the barren wall.

"How are we going to save her?"

"Save her?" He ground the heels of his palms against his eyes. I continued to glare at him. "I'm more concerned with saving you."

"I'll save myself. What about Charlie?"

He knocked his head back against the wall. The resounding thud vibrated beneath my feet. "Nothing."

I shoved him. "That can't be your answer."

"Right now it is. What do you want from me, Ally?" He pushed forward. My hands were still on his chest, but he drove me back. "If we want to keep everyone else here safe, then we have to pretend we weren't involved. We have to pretend we don't know what's happening and we have to distance ourselves from her."

"Just leave her on her own?" Goosebumps broke out along my arms.

"She's under lock and key."

"Do you know where the keys are stored?"

"Figure of speech. If we could stop things here, we would have a chance."

"A chance?" I scoffed and jogged down the first few stairs. Turning back to him, "That's all you have to offer me?"

He followed me down the half-flight of stairs. "I'm offering you a way to save yourself, to save me, to save your sister, and everyone else."

"An acceptable loss?" If my mouth hadn't become dry, I would have spit in his face.

"No." He grabbed my upper arm as I tried to leave. I started to yank it out of his grip, but he spoke again, softer, "No. Not a loss. We get her. Okay? I'll find a way for us to get to her. She's going to be in those cells for weeks before the red tape to do anything is complete."

"Weeks?"

"I know it sounds horrendous." He slid his hand down to my wrist. His touch light. He wouldn't stop me if I tried to leave again. "I really do, but we need to keep her brother safe. We need to do what she was trying to do."

"We're not going to dump all the trial materials."

He rolled his eyes. "We're going to find a way to stop them. A smarter way."

Pursing my lips didn't help me think, but it kept my mouth closed. He waited without any outward anxiousness. He needed to teach me how to do that. "Agreed, but we are going to get her." It wasn't up for discussion.

"We need to figure out how to move forward without attracting attention now."

"I certainly can't go down to Level 2." Something dark burned within me. Using the pain to fuel my focus was better than wallowing in it.

"Nah. Security was already increased. I actually have to keep a guard at the door."

"We still have security feeds coming in, though?"

"Yes, but we won't be the only ones reviewing them. I expect Jensen will request them, too." The next part Declan mumbled. "Even on Ground Level, he can be in my way."

"I was reading the last file of research for the test materials. It's different from the others, but I only have another fifteen pages or so left."

"Probably smart to finish that today. I could see Adam adding document restrictions once he discovers Charlie accessed a file."

"It makes sense for me to be reading the research documentation, though."

"It does, but it also brings attention."

"Fine. I'll finish this afternoon, then we'll regroup."

"You're going to have to pretend you don't know about Charlie being gone or what she's done."

I hit him, but it was without any real force. "You know I can't do that."

"Try." He grimaced. "I could have kept it from you, but the shiner I would have gotten as thanks for keeping a secret like that would not have been worth it."

"When we resolve this"—I pointed toward the floor—"we're still sparring. You will find your back on the mat."

"One more reason to get this done fast."

One more, indeed.

CHAPTER 43
TRADING UP FOR BIGGER PROBLEMS

The hallway outside Tomás's door was quiet, but I clung to the bottle of water in my hand like an anchor. The sixteen fluid ounces inside wouldn't protect me from him any more than it'd cleanse this place. Fear still flexed my fingers against the container like it'd slip my grip at any second.

Leah was the hostess of the Ramsey family. She knew how to take care of people. I knew how to protect—or I thought I had. Yet Charlie was gone, and now I stood outside her brother's door. I had failed her. And him. Water and a bag of crispy potato bites were not going to change that.

He needed someone to check on him. Charlie would like it to be me, I thought. The bottle slipped against my sweaty palm; I tightened my hold again. Get it together, Ally. I banged the side of my free hand against the door.

I counted to ten. Tomás didn't answer.

Thump thump thump. "Tomás? It's Ally. I've come bearing sustenance."

One. Two. Three. Four. Tomás appeared in the doorway. He was hunched forward, his body bathed in shadows. The hallway light lit his sallow face. The high-wattage bulbs showed more than the yellowing and sagging, they highlighted the crust of dried blood above his upper lip.

"Hey." He coughed his greeting.

I held up the water and the potato bites. "I thought you could use a snack."

He grabbed the food from me, and I tried—and failed—not to stare at his chewed-down nails. One more bite and he'd be bleeding there, too. He didn't say anything, but walked back into his room, leaving the door open. I accepted the silent invitation.

"How are you feeling?" The floor was a minefield of dirty clothes and empty water bottles. At least he'd been trying to stay hydrated.

"How does it look like I feel?"

Point well made. "Right. Sorry."

He curled on his side, knees to chest. "No, it's okay." He coughed a couple times and wiped his mouth with a tissue folded in his hand. Not sanitary, but I wasn't about to start that conversation. His voice was scratchy, but he kept talking. A good sign? "I'm going to the doctor tomorrow anyway. Maybe they'll fix me up."

"I thought Charlie told you to stay out of the infirmary?"

"Yeah. That was the plan, but I have the regular check-up. You know the drill."

No, I didn't and that was a big problem. "We haven't been here that long. How are you already due for a physical?" I kept my tone as light as I could, but my fear trickled in.

"Seriously?" He squirmed under my scrutiny. Only when I looked away did he keep talking, "I have to go every other week. They want to make sure I'm adjusting to the air change and blah, blah, blah. All the other guys I work with do the same thing."

"Oh." A string of curses fired through my brain.

"You probably tested out of it."

I arched my eyebrow and was impressed he could see it in the dimly lit room.

"Charlie mentioned your super breathing ability."

"I wasn't going to rub it in since you're King of the Cough." I cracked a smile. It wasn't the painful false ones I'd been showing around Cloud Nine the last couple days, but it wasn't real either. Hope did funny things to my face.

"Appreciate it. So, um, you heard about Charlie?"

My stomach sank down to my knees. This was her kid brother. "I heard they made her leave."

"The guy who told me—the one who came for her stuff—said she was going home, but I don't believe him." Chocolate turned almost hazel as the light caught his widening eyes. "You don't send people home in handcuffs."

No, they didn't. "Did they tell you what she'd done?"

"Messed with some test stuff, I guess. Not like they'd tell me." He sounded as bitter as I felt.

All I could offer him was a noncommittal *mhm*. My nails cut into my palms. He deserved more, but I couldn't give it.

"It's not like her to mess with that kind of thing." His ribs rattled when he coughed. "If she did destroy whatever, she had a good reason."

She did. My mouth opened to tell him, to tell him everything, but his sister was gone because I'd told her. She hadn't told him for a reason, and I wasn't going to be the one putting him at risk.

I pulled a couple of tissues from the box nearby and handed them to Tomás. They were thin and scratchy. Same as the ones we had on Ground Level. This place caused his cough and they couldn't even offer fancy, soft tissues to ease the problem?

"Do you need anything else? I can snag stuff from the pantry for you." I hated small talk.

He pulled a blanket up to his shoulders. "Nah. I grabbed stuff earlier, but, uh, thanks."

"No problem." I was already edging out of the room like the failure I was. "If you need anything, have someone find me. I'll help out."

"Right." He wouldn't reach out to me.

It was okay, though. At least I knew something now: The kids in the trials had to visit the medical staff twice a month. My search in the afternoon hadn't found records of test subjects' names in the Research papers, but the doctors had them.

I hoped Declan knew how to break into medical files.

————

Of course he did.

"That should have taken you longer." If he felt my scowl, he didn't show it.

Declan typed away pulling together lists of Cloud Nine employees who appeared on the infirmary schedule, past and future, at least twice a month.

Dec looked over his shoulder at me. "This should have been harder. I swear. Getting the camera recordings in this place requires more access."

He focused on the screen, then glanced at me. "Can you stop doing that?"

I stopped tapping my hand against my thigh, got up, and started pacing instead. "If they're so easy to find, why don't we have a list yet?"

"It's not as though there is a file labeled 'all test subject data.'"

"Fine." I kicked at the floor with the tip of my shoe. It squeaked. The abrupt sound soothed me. I could relate to sudden, painful outbursts at this point. The kind that left dark marks.

Declan was less pleased. "Could you maybe sit down?"

Instead of moving toward the couch, I edged behind him. "I probably could type faster than you." I rested my hands on his shoulders.

He looked up at me. Weariness cloaked him. He didn't need my needling; he was doing it to himself. Like I was. He opened his mouth, but I stopped him before he spoke.

I edged my hand up the back of his scalp. "Sorry. I don't handle inactivity well."

His grunt of agreement would have been met with a sharp tug to his hair if he hadn't pushed into my hand like a preening cat. The move was needy and my brain wasn't sure how to process it. My stomach, however, did a fluttery thing that made me think back to kissing him.

Backing away would have been smart, but I'd demonstrated a sincere lack of intelligence of late. Instead, I took comfort in knowing I could provide some ease to anyone at this point. It wasn't the same as stopping cruelty, but maybe it did something important for Declan.

I wanted to give him that.

Give it to myself.

"Okay." After minutes of silence, it rang like a proclamation. Declan spun and pointed across the room. "Couch."

Touching him might ease my nerves, but didn't stop me from throwing a foul look his way. He ignored it and headed toward the seating area. My pride made me sit at the far end of the couch. He moved closer. A minor victory.

Declan rested a tablet on his thigh and tilted it so I could see the chart on the screen. Columns for name, orientation date, and date of last visit were filled in. I scanned the list slowly, but Tomás's name popped out at me in a flash. My throat snapped shut. It wasn't until darkness crept into my vision that I remembered how to breathe.

An elbow to my ribs reminded me I wasn't alone and Declan had been talking. "Far more men than women."

I nodded. "Looks like all the trial subjects were recruited in the last six months."

"You're the only one 'recruited.'" I rolled my eyes, but he continued like I hadn't, "Don't forget that. But, yes, everyone else moved to Cloud Nine fairly recently."

"I think I know him." I tapped on Josh Florek's name, forgetting the action would make the screen zoom in. Declan wasn't angling for a fight, so he kept quiet while zooming the screen back out.

"Name doesn't mean anything to me."

"It wouldn't to me if my sister didn't have a crush on the guy."

He arched his brow.

"Yes. We talk about these things."

"You discuss boys with your sister?" He drew out boys in a singsong way that forced me to grit my teeth.

"No. Leah talks about boys. I sit there and endure." I shook my head. "You—we need to focus. Do you recognize any of the other names?"

"Several."

"Good," I said without a thought. I stood and began pacing a circuit around Declan's room. Motion would spur my mind into revealing the next step.

"Ally?" Hesitant and soft, I barely heard his voice. I didn't stop my lap of the room. "You need to see this."

His words shook like a chair missing a leg. I stopped next to the wall, but didn't dare step closer to him. Whatever he wanted to show me would only make things worse. I wasn't prepared for worse. "No."

"Your…" He stopped and I didn't know if I was livid or relieved. He didn't give me a choice, though. "Leah's on the schedule to visit the doctor."

My knuckles barely registered a tingle when I smashed them into the wall. The plastic didn't even dent. I whipped my arm out again. This time red marred the pristine wall.

I rocked back and snapped my jab out again and again. Not Leah. Blood trickled between my fingers. Cloud Nine could have it. They could have my blood, but they could not have Leah. I'd told myself her sickness was stress, new food, whatever. Excuses. She didn't work for maintenance. She didn't work solo. But I was an idiot.

The next slam of my fist finally left fracture lines on the industrial plastic. They modified foods here. I'd read the test materials. My sister was sick and I shared the blame.

Declan's hands gripped my shoulders, but his strength wasn't a match for the torque of my core. I nailed the wall one last time before he was able to still me.

"We can fix this." His words were gentle, the exact opposite of everything I was.

"How?" My dark laugh cut deeper than a curse.

"We just will." He pulled me back against his chest, solid and warm.

I stood there, blood dripping on his floor, and let him hold me. "They have my sister, Dec."

"No. They had her." His chest vibrated at my back.

He was right, but I didn't know how that fixed anything. I needed to keep her from working and out of those labs.

I pushed out of the cocoon of his strength and turned, taking his hand, and led him back to the couch. "You know a bunch of the other people on the list, right?"

"Yes." His fingers tightened on my non-busted hand.

"This is good." Feeling was returning to my other hand bringing a throbbing fire, but I could ignore it.

"Why is that good?" He pulled a black tee shirt from the back of the couch and wrapped it around my bleeding knuckles.

"Because we can tell them." I could have made the decision when I saw Tomás curled in that bed or when I heard Charlie had been hauled off or maybe when I saw a wastebasket brimming with bloody tissues on a video feed. It didn't matter. I knew what they'd done to my sister and it was time to act. Instinctively, I tightened my abs waiting for the 'Hell no' punch.

"It's not safe. You know what happened…" to Charlie. He didn't say it aloud, but the blow hit me just as powerfully.

"I do. If we hadn't made her keep a secret, we would be in a different situation."

"They could have taken her brother too?" His eyes widened as he threw his hand in the air. Declan was incredulity steeped in fear. They couldn't take Leah and I wouldn't let them touch me.

I rested my hand on his thigh. Heat seared me, but not in the head-tripping way it had before. This was about being a lone rock in the river. "If everyone knows the secret, then things change. We tell them all." My cheeks pinched as mischief curled my lips. "When they know they've been used, they'll be able to stop it."

He closed his eyes and breathed heavy enough that his chest could have shoved back a boulder on inhale. "If we do this, it needs to be organized."

"Organized." I liked when he agreed with me, so I tried to reciprocate.

A wry smile looked good on Declan. "I don't know if you mean that."

Humor left me. "I'm trying to mean it." Truly.

He sobered. "I know, but you're going to have to try and hold to this. If we do it wrong it won't just be you or I that's tossed out the window but a whole lot of innocent people."

"We are innocent, too, you know."

"We are, but we're stronger than them." It was the first time I'd heard him say something like that aloud. He let his size and strength speak for him so often.

I recognized the importance in his words. This was all on us. An undertaking of this magnitude needed more than one leader, and they needed to be stronger, faster, and braver. My stance on heroism hadn't changed—I didn't want the label—but it wouldn't keep me from doing what was necessary.

I inclined my head slightly, the acceptance of our new roles coming to me with trepidation. My resolve set a moment later, though. If I was going to do this partnership thing, I would do it right.

"I want to get the word out as soon as possible. We tell all the people on this list." I pointed to the tablet like it was our Bible. "And at the same time tell them to meet somewhere instead of Level 2 the next day."

"What are you thinking?" He didn't sound wary for once. The trust made something bright burn in my chest. It was a slow, smoldering heat. Not enough to distract me from the task, but the right amount to bolster my confidence. Declan did that for me more often than I realized.

"Sit in."

"Really?" I enjoyed his surprise.

"Yes. We can treat it like a strike." Normally non-violent resolutions weren't my thing. I could shut someone up a whole lot faster with my knee in their groin than by plopping down on a rug. However, with this many people involved that would only lead to danger, and Cloud Nine was doing good work. Well, it was capable of it. The projects needed to meet the ideals proclaimed on posters plastered on high school walls at Ground Level.

"If we pretend it's a strike, it'll make things easier to swallow if the government has to make changes." Declan was nodding. "No big publicity issues."

"And if they don't react quickly, then we make it a bigger problem." I didn't mind the possibility.

"If we go on strike, shouldn't it be everyone on the station, though?"

I scrunched my toes inside my boots. "I'm not sure."

"If we get everyone involved, they have to listen to us or nothing gets completed. I know they're testing on the computer kids, but they really are wiring electronics for other stations." His hands laid palms up in my lap, but the openness on his face caught my breath. Earnestness escaped his pores. The reversal on his emotional lockdown was almost enough to make me automatically agree. Almost.

"I want our message to be clear."

"Stopping all production isn't clear?"

"It would be clear that we're pissed, but it doesn't illustrate the exact cause."

"You can't expect everyone to keep it a secret from those not being pulled down to Level 2." Bewilderment didn't look right on Declan.

I would be solid for us both. "I don't expect that at all. I expect the rumor mill will fire on all cylinders."

"Then how will you stop everyone from joining in your protest?"

"Our protest," I corrected and was rewarded with a flash of a smile. "I won't stop people from joining, but I think you overestimate how willing people will be to stick their necks out for this. Particularly those already involved."

"You need to have more faith in people."

"You wouldn't have taken this on if I hadn't been here to spur you along." I fought back a surge of guilt for bringing it up. "Don't expect others to do the right thing, because they'll have to know the consequences if we fail will be disastrous."

He didn't meet my gaze for a moment; just shook his head. When he finally looked up, his eyes locked on mine. "I needed someone to kick me in the ass to take action. People will follow if you lead them."

"You think they'll bandwagon on to a screw-the-government plan just because everyone else is doing it?"

"Don't trivialize. They may have wanted to help but didn't know how. You'll be giving them that choice."

My head spun with the possibilities. The cushion behind me kept me upright, but it wasn't what was keeping me grounded. If he was right, there was a chance to pull this off. I much preferred offering a choice to people, especially because these people hadn't had that freedom in longer than they realized.

"Okay." I dropped that word with all the finality I could muster. "How do we keep Jensen and cohorts from taking the shuttle up here right away, though? Doesn't he have the backing to come in gangbusters?"

"Smart woman." The tension in his body eased and was replaced by a snapping undercurrent of excitement. "I'll handle stalling the shuttle."

"Good." My mind was already three steps ahead playing the worst-case scenario. "What about Adam?"

"He cannot stop the shuttle."

I smacked Declan's leg harder than necessary.

"You give him too much credit. Even if he hears about what's happening, he's too much of a coward to take any action."

"Maybe you give him too little credit."

"Doubtful. At best, he's going to come to you and ask you to stop things."

Sourness filled my mouth. I needed to stop trading up for bigger problems.

For now, though, I'd focus on simply telling the truth.

Secrets offered no favors. It was time for Cloud Nine's dirty one to be laundered.

CHAPTER 44
ALL EYES ON ALLY

f someone told me I was being secretly doused with chemicals, my reaction would be bloody. For the messenger and those using me. Compared to that benchmark, the talks with the test subjects went better than expected.

One of the girls in food prep, Megan, broke out in tears as soon as I started talking. It was plausible they'd been testing on her for months, and at that truth, she began hyperventilating. Her sobs softened once I told her there was a plan.

She wasn't the only one who turned to tears, though. With Charlie gone, I knew I had to tell Tomás. It was awkward. He was still pale and too thin. I worried his cough would knock him over, but he found a seat as I explained what I thought was happening. He cried when he put together his sister's actions with what I told him. I wrapped my arms around him like he was family and held him until his sobs softened. He was hurt more than anyone else I'd met by the CAD program's testing.

He signed on for the sit-in without a second thought. Charlie would be proud.

That should have been the most uncomfortable of my interactions, but Leah's friend Tina nearly vomited on my shoes. I understood fear, but my sympathy only went so far.

Really, the only person who handled the news well was my sister.

I went to her room in the morning, as usual. My knock on her door earned me a muffled, "I'm not hungry. Go away."

I kept thumping my fist against the door knowing she'd eventually answer. When we moved here, I'd wanted her to see this wasn't a safe place. Only now that I had proof, my chest tightened with the dread of saying I told you so. I'd never hated being right so much.

When the door flew open, Leah was ready to argue. Her hair was a knotted mane and her face red with deep lines from her pillow cutting across her cheeks. "What?"

"I need to talk to you." I didn't sound half as guilty as I felt.

Her voice was still waking up, but she eked out, "Now?"

"I wouldn't wake you this early if it wasn't important." No one else was in the hallway, but I couldn't help checking both directions. "Can I come inside?"

She shuffled backward and stayed by the door as I entered her dorm room. I sat on her bed and waited for her to join me.

"There's a problem here." I swallowed a lump of fear. "On Cloud Nine."

Her shoulders sagged, defeated. "Not this again. I thought you were past the conspiracy theory crap. I told Mom you were past this."

My sister stared at the ceiling. I welcomed her irritation. It was better than what would have to come next.

"I was," I admitted. "Kind of. Then Tomás got sick."

"He's got some respiratory thing. I'm sure they're giving him cold medicine or something."

"Can you not interrupt? This is important." I scrubbed a hand over my face. I hadn't meant to snap.

Her scowl faded when she finally looked me in the eyes. "Okay."

"I started looking into what might be happening. Wait." I held my hands up in placation, took a deep breath of the rich air and let it saturate my lungs, and then exhaled. "The how doesn't matter. The station is testing biosynthetics on him."

I took another deep breath, preparing to tell her she was a victim, too, but she cut me off.

"They're testing chemicals on him?"

"Essentially, yes. He's not the only one."

Leah sucked her bottom lip into her mouth and bit down. My sister was smarter than I gave her credit for. She knew where this was going. "Who?"

"Most of the maintenance staff and it looks like food prep, too."

"So, me?"

"Yes, you." Words fell out of my mouth faster and faster like if I were to say everything at once it'd all be over. "I think it's why you're having stomach problems. I haven't been able to find all the information on your specific trials, but Declan and I have been researching it and then I told Charlie and they took her away, and I can't let them do this to you."

She hugged me. I should have been holding her, but my little sister wrapped her arms around me because she knew I was about to lose hard-fought composure.

"We won't. I'm not feeling bad today anyway."

I gave her a weak smile and a firm hug back. "I will fix this."

"At least you didn't say 'I told you so.'" She released me, but remained at my side.

"Don't get used to it."

She bumped her shoulder against mine. "Fine. So, what's your big plan, because I know you have a big plan."

She believed me without question and was on board with the sit-in plan before I'd even explained the whole thing. Maybe we were cut from the same cloth, after all.

Leah had better luck telling the others, too, as I knew she would. She coddled people through the shock with more than carefully chosen words, which was all I had been able to offer when explaining the situation.

Despite all the drama, the cafeteria was packed that night. The tables were full, and those who were eating had pre-packaged snacks. It was nearly 8 p.m. and the world hadn't yet crashed upon my skull. My brain was keeping my body locked in a full adrenaline assault, every tendon snapped so tight I would break something if I stumbled into the furniture.

Declan laid a hand on my arm, and I jumped. Several eyes in the room turned toward me. Dec stroked his fingers down my locked-tight arm and whispered in my ear that everything was under control.

Facing away from the amassing crowd—more than just those being tested upon arrived, score one for Declan—I whispered in his ear, "Did you disable the shuttle?"

"There's a malfunction set to trigger in another minute." I pinched the bridge of my nose and he pulled my fingers away. "I wanted the cameras to show me here when it failed. Not because I don't want them to know I did it, but because I like reminding them of the control they've given us."

Laughter bubbled out of me. "Nice."

"We should probably get this show on the road, right?" His body didn't belie his nerves, but I could see the trepidation behind his eyes. We were actually doing this and it scared him. It was a fear we shared, and one we'd both bury in some black hole near our livers.

There was no turning back.

I bobbed my head, but neither of us made a move. These people didn't know me. Sure, that was my fault, but at that moment it was an excuse not to turn around and address them.

I nudged Declan. "You should say something."

He huffed. "I'm the guy who gets them in trouble. They probably hate that I'm here in the first place."

Perceptions rooted us. Leah had buzzed about the room, checking on people like this was going to be a sleepover party just a few minutes ago, but now I couldn't find her in the chaos. The urge to make her call everyone together sang in my veins. My sister was a siren for group activities. She was not, however, the one in charge here. I didn't want her to be. She didn't need the burden of others' fears thrown atop her shoulders. Our mom would be angry I'd involved her at all. That's what you get for sending her with me, I suppose.

The room's setup was for quickly serving food and consuming it. There was no obvious front to the mess hall. My move to the counter where I snagged breakfast every morning was arbitrary, but I figured everyone knew the focal point. My feet didn't want to stay still, but I rocked onto the balls of my feet and pushed downward as though I could pin myself in place. Nerves did not become me. I cleared my throat in preparation to yell over the soft din of the room.

I underestimated their awareness of me and, I guessed, my role. The quiet cough brought the room to a standstill. Conversations died. Chairs were turned to face me. At least seventy sets of eyes stared at me, pelting me with their hope.

I clenched my jaw. Hope? How had I become the beacon of hope? I was the one they gossiped about. I was the person who they avoided in the hallway. Now they looked to me like I held all the answers.

I did have answers, not all of them, but enough to make me the leader. The surge of confidence cooling my skin wasn't due to the power of holding the room rapt; it was the result of knowing I could do this. There was a reason I was commanding attention and it wasn't because I held something over their heads, but because I would do what it took to help them.

I would not let them down.

Not now.

I inhaled until my lungs burned with the clean air Cloud Nine boasted on every poster.

"Thank you for coming. Everyone." I scanned the room making contact with familiar faces as I did. "Declan, Leah, and I did our best to lay out the basics for you today."

A hand shot up in front. I raised both of my own in placation. "I know there are more questions. There should be more questions, but we need to get a few things done quickly." No point in sugarcoating any of this. "The Clean Air Development Program has been using the people on Cloud Nine as test subjects for new research. If you have worked on Level 2, you have been tested on."

The sentence hovered. When it finally sank in, the cadre of whispers tickled my skin. I let them have this. Slowly, attention returned to me. I nodded, acknowledging their trust.

"If you've been coughing, having trouble breathing, or anything like that, find Declan"—I pointed to him—"in a moment. We're working on a counteractive medicine, and we'll need your help."

A few people started to shuffle toward Declan, but I kept talking before I lost the whole room. "For this to work, we need to stay in this room. Obviously, we can take food and drink from the adjoining kitchen and hit the bathroom in the far back corner, but do not leave. For our stand to work, we have to stay put."

A guy near the back yelled out, "Won't they just send new people?"

Declan's holler answered with authority, "Transports to and from Cloud Nine are on hiatus, a status that can only be corrected from our end."

Keeping a smile off my face was harder than predicted. His arrogant tone was what these people needed to hear. "We have it covered. If they aren't already on Cloud Nine, they won't be joining us. In the meantime, get comfortable and I'll be around to answer questions one-on-one soon."

It might have been easier to give a long speech explaining what we were up against, the details of the trials on Level 2, and just what our plan was, but opining wasn't my thing. I'd answer direct questions. I'd do my job. I'd try to keep them safe.

That's all I could promise.

The room reverted to a more social vibe and several people were working their way over to Declan. I ducked around the corner into the kitchen area and snagged a bottle of water. Sauntering back into the main room, I looked down as I twisted the cap off.

"What in the hell do you think you're doing?" Adam's voice crashed into me. I lifted my head to see his face red with exertion, or maybe anger. It made the white in his eyes pop. His hand was wrapped around the edge of the door, as though he might fall over if he let go.

I casually edged a few steps closer. "I'm doing what you didn't, and taking care of these people."

"You have to stop this now. I can't—"

"You can't stop us? I'm aware. We're going to change things for the better."

"No!" He gasped, swallowed, and tried again. "You don't understand. You can't stop this."

Declan rushed forward and slammed his forearm across Adam's collarbone, pinning him to the wall.

I acted like nothing had changed. "I won't let you or anyone else use people like they're things." I spat the word and wished it would make him feel as filthy as the thought did me.

His lips pulled tight, but he kept them closed. He instead snorted heavy breaths through his nose like a wounded bull.

I started to turn my back to him when the heavy stomp of boots pounding on tile stopped me. I rounded back and my shoulder had just cleared the line of the doorway when Jensen came barreling through. I widened my stance and dropped my weight down in time to steady myself before his full weight slammed into me.

My bottle of water crunched against the tile, its contents splashing over my feet.

I let Jensen's weight move me backward, keeping my feet wide until I finally planted my back foot enough to shove into him. It didn't knock him off me, but jarred him. A hard punch landed on my shoulder. His aim was sloppy, and I planned to use that.

An ill-timed head-butt earned me a bloody nose. Focus, Ally.

Jensen tried to shift his arms around me, pulling my body toward his. He could try, but this guy had underestimated me before. I snaked my right arm in between our bodies until my forearm was pressed against his collarbone and my hand curled over his shoulder like some human-T-Rex mutant.

Declan was moving toward us, but my glare stopped him mid-step. I needed to do this.

Jensen's hands grabbed at my waist. Please. My left palm connected just above his elbow to pin his arm to his side at the same time I dug the nails of my other hand into the flesh of his shoulder. I twisted my hand and his shirt dampened around my fingers. He yipped and tried to pull backward.

It was the wrong move. He knew it, too.

His fist slammed into my side once before I got a shot in, but then I was yanking him down—using his skin as my holding point—onto my knee. I made my leg into an arrow with the patella at the point and drove it between his legs.

His next body shot came before he began to fold. It was weaker, but he managed to curl it upward to catch under my ribs. I hadn't tightened my muscles enough and even biting my tongue didn't stop the roar of pain from escaping my mouth.

I shoved him backward. Hard. Using the arm at his neck to force him to obey. He looked up at me. Seething. "You will stop this."

His words meant nothing to me. I was done with guys like him thinking they could order everyone around without question. He couldn't treat others however he liked. He couldn't use these people. And he sure couldn't stop me from saving them.

I dropped my shoulder for a moment. I wanted a clear view of his face spattered with my blood and his own. "Wrong."

I lifted my hand from his body. The white tips of my fingernails were coated red. I balled my hand into a fist. Jensen's jab connected with my nose before I could strike. I heard the snap of bone, but it didn't matter.

Face shots were bloody, but they didn't hurt until afterward. I twisted my upper body, letting the tension release as I slammed the side of my hand into Jensen's neck, just below his ear. I wasn't done yet.

He curled down trying to protect his head. I let him, and then brought my fist down like a swift hammer on the back of his neck. He dropped to the floor.

On hands and knees, he still had bravado. "You can't win this, honey. Someone else will beat your ass down and I'll laugh the entire time."

I shouldn't have done it, but I wasn't always the better person Declan thought I could be. I stomped down on the back of Jensen's knee as hard as I could. He screamed the piercing cry of a man who just felt bones shatter and meat merge. He crumpled on the ground and whimpered.

Adam rushed to his side. At least I knew where he stood.

Declan came to mine with a simple white cloth that he pressed under my nose. "It's broken, you know."

Now that my blood wasn't pumping in my ears, I heard the soft whistle my nose made as I breathed.

"So it is." I pressed the cloth more firmly to my face and sat down in the closest chair.

"Was all that really necessary?" He was close to my ear, the words meant only for me.

"The knee wasn't. Everything else? Hell yes."

The weight of his hand on my shoulder was the silent approval I craved. After another few moments of staunching the blood flowing from my face, I asked for a bag of ice for my ribs. At the very least it'd soothe the internal wounds, but I needed to cool more than that.

Jensen had been right about one thing, there were people on Cloud Nine who would be loyal to the government. People who would rather do what was best for themselves than what could protect their friends.

I pinned the makeshift ice pack to my side with my elbow.

I didn't have long before the pain in my face became a sincere distraction. There wasn't a good place to discuss things with Declan privately. This teamwork thing was complicated.

A simple incline of my head brought him to my side again, though. I wanted to send a message to those who would treat us like things instead of people. Declan hesitated but sent Tomás to get the necessary equipment.

I steadied myself for the bold move by watching Jensen writhe on the floor.

I could take one down, why not them all?

CHAPTER 45
THE DECLARATION

Cloud Nine had cameras in every hallway. In every workspace. In the dining area. Everywhere.

I understood that, but this was the first time I wanted to be caught by them.

The mess hall's far camera was adjusted to point directly at me. The bloody rag and bag of ice used to quell my injuries were out of the shot. Anyone watching the video would see what I wanted them to see: me and Jensen, both bloody and disheveled. They'd also see the mass of people behind us, silent and solid. Unified.

While the surveillance on Cloud Nine didn't capture audio, it wasn't for lack of ability. Right now, that small lens and the microphone embedded on the camera's side would capture my every word. There was something familiar in the pressure of the moment.

Jensen kneeled next to me. He was too out of it from injuries and wounded pride to argue. I knew they'd recognize him, and I didn't bother introducing any of my people, either. They had files on each of us. Our strengths, weaknesses, families, pasts, hopes, and everything in between.

I didn't question for a moment they would know exactly who I was, so I kept my message simple.

"We want to save you," my voice echoed in the hall, all the bodies moved behind me, "but we won't be used. Be honest or we will not leave, we will not work, and you may not survive."

I paused and imagined the adults scrambling as a teenage girl put them in their place. The urge to wet my lips hit me, and I buried it.

"If you're willing to change, we want to hear it. We'll be open to negotiations in two days. Until then, keep your distance." I looked down at Jensen pointedly.

Our message ended. Declan told me he'd have the video clip relayed directly to the head of the EPA, the director of the Clean Air Development program, and the Cloud Nine Ground Level delegation. He knew more about the political side than I had ever imagined. He had so much to teach me before we met with anyone about making changes here.

Fear and anxiety came with freedom. I'd take them every day for the chance to make my own choices.

I didn't know if my plan would work long-term, but no one was locked in a room being tested against their will on Cloud Nine anymore. That was my first, huge step toward a revolution.

———

The thrill of finally acting and the fear of the consequences hummed in my muscles even as the pain from my fight with Jensen began to register.

The group began to disperse throughout the room.

"I'm going to lock these two up in the kitchen. Keep them close. Any objections?" Declan already had Jensen's biceps in his hand. My attacker slumped on the floor with less style than a bag of laundry. A little tug would have the guy on his feet.

I nodded my approval and turned my attention to Leah's friend Megan before she disappeared into the sea of people. "Have you seen Leah?"

"Not since earlier." Megan wasn't so helpful, but we'd had a long day.

"Any idea where I might find her?" I asked in my most placating tone.

"Last time I saw her she said she was going to Level 2 to pick up any stragglers."

No.

I nudged Megan out of my way and lunged between the first set of tables. I darted from table to table calling out Leah's name. No one had seen her.

How had no one seen my sister? Everyone saw her. Always. That was her nature.

I plowed face first into Declan. How was he back already? "I need you."

My need to find Leah was mashed into the pit of all my lost thoughts the second the gravity in his voice penetrated. "What?"

He started to reach for my arm to escort me out, but thought better of it. Smart man. Instead, he urged me out into the hallway. When we were out of earshot, but could still keep an eye on our people, Declan pulled a small tablet from his pocket.

"They responded." The earlier thrill was gone. Declan's hand shook as he held the device in front of us both. I slipped my left hand under his to steady him. And myself. What scared him so deeply? I had hit my limit of devastating news for the year.

I tapped the screen to start the video.

I didn't scream. That would have been useless.

I didn't run. There was nowhere to go.

Instead, I squeaked like some pathetic mouse and forgot to breathe.

A barren room—a prison cell if there ever were one—filled the screen. In the center was Leah. Bound to a simple white chair. A ragged cloth covered her mouth. She wasn't moving, but I made out tears streaking her cheeks.

The image disappeared and I snapped my other hand to the tablet so hard the screen should have shattered. A white square took over. Then the four words I didn't need to see appeared: *We have your sister.*

There were no demands or instructions. Just four terrifying words in unassuming black.

We have your sister.

The squeaking stopped. I returned my hands to my sides where they could make tight fists.

"We'll get her back." Declan was miles behind me.

My vehemence surprised me, but the depth of my rage required it. "I will get her back and burn down this program in the process."

I turned back toward the others and started to plan.

ABOUT CHELSEA MUELLER

Chelsea Mueller writes gritty, twisty fantasy and thriller novels for adults and teens, including the critically acclaimed Soul Charmer series and the YALSA Reluctant Reader Pick *Prom House*. She loves bad cover songs, good fight scenes, and every soapy YA drama Netflix can put in her queue. Chelsea lives in Texas and has been known to say y'all.

For the latest updates, join her email list at ChelseaMueller.com or follow @ChelseaVBC on Twitter and Instagram.

ALSO BY CHELSEA MUELLER

Prom House

Casual Conversations About Love and Murder

SOUL CHARMER

Borrowed Souls

Rogue Souls

Lost Souls

www.ingramcontent.com/pod-product-compliance
Lightning Source LLC
Chambersburg PA
CBHW030806210726
48290CB00002B/445